IN THE GROUND

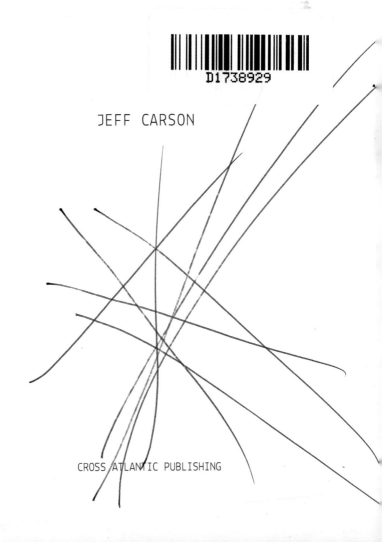

JEFF CARSON

CROSS ATLANTIC PUBLISHING

CHAPTER 1

THE UNMARKED SLUICE-BYRON County Sheriff's Department SUV brushed the underside of a cloud as it drove through the saddle between two thirteen-thousand-foot peaks on County Road 621.

Air blew through the window and although it was late June, a few days into summer, to Sheriff David Wolf it felt as if he had his elbow propped inside an open freezer. He could have unzipped his jacket, rolled up the window, and set the inside temperature to seventy degrees, but then what was the point of getting out of the office?

Once beyond the road's apex, he let his foot off the gas and coasted. He felt the cab rumbling deep in his chest as the tires skated over more washboard and potholes—a soundtrack that never got old.

The mountain on the right side of the road abruptly dropped away, revealing the majesty of the Colorado high country landscape behind it. The Dredge River sparkled in the seam of the valley below, cutting through a carpet of trees on its way east, out into the green, shadow-speckled high plain Dredge

Valley. Beyond that was another wall of snow-laced peaks in a seemingly endless sea of mountains.

A rock pinging off the bottom of the SUV brought Wolf back to the task of keeping from tumbling off the roadway's edge.

He checked his speed and leaned over toward the passenger window, catching a glimpse of the mining operation far below. Pinprick reflections glanced off of a group of county law enforcement vehicles amid a handful of civilian trucks. A cluster of tiny white-clad ants—CSI investigators—swarmed a piece of red machinery that looked to be the wash plant. Deputies in dark jackets stood in clusters or wandered the area.

After the first hairpin turn, the spectacle came into view without him having to risk death. The mine was a small operation compared to some surface mines Wolf had seen. Earth movers had cleared a few football fields' worth of forest and gouged their way into the mountain on either side of the river. There was a retaining pond, unnaturally turquoise, a lower cut where a single excavator sat idle, and a flat upper area where four trailers were lined up.

A row of pickup trucks in front of the trailers stood out among the other official vehicles, which were all labeled with the SBSCD logo and paintjob and parked more haphazardly.

In addition to the trucks sat three four-wheel ATV vehicles, the kind with bucket seats, roll cages, and flatbeds, used for navigation within the mine space.

Wolf had visited a few gold mines growing up, as the former landlord of his family's ranch had been a mining magnate himself, so he could now confirm the large red machine sitting at the edge of the flat area below as a wash plant. The bulky section of the gold-extracting-machine was about the size of a semi-trailer. Out of the top yawned a rectangular covered opening called a hopper, where dirt was dumped in by excavators. Then the earth tumbled through a series of chutes with the aid of running water, depositing the heavy gold contained within into riffles beneath sifting screens. The remaining dirt, now free of the sifted gold, was gathered into another chute and deposited into the turquoise pond.

As Wolf reached the bottom of the hill his eyes flicked for the dozenth time back to the hopper with its iron bars covering the opening to stop larger boulders from entering the machine and tearing it from the inside out, because that's where the dead body lay sprawled to the sky.

He parked and got out. Stretching his arms overhead, he felt a crick in his back from sitting too long behind the wheel, or too long behind the desk before that.

Closing the door, he sucked in the thin mountain air laden with the scent of pine and running water.

He could hear the whoosh of white water flowing off the snow-veined peaks down in the crack of the valley, over that the faint sound of radios scratching and people chatting. He unzipped his rain jacket to let his neck breathe, alert to the sound of quick footsteps heading towards him.

Wolf crunched through the wet gravel, down a small embankment and met the footsteps halfway.

"How are you, sir?" Chief Detective Heather Patterson asked.

"Patterson." Wolf's eyes scanned the cut in the land below, the muddy road the earth movers used, the big red metal wash plant, the scrum of bodies bustling nearby.

Wolf had parked slightly upslope and above the flattened upper area of the mine, and as they walked down toward the action Patterson gave him time to take it in.

The dead body lay atop a flat grate on the red machine. Face up, on his back with arms sprawled to the sides, the corpse looked placed for the gods atop a red iron altar.

"What have we got?" Wolf asked.

Patterson drew closer. "Deceased is a thirty-two-year-old male named Chris Oakley. He was a worker at the mine who has been missing since Friday night. Shit."

She stopped and picked up the notebook she'd just dropped.

"Sorry. Damn thing." She stood straight, flexing her left hand, displaying her below-elbow cast poking out the bottom of her jacket sleeve. The Chief Detective was a fifth-degree black belt in Kempo karate, and two weeks ago she had learned that five boards were the maximum she could karate chop through with her left hand without breaking her ulna.

"Where he's lying is a hydraulic grate covering the ... uh, hopper, they were calling it, which, that front-end loader right there drops the dirt into," Patterson gestured towards a yellow excavator with a large scoop parked silently. "The dirt enters the wash plant for processing, and the grate catches the bigger rocks that would otherwise damage the plant. When there's a sufficient buildup of rocks on top of the grate, the operator of the front-end loader uses a remote control switch he keeps in the cab with him to hydraulically lift the grate."

Patterson continued to read through her loopy handwritten notes.

"Earlier this morning, at approximately 10:30 a.m., a worker named Casey Lizotte put a load from those piles there," she gestured to a series of heaping piles next to the wash plant, "onto the hydraulic grate and noticed that a body rolled out of his scoop. He backed away. Stopped the front-end loader right there, he says, and that's when they called the Sheriff's department."

"It's Monday," Wolf said.

"That's right, sir."

"He's been missing since Friday and we're just hearing about it when they uncovered his body?"

"He's been missing since Friday, but they're saying they didn't know it until this morning."

Patterson nodded toward the line of trailers. At the end of the row of buildings stood a small canvas tent where four men sat in camp chairs talking with Rachette, who looked up from his note taking and nodded to Wolf.

"That's them."

"Only four of them in the operation?"

"Correct, sir."

"So how does that explanation work?" Wolf asked. "Why are we only hearing about this now? Why not earlier?"

She sighed and folded her arms. "I asked the same thing. Mind you we're still waiting to interview them separately, but from what I'm gathering apparently Chris Oakley, our deceased up there, worked the night shift Friday night. It's normal for them to sleep through the next day if they're on the night shift the night before. So they suspected nothing out of the ordinary Saturday when he didn't come out of his trailer. Come Sunday they weren't worried either, because apparently there had been some kind of argument. The owner, his name's Eagle McBeth, told us he thought he was sulking in his trailer the whole time."

Patterson shook her head. "It's pretty convoluted after that. I guess the owner, Mr. McBeth, was angry at the deceased and went down into town, hired a new guy to replace him."

"And then?" Wolf asked.

"McBeth says come this morning they started getting worried. Knocked on the deceased's trailer door, no answer. Went inside, he wasn't there. They called deceased's girlfriend, and she hadn't seen him all weekend, not since she left Friday night, again, something to do with the fight. According to their story they were about to call the sheriff's department to file a mis-per this morning when the new guy dug up the body from those piles there and..." Patterson clucked her tongue. "Here we are now."

Thunder rumbled in the sky toward the saddle between the peaks. Dark clouds had been building in Wolf's rearview mirror the entire drive from Rocky Points to Dredge. Judging by the forecast and the five previous afternoons, they were going to get a good soaking shower.

Wolf walked toward the wash plant, Patterson at his side.

"How was the Council meeting this morning?" she asked.

Wolf had consumed the morning with the County Council going over a budget proposal he and Patterson had spent many hours creating. It was the reason he had arrived at the scene here and now. "It didn't go very good," he said.

"What didn't they like?"

"Just a few of the line items."

"The Leadership Fund?"

Wolf shrugged. "They just wanted to know more about it."

"So that's no problem. We'll put something to—"

"What else?" Wolf nodded toward the wash plant.

"Right. Um...the miners are from Jackson Hole, Wyoming," she said. "Hence the name".

The words *Jackson Mine* were stenciled in white on the wash plant.

"Sir," Rachette jogged up.

"Where's Yates?" Wolf asked.

"Over with the miners."

They stopped and looked up at the body splayed on the big machine.

"You see the stiff yet?" Rachette asked.

"Not yet," Wolf said.

"Got a hole in the chin and at the top of his head. Looks like the head is the exit wound if my memory of forensics and ballistics class are not failing me."

Wolf eyed Patterson for confirmation.

She shrugged. "I haven't been up there, sir." She flexed her cast hand.

"What else?" Wolf asked Rachette, deciding the vagueness of the question was warranted at this early stage.

"The names of the four miners are," Rachette looked at his notebook, "McBeth, Koling, Sexton, and Lizotte. McBeth and Sexton are thirty years old. Koling is thirty-two. Eagle McBeth is the owner. They all seem to be pretty tight. Grew up together up in Jackson Hole with Chris Oakley, our deceased. Lizotte's the odd man out. He's the new guy from this morning hired to replace the deceased. He's twenty-seven years old.

"I'm not sure what Patty's told you yet, but they say Oakley had the night shift Friday night. Before that, they had all gotten into some sort of argument. McBeth says it was about the lack of gold in the box. I take that to mean they're not finding much gold? McBeth, and the other two, also mentioned Chris Oakley's girlfriend being present earlier in the night.

"McBeth says the argument started when they all came out to see why Oakley was yelling at her. I guess it was a big blowout, she stormed off, drove away, and the argument turned between the miners about the gold." Rachette turned a page. "I guess they all thought this guy Oakley was in his trailer this whole weekend, pissed off and keeping his nose out of the work they'd been doing out here. They thought he'd up and quit."

Rachette flipped another page and squinted. "What the hell? What does this say? Trails? Tails?" He checked the blank side of the page, then flipped it back.

Patterson ripped it from his hand. "My God, who wrote this? TJ?"

TJ, Tom Junior, was Rachette's oldest son, who had graduated kindergarten that spring.

"I wish." Rachette took the notebook back. "Anyway, we

need to get them to the station and talk to them separately. They're just feeding off one another down there. I can't get a sense of if they know anything more they're not telling us or not. But it's definitely foul play. Gotta be, right? If it was suicide, how was he buried? Guy's covered in dirt. He came tumbling out of the loader."

"Do we have a weapon?" Wolf asked.

"No, sir." Rachette gestured. "Could be anywhere in that wash plant, or in one of those piles of dirt."

Wolf saw there was a group of forensic technicians near a particular mound. "Is that where Oakley's body was taken from?"

"That's what the new guy, Lizotte, thinks. He's not one hundred percent sure, though."

A forensic technician was scanning one of the piles with a metal detector.

There was a loud ping on the metal side of the wash plant. They turned and watched a lanky figure clad in a white forensic suit climbing off the flat-topped hopper and down a set of ladder rungs welded to the side.

Dr. Lorber, the county Medical Examiner, took the flight of metal stairs and headed toward them.

"How's it going up there?" Wolf asked.

Lorber lifted up a pair of goggles, revealing steamy John Lennon style glasses underneath. He plucked them off his beak nose, pulled a microfiber cloth from inside his suit and wiped them clean.

"Body is still plenty dirty, being he was deposited with a load of paydirt from that tractor, so I haven't had a chance to thoroughly check him, but it's looking like a gunshot to the chin, exit out the top of his head."

Thunder rumbled again, this time louder, and all eyes

turned toward the top of the valley. Another flash lit the closing darkness behind the peaks Wolf had just driven down.

"But we've got a bigger problem right now," Lorber said. "That storm is going to be a soaker. We have him wrapped up, but I'd rather get him down and into the meat wagon before it hits."

Wolf eyed the wash plant, the body on top, and the sky behind it all. "Grab a couple throw-bags," he said to Rachette. It was standard issue for each vehicle among the SBCSD to be stocked with a seventy-five-foot, quarter-inch rope throw-bag for emergency rescue.

"Yep." Rachette turned and ran away.

"I need to speak to the owner," Wolf said to Patterson. "Which one is he again?"

"Eagle McBeth," she said, leading him to the open-sided tent where the four men from the mine were still milling about.

"Which of you is Eagle McBeth?" Wolf asked, reaching them.

The shortest of the three, a man with black hair and dark skin, stepped forward. "I am."

"We need to get your employee down before that lightning hits. We'll use ropes, but I want to know how to angle that hydraulic gate upward. How do I activate it?"

McBeth blinked rapidly, thinking for a minute. "You want us to fire up the front-end loader?"

Wolf considered sending the body for another ride in a metal dirt scoop versus a gentle lowering by rope. Then he considered how McBeth had suggested the idea in the first place. It seemed rather insensitive. Or maybe the man was ruthlessly practical.

"No thanks. We'll lower him down."

McBeth nodded. "The remote control is inside the loader.

And there's a manual button on the side of the wash plant as well."

"Show us please."

McBeth walked briskly toward the front-end loader, and when another flash lit the sky he broke into a run. Wolf and Patterson followed close.

The man expertly climbed up into the cab of the hulking machine and leapt down with considerable grace. An athlete hid beneath the dirt, hair, and layer of fat on McBeth's body.

"Here's the remote," he said, handing it to Wolf. It looked like a simple garage door opener. "The left button opens it, the right one closes it. You do not want to touch the left one with anybody up there. You'll launch them off. Thing is very strong, and I have to tell you, it's not smooth at all. That's something we've been meaning to fix."

Wolf reconsidered his plan. "Can I open it only a fraction? Or one push opens it all the way?"

"A left button push starts it opening. If you're quick enough you can push it again and it will pause the opening."

Wolf looked up at the two forensic technicians on top of the grate with the dead body, feeling like he held a detonator and the hopper was wired with explosives. "Let's go."

Lorber headed towards the wash plant, his giant strides covering the ground quickly. He climbed the one-story high red-metal stairs, skipping two steps at a time, Wolf followed, skipping every other step. The large machine echoed and boomed with each footfall his boots. The railing was ice cold to the touch.

Lorber reached a catwalk and walked to the other side of the rectangular hopper chute, where a rebar ladder had been welded to the side, leading up to the grate that was a good ten feet above them.

Wolf looked over the edge of the railing, into the guts of

the wash plant. Three chutes ran downward, covered in mud strips that had caught on riffles. He knew that was where the gold sat, or lack thereof. Water hoses mounted at his feet were shut off but still dripped. It smelled like wet earth and diesel fuel.

Wolf turned around and saw Lorber had already climbed the ladder to the top.

He poked his head over and waved Wolf up.

Wolf held the garage opener. He dared not put it in one of his pockets and accidently press a button on the way up. He pictured the grate opening like a mouse trap arm, sending everyone atop it flying off.

"I'll take it."

Wolf looked down and saw Patterson was standing next to him.

"Yeah. Please. And...please don't touch it."

"Yes, sir."

"Hey," Rachette said, appearing next to her. "You want these?"

Wolf took the two mesh bags containing the stowed ropes. He grabbed onto the first rung of the ladder, cold and slick with mud from the shoes of those who'd already climbed it, and realized why Patterson had decided to stay on the ground. It was tough enough climbing with two good arms.

Wolf reached the top and grabbed one of the grate's dented slats. The good news was they'd already done a lot of work. The corpse was inside a bag, strapped down tight onto a spine board.

The bad news was the wind started howling off the mountain, hitting them in full force. Daphne Pinnifield, Lorber's assistant, and another technician were on their hands and knees next to the body, Lorber crouched behind them. It looked like a dance party was happening on a postage stamp.

"We need everyone off here but me and Lorber."

Wolf climbed back down to make way for the two technicians, then climbed back up to join the M.E.

Wolf's hands gripped tightly on the steel grate, the slats digging in painfully to his knees as he climbed aboard a second time. The occasional sharp burr from where a boulder, or a thousand boulders, had landed dug into his palms. The wind doubled. Another bolt of lightning flickered, followed closely by a clap of thunder.

The dead man appeared to weigh at least two hundred fifty pounds.

"The dude's a rhino," Lorber said. "Took us an hour to get him wrapped up."

Thunder rumbled again. They had little time.

"Careful!" Wolf said, gripping the steel bars harder.

Lorber looked like he was almost blown off the edge as a gust hit him, but no fear shone behind his Lennons as he gripped the slats with long, sure fingers. The county Medical Examiner was an expert rock climber in his non-professional life, a legend in psychotic outdoorsman circles Wolf seldom frequented.

Oakley's face was still poking out of the top of the body bag, which was unzipped for a reason only Lorber knew.

Wolf had seen plenty of dead bodies before, but it never got easier. Except for the gaping mouth packed with dirt, this one body was relatively benign. There was no visible sign of injury other than a swath of red on the top of his head. The eyes were closed. A dark beard a quarter of an inch long carpeted the lower half of his face. His hair was a matted mess on top, so caked with mud it barely moved in the wind.

"Zip it up, let's get this guy down," Wolf said.

Lorber zipped up the bag, and Wolf tied one of the ropes around the upper portion of the body, threading through and wrapping the handles of the spine board. Lorber did the same on the lower portion.

Wolf pointed down toward the ground, and the pile of discarded boulders below. "He slides off that way when we open the gate." Wolf extracted some rope from the throwbag and dropped it over the opposite side where Rachette, Nelson, Yates, Hanson, and Patterson stood below on the catwalk. Lorber did the same.

"Okay, let's get off of here!" Wolf said, shooing Lorber past him.

The skies opened up. First it was a ping here and there on the metal, then larger, louder clanks as hail started dropping. Soon the wash plant and everyone on it were getting pelted by a rain-snow-hail combination coming in at a forty-five-degree angle.

"Be careful on the way down," Wolf said, more to himself than to Lorber, as Lorber disappeared over the side with the ease of a long-legged spider.

Wolf shimmied his way over, slid over the edge, and climbed down the rebar rungs, his hands chilled to the bone now as water cascaded from the sky.

"Here you go!" Patterson handed over the remote control, and once again Wolf felt like he was holding a bomb trigger. He spotted the mine owner, McBeth, standing below. He pointed at him. "I need you to operate this!"

McBeth pointed at his own chest.

"Okay, hang onto that rope and lower him down everyone. We're going to pop that grate, and according to the mine owner it's abrupt. He's big, so grip tight."

Rachette whooped, smacking the others on the shoulder hard. "Let's do this! Patty, move back."

Wolf squeezed past them, went down the stairs and around the other side of the plant to where the boulders were piled below the hopper grate. McBeth joined him, more than a little trepidation in his face, but there was a glimmer of steel in his eyes as he took the remote from Wolf's hand.

"Ready?" Wolf asked loudly up to the catwalk.

They nodded.

"Three! Two! One!" McBeth pointed the remote and pressed the button. Immediately there was a thunderous boom as the hydraulic door lifted up about a foot in less than a second. The body above it lurched and bounced hard. Rachette, Yates and the others leaned back in their stances.

The corpse bounced heavily, getting a foot or two of air before it settled back onto the now angled grate.

"All good?" Wolf yelled.

"All good!" Rachette said.

McBeth pressed the button again, and this time the gate swung all the way up at a steady, slower pace.

"Whoa, whoa, whoa!" Everyone within radius shouted at the same time.

Oakley's upper torso was now pointing sharply downward. The rope attached to his lower half was getting hung up on something.

"Shit," Wolf said under his breath. He thought of the sharp burrs on the steel that were undoubtedly digging into the rope. "Okay, how good are you with that loader?"

McBeth shook his head. "Not as good as Sexton."

While Wolf considered his options, another flash of lightning hit the side of the nearest mountain. "Get him in that thing."

"Sexton!"

Wolf watched a man dart from the crowd toward the front-end loader. With practiced precision he lunged up the side, popped inside the cab and fired up the engine.

It lurched, growling to life. Black smoke poured out of the

exhaust pipe, smothered immediately by the downpour, as Sexton drove quickly forward, jammed the brakes, turned a quick two-point turn and sped past Wolf and McBeth.

Bouncing hard over boulders, he went at a full clip toward the plant, at such alarming speed that he looked like he might ram it with the raising boom, the angle of the scoop changing at the same time so that the shiny metal teeth would bite clean through the dirt chute, killing everyone on board the other side with the force of the impact.

Oh God. What had he done? Wolf's heart stopped.

But so did the loader.

Expertly, Sexton careened to a stop with the scoop on the loader mere inches from the metal façade, only a foot below the dangling body.

Sexton edged the boom up, placing the scoop under the spine board like a mother cradling her baby.

"Good?"

Wolf looked into the cabin of the loader and saw the single word had come from inside. Sexton was staring at Wolf for approval.

Wolf gestured up with his thumb, then showed a few inches with his other hand.

Instantly Sexton adjusted, and the boom raised. Sexton seemed to not need more coaxing at that point, because he turned his attention forward again and raised the boom in a slow continuous motion, capturing the entirety of the body into the upraised scoop.

"Let go of the ropes!" Wolf said.

Rachette and the other deputies dropped their ropes at their feet.

Sexton backed up, then came to a stop when one side remained stuck on the grate above.

"We have to cut that!" Sexton said, looking at Wolf again.

Wolf held up a finger and sprinted back toward the plant, this time skipping two steps at a time as he shot up the stairway.

"Wait!" McBeth called.

Wolf looked over his shoulder.

"I'll drop the gate! Everyone get ready!"

"He's dropping the gate again," Wolf said as he reached the catwalk.

Lightning flashed, thunder clapping unnervingly close, and an even bigger explosion of sound came crashing down, rattling the machine and his brain inside his skull. Particles of rock and dirt joined the rain landing on them as the hydraulic gate slammed down with zero grace.

"Shit! What's happening over there?" Patterson asked as Wolf squeezed past again.

"Everyone down! Now!" Wolf shouted as he climbed up the ladder.

He reached the top and scrambled onto the grate. He went to the edge and looked over into the scoop of the loader. Oakley's body lay face up in the center of the scoop. One of the ropes lashed to the board was caught on a burr in one of the metal slats. He unsheathed his Leatherman multi-tool, flipped out the serrated blade and cut both ropes, dropping the line down onto the body.

The loader revved angrily, sounding like a semi-truck as it backed away. The boom came down, the scoop maintaining its angle relative to ground with practiced precision.

"What happened!" he heard from down below.

Wolf climbed to the other side. "Okay, we're finished! I said get down! Get off this plant and into your vehicles now!"

Another lightning strike flashed somewhere in his peripheral vision, and Wolf decided to take his own advice. Keeping his four limbs attached to the rebar ladder at all times, he slowly climbed down to Rachette who waited for him on the catwalk, pointedly ignoring his earlier order as the others had already scrambled away.

"Let's go!" Wolf said.

Wolf followed him to the steps, running into Rachette's back as he came to a sudden halt.

A crowd had gathered in a tight circle below. In the middle lay Patterson. She gritted her teeth while her good hand clutched at her ankle.

CHAPTER 2

WOLF JUMPED down the last couple of steps. "Everybody back! Give her some air. What happened?"

"Somebody pushed me from behind," Patterson said. "Ah, shit. Right there. Right there. Yeah."

"I'm so sorry," Deputy Nelson knelt next to her. "I was just trying...I slipped, and I slipped into her. Sorry, Patterson."

Rachette pulled Nelson back toward the group. "Back up, man, give her some space."

"Don't worry about it," Patterson said. "You didn't mean it." She let loose a stream of curse words through clenched teeth, her eyes screwed shut.

"Everybody back up," Wolf said. "I want everyone to take shelter from this storm. Get in your cars, now."

Reluctantly, the crowd dissipated, all except Rachette. Another woman who had been kneeling next to Patterson and cradling her leg also remained. The hood on her SBCSD jacket covered her head and shielded her face, making it impossible to see who it was.

Wolf tapped her shoulder. "Deputy, thanks for your help, but I need you to get into your car."

"I'm a trained medic," she said.

"Join the club," Rachette said. "Let's move!"

"What about here?" the woman said, prodding Patterson's shin.

"Ahhhh, yeah. That hurts."

"More than here?"

"No. Just as much. It all hurts."

Rachette put his hands on his hips and gestured to the hooded figure in theatrical fashion.

"What's your name?" Wolf asked, kneeling down on Patterson's other side. He finally caught a glimpse of her face beneath the hood.

"Deputy Cain, sir. Dredge Satellite Unit."

Her eyes were large and dark brown, almost black, as if God had skipped the iris and gave her all pupil. She looked familiar, like he'd met her before, but...no. He would have definitely remembered meeting her, he decided.

"... to be careful."

Wolf blinked, realizing she'd just said something and he'd missed it. "What?"

"I said she'll definitely need X-rays," she said.

"Right."

"Ah!" Patterson leaned her head back to the pouring rain. "What the hell? What's happening to me!"

"You think it's a fracture?" Rachette said. "What was your name?"

"Deputy Piper Cain. I'm not sure if it's broken. It seems to me like a hard sprain, but of course, it's better to be safe than sorry. There're a lot of bones in the foot."

"It's not the foot, it's the ankle." Patterson groaned.

"Sir, I'd be happy to drive her into the ER," Cain said. "Or... obviously...you could take her."

"You're driving me in," Patterson said. "I'm not listening to Rachette's bullshit all the way to the ER."

"Hey." Rachette frowned.

"I could take her," Wolf said. "I drove, too."

"I'll go with her." Patterson's tone conveyed the matter was settled and they'd get a foot up their asses if they said anything further.

"Help me up." Patterson shot out her good arm and clutched onto Rachette's pant leg.

Rachette wobbled, almost falling over, but then steadied himself and pulled her up. "Now she wants my help."

Wolf watched as Cain helped on Patterson's other side.

"You got her?" Wolf stepped in close.

"I got her." Cain swiveled around, pointing them toward the line of vehicles. "I'm the Jeep Cherokee."

Yates jogged up, appearing out of the rain. "What happened?"

Patterson, only five foot four and less than a hundred pounds, even with her clothes soaking wet like they were right now, floated between Rachette and Cain. Cain supported Patterson's injured leg at the knee.

"She hurt her ankle," Wolf said.

Yates shuffled alongside the procession. "Patty, you okay? What happened?"

Wolf studied Cain as they walked. Where did he know her from? He knew he'd seen her before. The hood drawn over her head added to the mystery. He was the sheriff and she was one of his deputies. That was a good enough reason she looked familiar, he supposed. But, then again, he was only interim sheriff, and he hadn't set foot in Dredge in the year since he'd taken office. On top of that she had to have been new, he decided.

He found himself studying her up and down on the way to the vehicles. Wet strands of dark hair were lashed across her face and stuck to her skin. She had perfect teeth, he noted, as he watched her speak to Patterson.

"Get the door?"

"What?"

Rachette looked over his shoulder. "Sir, can you get the door?"

"Right."

But Yates beat Wolf to it, popping open the passenger side of Deputy Cain's Jeep.

"No, we should put her in back," Cain said, "so she can elevate her leg."

Wolf opened the rear while Yates closed the front.

A feminine scent spilled out, wafting past his nose, and he decided it was the opposite of opening his own car door.

They got Patterson inside, and she groaned her thanks. "Ah." She appeared to be in agony as she tried to settle on the seat.

"Should have gone in the other way," Yates said.

"Let's pull her back out," Rachette said, putting his hands under her armpits.

"Get off!" Patterson swatted him away and propelled herself forward.

Cain sprinted around and got into the driver's side. She nudged the hood back, sending raindrops flying, revealing long thick hair pulled back in a ponytail.

For an instant Wolf looked in and locked eyes with Cain in the mirror, before she turned around to face Patterson. "We're ready to go."

"Shut the door," Patterson said.

Rachette pushed the door closed. Wolf backed his head out of the way just in time, the door grazing his nose on the way past.

Wolf knocked, "We'll see you there!"

Without looking, Patterson gave a thumbs up. The Jeep

sped away, past a line of parked department cruisers, out onto the exit road and up the valley until it disappeared into the foggy veil.

Wolf, Yates, and Rachette walked to the open-sided tent where the miners stood huddled out of the rain. They spoke excitedly, duffel bags and backpacks slung over their shoulders.

Wolf pulled his hood up over his head and walked toward them.

"My name is David Wolf. I'm the sheriff."

The tallest of the men nodded. "My name is Kevin. Kevin Koling." He extended a big hand that wrapped easily around Wolf's.

"I'm Lizotte. Casey Lizotte," the shortest of them said. He stood noticeably apart from the other three. Wolf remembered he had been the one who dug up the body. The new worker.

"You're Sexton?" Wolf nodded to the man next to McBeth.

"That's right."

"That was some good tractor driving over there."

Sexton nodded, saying nothing.

"Told you he was good," McBeth said, his voice barely audible over the rain drumming the top of the tent.

Wolf nodded. "Well. Thank you. I know that couldn't have been an easy thing."

The big man, Koling, stared hard at him. "I don't understand it. How did he die? It makes no sense. Eagle said there was blood on his neck and his head. What would do that? It had to be some sort of accident. Something to do with the wash plant. Or a rock falling on him?"

McBeth, Sexton, and Lizotte waited for an answer.

"We're not exactly sure yet," Wolf said, deciding to hold back on the truth until they got these men separated and into an interrogation room.

"Where did you pick him up from?" Koling asked Lizotte. The big man leaned toward him. "Was he buried?"

Lizotte opened his mouth, his eyes darting from side to side. "I...I don't know. I just looked up and there he was, coming out of the scoop. I told you, Kev."

"Listen," Wolf said. "We'd like to talk to you each separately. We'll get to the bottom of this and find out exactly what happened, you can rest assured about that. My detectives inform me you've gathered some clothing and supplies from your trailers for the next few days." Wolf gestured to their bags slung over their shoulders.

"Few days?" McBeth asked with a scoff. "They said they needed to search the place for clues. They never said anything about a few days."

"We're not sure how long it will take, sir," Wolf said. "It could take one day, it could take a few. We're just worried about getting all the information we can so we can sort this out. That includes searching every bit of this property. And I'm sorry you cannot be present while we do so."

McBeth and Koling exchanged a glance and shook their heads. Sexton stared at Wolf.

"So, where are we going to stay?" McBeth asked, gesturing to his men. "Casey lives down in Dredge, so he can go home. But what about the rest of us? The only other places we have to stay are up in Jackson Hole, Wyoming."

Detective Yates cleared his throat. "We have a relationship with a local hotel in Rocky Points. They'll give you cut rates if you're staying there because of an investigation we're conducting."

Koling barked a laugh. "As if we have money for that right now. Discount or not."

McBeth looked at Wolf. "Things were tight enough here at the mine to begin with. I'm not sure that's an option for us.

We'll probably head back up to Jackson if it's all the same to you. The way I see it, we called you guys in because we found our man. Now you're kicking us out so you can look for evidence? You think that we killed him? Sorry, but that doesn't sound like something I'm interested in sticking around for. How about you guys?" He looked at his other three men. Koling and Sexton nodded agreement while Lizotte, the local new man, looked less sure how to act.

The truth was Wolf was hoping to get these men into the station right then and there for questioning, before they could come together and concoct a story. The other truth was he couldn't make them stick around, or make them talk.

They started walking away.

"Whoa, whoa." Wolf held up his hands, stopping them. "Listen. You're absolutely right. That certainly doesn't sound like a good deal for you guys. Listen, we're trying to get to the bottom of what happened to your friend, and we need your help. How about this? We'd really like to talk to you guys at the station down in Rocky Points. I was going to say tonight, but I know you've had a long day and the last thing you guys want to do now is sit in a stuffy room and talk to us. How about we put you up at the motel in Rocky Points. It's clean. Comfortable." He noted the filth caked onto their skin and hair and the permeating scent of men who hadn't cleaned themselves in days or weeks. "You guys can get a nice hot shower. Watch some television. And in the morning maybe we can chat down at the station."

Koling looked at McBeth. So did Sexton. They're leader clearly held the responsibility to make the decision now, and he looked to ponder it reluctantly.

"There's a good pizza joint right next to the motel," Rachette said. "Got craft beers."

Wolf shrugged, watching McBeth. McBeth flicked his eyes

to Wolf again, this time looking resigned. "What time tomorrow?"

"How's nine a.m.?"

McBeth looked at the others in turn. They shrugged, and then Koling nodded.

"And then what?" McBeth asked. "When do we come back here? You can't just put us up at the motel forever. I know you're not going to pay for that."

"Right now let's not worry about that," Wolf said. "We'll talk about that tomorrow."

McBeth looked at him, his face blank. "Okay, fine. So what do we do?"

"I'll call now and reserve three rooms at the Edelweiss Inn in Rocky Points. You three go there and get some rest. We'll see you tomorrow at nine so we can chat."

They broke away without another word and walked out into the rain. The three original Jackson Mine men climbed into three full-sized Ford trucks, two blue, one black. McBeth's was black.

The new guy, Lizotte, got into a Jeep CJ-7 with a hard top that looked less than weatherproof.

All four vehicles fired up their engines, and in a cacophony of sound moved out and up the road.

Wolf, Rachette, and Yates stood under the tent, watching the rain intensify.

"Dang," Rachette said. "Didn't know you were such a good salesman."

Wolf shrugged. "Get on the phone with Tammy and set up those rooms."

"And if there's no availability?" Rachette asked.

"Then put them in the Super 7 north of town."

"And if there're no rooms there?"

Wolf looked at him. "Then find somewhere else or we don't have anybody to talk to tomorrow."

"Yes, sir."

"Let's get in my cruiser and warm up," Yates said. "Do you guys use this?" He elbowed Rachette.

"What?"

Yates pulled out his key fob and pressed the center button. The lights on his SUV flashed and the engine roared to life. "There's remote-start on these babies."

Rachette fluttered his lips. "I invented remote-start."

"So you haven't seen it."

"No."

They walked to Yates's humming SUV. Rachette sat in the front with Yates. Wolf sat in back and unzipped his rain jacket, savoring the heat already pumping out of the vents as it wicked the moisture from his flannel.

The dash clock read 5:05 p.m. Outside Lorber and his crew had the body loaded and the forensic van rolled out of the lot. There were still a half dozen deputy vehicles parked and idling, warming their inhabitants. Wolf rubbed his hands together in front of the rear vent.

"I'll tell you what," Rachette said, turning to Yates, "if I wasn't married, I would be all over that chick."

"Who?" Yates asked.

"Deputy Cain."

"If you weren't married, she would be all over a restraining order on you."

"Says the guy who hasn't been laid in—"

"Let's watch the language," Wolf said.

"Yes, sir."

"Have you searched the trailers yet?"

"Not yet, sir," Yates said. "We'll get inside them once this blows over."

Outside, the rain lashed sideways. A web of whitewater runoff laced between the vehicles and down the sides of the mountains in every direction.

"But they each reported having guns inside their trailers. I had them each show me where they were when they got their overnight bags."

"How about Casey Lizotte?" Wolf asked.

"He says he does not own a firearm," Yates said.

"And he lives down in Dredge?"

"Yes, sir."

The rain began to slow, and just as quickly as the storm had hit, it was letting up. The last of the deluge swept down the valley, swallowing the view in blackness. The sun poked out, lighting a rainbow on the rear of the storm.

Deputies and forensics workers were popping open their doors, meandering back into action outside.

Daphne Pinnefield, Lorber's assistant ME, walked toward the trailers, carrying a kit bag over her shoulder. She donned latex gloves, popped open one of the doors and disappeared inside.

Wolf opened his door. Yates and Rachette climbed out, too.

"You headed to the ER?" Rachette asked.

Wolf gave him a thumbs up and headed up the incline to his SUV. "I'll see you guys later."

CHAPTER 3

WOLF DROVE west on Highway 641 for half an hour, his wipers on as yet more rain beat down. He bypassed Highway 74, which would have led him to the southern edge of Rocky Points and continued south toward Ashland instead.

The curves of the county road along Arapahoe Creek were tight and heavily wooded, eventually straightening out and dropping in elevation, spitting him out into the wide, flat Ashland Valley south of Williams Pass. The sage-covered landscape was doused in the shadow of the thirteen thousand-foot peaks as the late-afternoon sun dipped out of sight for the day.

Once he reached the Sluice-Byron County Hospital parking lot and shut off his engine, he took his time strolling into the brightly lit glass building, savoring the rich scents coming off the sage-dotted fields after the heavy rains.

Or was he stalling?

It had been over a year since he'd been inside this building, when he used to come over on lunch breaks to see Lauren. He wondered if he would recognize any of her friends and colleagues. If they would recognize him. And if so, so what?

As he stepped through the still wet parking lot, his mind shifted back to Deputy Cain's obsidian eyes.

He walked through the automatic sliding glass entrance, into the familiar smell of cleaning products that reminded him of Lauren's scent when she used to come home from long shifts.

Inside, Deputy Cain faced away from him, scratching the back of her head. She wore no rings.

"Hey, how's she doing?" he asked.

"Oh, hello, sir. They're just admitting her."

Patterson sat in a wheelchair, one of her legs propped up while a nurse removed her shoe.

Patterson gritted her teeth.

"You okay?" the nurse asked. Patterson closed her eyes and leaned her head back in response.

A female doctor Wolf recognized walked up to them. "Sheriff." She nodded.

"Hello, Dr. Johnson."

Deputy Cain introduced herself and they shook hands.

"I hear you fell."

Patterson put up a thumb, keeping her eyes closed.

"Looks like you hurt your arm, too." Dr. Johnson swiped at her tablet computer. "Did we treat you for that?"

"Nope, I went to the urgent care up in Rocky Points."

"When was that?"

"Two weeks ago."

"Well. That's not good." Dr. Johnson chuckled.

Patterson looked up at her, and Wolf felt his insides go cold.

Dr. Johnson swallowed. "Right. Well, Lisa's going to take you up to get some x-rays. And then we'll go from there. We'll try and get you taken care of as fast as we can so you can go home."

With Patterson wheeled away, Wolf turned to Deputy Cain. "Have you informed her husband yet?"

Cain nodded. "Heather called him on the way here. I mean, Chief Detective Patterson, sir."

He cracked a smile. "If you two are on familiar terms now that's no problem with me. Thank you for driving her in, by the way."

She nodded, her eyes deliberately straying from Wolf's.

He found his sheriff title made some people nervous. Or maybe being a satellite deputy she was unaccustomed to rubbing elbows with this many people in one day.

Wolf's phone vibrated in his pocket and he pulled it out.

Charlotte Munford-Rachette, Detective Rachette's wife and deputy within the department herself, was calling. With Undersheriff Wilson out of town for the last two days and due to be on vacation for the next seven, she'd been helping him with administrative work. He sent her call to voicemail.

"I don't think we've met before."

"That's right." She gave a tight smile.

"It's crazy, it's been a year since I took over and I'm still meeting people for the first time. It's a big county...for being one of the smallest counties." He smiled. "You must be new, am I right?"

She looked at him with a puzzled look and then skipped her gaze out the window.

Silence fell between them, and at that moment he got the distinct feeling she was not nervous, but, rather, that he was missing something else entirely.

His phone vibrated again. He pulled it out and read a text message from Charlotte.

You forgot to sign the 10D-104s. White needs them by tonight.

On cue, his phone rang, this time showing District Attorney White's name. Wolf walked to the windows and put the phone to his ear. "Hello, Sawyer."

"Hey, you never sent the 10D-104s."

"Yeah, I know. Sorry I forgot. Something came up here at the mine in Dredge."

"So I heard...but I still need those, and by the end of today. We talked about that. Without Wilson or Patterson here I need your signature. Can't use Charlotte."

"I know, I know." Wolf checked his watch. It was already 5:40. "I'm at County. I can be back in about 30 minutes."

"County? Why?"

He told White about Patterson.

"You kidding me? Woman needs to ride around in an ambulance." White sighed into Wolf's ear. "Well, I'm heading home. Katie will be waiting for you." Katie Hepler, one of White's assistants, had a daughter in second grade and a husband who worked for Chautauqua Valley Water. Wolf hated the thought of making her miss dinner with her family so he could sign three pieces of paper. Wilson wouldn't have forgotten to sign them. But Wilson was out of town, of course.

"I'll be there as soon as possible." He hung up and went back to the waiting area.

When he found Deputy Cain was gone, he walked to the automatic doors and stepped outside, catching sight of her just as she climbed into her Jeep Cherokee.

Wolf raised a hand to wave as she drove out of the lot, but dropped it. She was speaking into her phone, looking in the opposite direction.

As Cain accelerated south on Highway 734, Scott Reed, Patterson's husband, rolled into the parking lot from the opposite direction. Their five-year old son, Tommy spilled out of the back seat.

"What happened to Mommy?" he asked.

"Aw, she'll be okay," Wolf said. "She just messed up her ankle."

"Messed up? What does that mean?" Wolf couldn't help but smile. The kid was his mother's son.

"I'm not sure. That's what the doctors are figuring out right now."

Tommy nodded, clearly unsatisfied with the answer.

Scott scooped Lucas, the two-year old, out of the car seat in back while Tommy stepped in front of Wolf. "Does that mean... is she going to...have a different, other cast, but on her foot now?"

"I'm not sure. We'll have to see."

Another SBCSD cruiser drove into the parking lot and parked next to Scott. Deputy Hanson stepped out.

Scott gathered a shoulder bag out of the hatchback, turned and shook hands with Wolf. "How's she doing?" Scott looked dead tired. "Hey, Hanson."

Hanson stepped up. "Hey there. Hey kids. How's Patty doing?"

"She's doing okay," Wolf said. "Not sure if it's a break or a sprain. They're taking X-rays right now."

"Well, I guess it could be worse," Scott said. "Like that guy you found up at the mine."

Wolf nodded.

"What guy at the mine?" Tommy asked. "You found a guy up at the mine?"

"No," Scott said, rubbing Tommy's head. "I said a guy found gold up at the mine."

Tommy shot him an angry look. "But you said it could be worse."

"Let's go see Mommy. Come on."

"I have to head back to the office," Wolf said. "You guys go give your mom a hug."

Feeling mildly guilty for leaving, he extricated himself after saying goodbye and climbed into his SUV.

Heading north on highway 734, the lingering clouds overhead turned orange, slowly fading with every mile. With the fragrant air flowing through the vents and sparkling landscape outside, he felt more alive than he had in months.

He tried to remember the last time he'd spent so much time outside. It was like old times, back when he was a deputy, patrolling the far reaches of Sluice County.

In those days he used to daydream about what it would be like to be sheriff as the miles turned over on the odometer. His father had been sheriff before him, but in a simpler, smaller time. Now the department covered double the square miles, with ten times the number of deputies.

Once back in high school he'd done so well on a physics test that his teacher, Mr. Hogan, had recommended he pursue higher mathematics as well. Mr. Hogan had pulled some strings and landed Wolf a spot in an AP Calculus class. At the time Wolf had been thinking that would look good on college applications so he'd gone along with it.

After a semester of working his mind numb, Wolf had just managed to get a passing grade in the class, but he'd rarely ever felt on the same page as any of the other kids. He'd always been playing catch up with all the problem sets and homework. And during class? He'd always been that silent student in the corner of the room wondering just what the hell was going on, resolving to figure it out for himself later. Which he would then sometimes do, sometimes not, but always at the expense of having a social life or doing something else more enjoyable.

That's how being sheriff this time around was beginning to feel. He was working his fingers to the bone, or, more accurately, his backside through the cushion of his office chair, trying to keep this huge machine called the Sluice-Byron County Sheriff's Department running smoothly. And apparently paperwork was the grease for this machine. Mounds of it. They were more problem sets. More homework.

And here he was hauling ass back to the office because he'd missed something, playing catch up again. He could only be thankful this time around was almost over. Did he get a passing grade? Frankly, as long as he was back behind the desk as Chief Detective come the end of it all, which, according to MacLean was exactly what was going to happen, he didn't care.

He cracked the window, letting the cool breeze blow away his negative thoughts.

The echo of Patterson's two kids' voices still bouncing in his head, his thoughts shifted to his own son Jack and daughter-in-law Cassidy. And to little Ryan. Although Wolf was barely in his fifties now, becoming a grandfather to Ryan was a role he settled more easily than he could have imagined possible.

Wolf longed to see Ryan again, with his joyous smile and waddling walk. They were only a few dozen miles away, but there was a mountain range between them that took an hour and a half to drive up and around. It had been weeks since he'd last seen them.

He picked up his phone and dialed Jack's number.

The digital ringtone purred through the speakers of his cruiser.

"Hey Grumpa," Cassidy answered, using Ryan's name for Wolf.

"How are you?" Wolf asked.

"Great." There was clinking and noises of the kitchen in the background. "Just cooking up some dinner. How about you? Sounds like you're driving."

"Oh you know, keeping busy."

"How are your final weeks going as sheriff? Are you going to miss it?"

"It's going well. And I'm not sure I'll miss it that much."

"Really? Wow, Jack never told me that. I'm glad it's almost over for you, then."

Wolf listened to the sound of her cooking. Now in their early twenties, Jack and Cassidy were following in the footsteps of Wolf and his deceased ex-wife, Sarah, having a crack at married life and raising a kid at an early age. They were doing a better job than he'd done.

"Hey, speaking of not missing things that much," Cassidy said, "I was down in Aspen yesterday and went past Lauren's art gallery and saw it was closed up."

Even with all the therapeutic sessions with Dr. Hawkwood over the last two years, Wolf still felt a small shock pulse through his system at the mention of his former fiancée. He had not seen Lauren or her daughter Ella since that afternoon they'd ceremoniously buried Jet, and, symbolically, their prospects of ever getting back together. He often wondered what they both looked like now but hadn't gone so far as to drive down to Lauren's art storefront in Aspen to find out. He'd intentionally remained farther north in the Roaring Fork valley, closer to Carbondale, where Jack, Cassidy, and Ryan now lived.

"Anyway," Cassidy continued in her conspiratorial tone, "I heard from one of my friends there that she met some guy and moved out to San Francisco with him."

The phone rustled, and then the muffled sounds of conversation filtered through the speakers.

"Hey!" Jack's voice filled the cruiser.

Wolf blinked, the fog of Cassidy's news slowly lifting. "Hey, how's it going?"

"Good. You?"

"Not bad. Just working, you know. How's life at the station?"

Jack said nothing, and the kitchen noise disappeared in the background.

"You there?" Wolf asked.

"Yeah, sorry. I was just leaving the room. Hey, sorry about that. You know Cassidy when she has a piece of juicy gossip."

"It's okay," Wolf said. "It's..." why was he still talking? "It's okay. I said how's life at the station going?"

"Oh, it's great. Chief says I'm doing well. Had a car crash the other day I wish I hadn't seen, but...part of the job, you know?"

Wolf nodded. "Yeah. Definitely part of the job."

"It's wet out, so that's good. How about you? What's new in Points?"

"A lot, actually. Some mine workers outside of Dredge called in a DB. It's one of their own."

"Really. And it's foul play?"

"Looks like it." Wolf liked having these professional chats with his son, which were more frequent with Jack's career change. Jack had majored in geology in college, but once out had decided to serve as a firefighter. Either job choice would have been fine in Wolf's eyes, but he had to admit he was happy with Jack's decision.

And he was equally proud of how Jack had gotten the position. Wolf had known the fire chief personally over in Carbondale, but Jack had threatened to disown him if he said anything behind the scenes to help. Wolf had followed orders, and although it had been a long, grueling process to get hired, Jack had landed the job.

"Ryan, come here!" Jack's phone rustled. "It's Grandpa. You want to talk to him?"

Wolf smiled in anticipation, already hearing "Grumpa! Grumpa!" in the background.

"Okay, here he is." Jack put them on speaker phone.

"Grumpa!"

"Hi there, buddy! How are you doing today?"

He responded with a sentence about kicking something, and running fast? Wolf had no clue.

"Really? That sounds amazing."

Cassidy's voice called in the background. "He's says he's learning how to play soccer. He learned how to kick today and he's really fast."

"Oh, okay, wow! That's great. So he went straight from walking to playing soccer. That was quick."

"I love doggies!"

Wolf smiled. "Doggies are great. Maybe your mom and dad—"

"—Maybe not quite right now!" Cassidy yelled.

"Right, sorry," Wolf said. "So, hey, how about this weekend? You guys still coming over?"

The speaker phone cut off and Jack was back on. "Actually my shift is changing, so it's not looking good. I'd be dead asleep the whole time. How about next week? I'll be off then."

"Yeah, sure," Wolf said, hiding his disappointment.

Ryan was screaming in the background. "Okay, Ryan wants to talk to you again."

"Put him on."

Another stream of unintelligible syllables came through the speakers, but this time it was because of reception.

"Hello?"

A single blast of noise carrying Cassidy's voice came through the speakers and the call cut out. He was climbing the southern side of Williams Pass, which was never a good spot for cell reception. After another pop of static he slowed to the side of the road.

"You guys are breaking up," he said.

Cassidy's voice came through again. "...I just thought he'd want to know...she moved on...I don't care, he needs to hear it—"

The phone call ended.

He sat still in his seat, engine idling on the emergency pull-off halfway up the pass. A single vehicle coasted by.

He rolled down the windows and shut off the engine. Silence enveloped the car, save the faint whoosh of the vehicle as it turned out of sight in the sideview mirror.

He thought of Lauren and Ella out in San Francisco, a place he'd never been, living with a man he'd never met. She had moved on. Good for them, he thought. And he meant it.

There was a rustling in the trees off to the right and a deer climbed up the embankment to the edge of the road. The animal tiptoed into his lights and stopped.

Wolf put an elbow out the window.

"Hey," he said.

The deer turned its head, ears high. Its oil-drop eyes stared. Big ears flapped at swirling bugs.

They sat like that for a while—Wolf staring at the animal, the animal staring at an alien machine—until some synapse fired in its brain. The deer lurched a tentative step, then broke into a trot, and then sprinted across the road, up the steep cut on the other side. Underbrush crashed violently as the deer disappeared into the dark forest above.

Wolf checked the mirrors and leaned to check out the passenger window. When he found nothing out of the ordinary, he looked at himself in the rearview mirror. His eyes were bloodshot. The skin of his face seemed to be of a stranger's it was so pallid and wrinkled looking.

He fired up the engine, rolled up the windows, and drove.

CHAPTER 4

THE AIR IS hot foam in Wolf's throat. The grate of insects whining almost drowns out the voice in his earpiece.

"West, clear."

"South, clear."

"Wait a second," Wolf says. "I'm seeing some movement at the edge of the forest."

Encounters with Sri Lankan elephants are not uncommon in these parts of the country, but it seems strange that one would be testing the edge of the raised meadow so close to an idling CH-47 Chinook helicopter.

The movement is human, Wolf realizes, as a boy with a heavy backpack emerges from the jungle wall and into view in his scope.

"Shit. There's a kid walking out of the jungle."

Wolf tracks the child for a few more steps, then tracks back to the edge of the lush forest where two men are making shooing motions with their hands.

When Wolf tracks back to the kid the boy has disappeared, replaced by a girl with long clay-red hair and gangly limbs. The backpack is no longer earthen in color, but vibrant pink.

"Sir!" The voice in Wolf's earpiece makes him flinch. "Sir!"

A bird-sized insect jumps from the grass and lands on his face. The pinpoint claws of the bug dig in.

The image of the girl bobs. Wolf cracks open his other eye and sees she is nearing the helicopter. One of the women standing in line to board is pointing at her, looking just as startled by her appearance as Wolf.

She is carrying a bright red pencil in her hand, thumb poised over the tip like it's a detonator in her hand.

"Sir!"

Wolf squeezes the trigger and the gun kicks against his armpit.

Wolf snorted, choking on saliva. He sat up hard, slamming his skull against something hard.

"Shit." He clasped both arms around his head as pain reverberated in his head.

"Are you okay?" Heather Patterson was bent over him, holding a pair of crutches in one hand, reaching out for him with the other.

His eyes fluttered open and he got his bearings. With his arm he wiped a stream of drool off his face, feeling the imprint of carpet on his skin. A dagger of pain stabbed between two of his lower vertebrae as he sat up.

"Are you all right?" she asked.

"Yeah. What's up?"

Patterson backed away and gave him some room to crawl out from under the edge of his desk and off the floor. When he slithered out of the cloth sleeping bag she turned away. "Geez."

"Sorry," he said, grabbing his Levi's from his office chair and slipping them over his boxer shorts. "What time is it?"

"7:10."

Damn, it was late. He rubbed his eyes, scanning her foot. It was wrapped with a flexible bandage.

"What's the prognosis?"

"Sprained ankle," she said. "Nothing broken."

"That's good."

"Still hurts like hell. Why are you sleeping on the ground in your office?"

"Uh, just...catching up on emails and paperwork last night and it got late."

She popped her eyebrows and looked at the pile of paper inside the wire basket marked "inbox" and the overflow stack next to it. The layers of reports and forms looked denser and taller than the sedimentary layers up in Glenwood Canyon.

"I see you made some good headway."

He reached into a cabinet behind his desk, pulled out his overnight bag and dropped it onto his desk, sending a sheet fluttering to the floor.

Patterson picked it up and slapped it onto one of the stacks.

"Geez." She thumbed one of the piles. "Wilson's gone for two days and you're this swamped? Wait. These are from last month. I thought Wilson was going to have a talk with you about the RS-1oF reports."

"He did." Wolf dug through his overnight bag, finding the tube of toothpaste and toothbrush. When he looked up, Patterson had her mouth open and her eyebrows in the W-T-F position.

"I'm getting to them. And those are dated after the twentieth of last month, so they're not late."

She opened her mouth to say something, then closed it.

"What?" He pulled out his toothbrush and toothpaste.

"What exactly did Wilson tell you about the reports?"

Wolf screwed his face up in thought. The conversation with his undersheriff about various paperwork system implementations was nothing more than a garbled voicemail that replayed in his mind—most of the good stuff lost due to poor reception. "I remember something about the RS-10F reports, but the specifics are eluding me right now."

She nodded slowly, patiently. "It's just that waiting so long to do these specific reports is causing some backup in other departments."

"Oh." He looked past her, through the windows to the squad room. "Like what kind of backups, again?"

"Like, when you're late on these reports—"

"But I'm not late."

"Okay, yes. But, when you're, I should say, pushing the deadline limits of the reports, that pushes the deadline limits of everyone below you for the things they need to do that rely on the completion of these reports. Does that make sense?"

"So the deadline is really for the last person in the chain," Wolf said. "So shouldn't my deadline be earlier?"

"That was precisely what Wilson was supposed to talk to you about. Pushing up your deadline on these. Right now there are four or five days a month where people are scrambling late nights to catch up."

He stared at the reports. "Okay. Got it. I'll get those done ASAP, thanks."

She nodded. "Good. And I'll send you an email with the updated deadline."

"Great. Thanks."

He pulled out his towel and tucked it under his arm. Patterson remained in front of him.

"What's up?" he asked.

"We never got to talk about it yesterday," she said. "You said that they didn't like the budget?"

Wolf put down his stuff. "Oh yeah." He turned around and stretched his arms overhead. The exterior window blinds were drawn up, letting in subdued light that reflected off the western wall of the valley. A white strip of fog clung to the pines, tendrils swirling off of them like spiderwebs in a breeze. "They balked at the Deputy Leadership Training Fund."

"Helms balked at it." Patterson said. It wasn't a question.

Wolf turned around and nodded.

"The bastard," she said. "He's in town two years and he thinks he's king shit of Rocky Points. Why? Because he's the county accountant?"

"Treasurer."

"Asshole."

Wolf turned back to the window again and gazed outside, thinking of their push to train many of their staff. Back in March Wolf had witnessed the annual performance reviews for the first time sitting in the Sheriff's office, which had given him access to all the results throughout the entire department.

Every year since the SBCSD resided in the new, larger building, every March something called a Three-sixty Peer Review had been conducted within the department. *Three-sixty*, meaning three-hundred-sixty degrees, meant department heads rated their subordinates on performance, while staff rated their managers at the same time.

This time around the results had been anything but impressive. The data showed over ninety percent of deputies were suboptimal at their jobs according to managers, and eighty percent of managers were failing abysmally at their own jobs according to their subordinates.

Sheriff Will MacLean had found the same numbers being reported over his last two years in office, but he'd written it off as fluke anomalies, ignoring the stats. *Bullshit surveys*, as Wilson had said he'd called them.

When Wolf had shown curiosity at the latest review results, Undersheriff Wilson had pointed out the drop-in performance closely matched a re-shuffling of much of the staff positions two and a half years ago. MacLean had put seven new managers into positions they'd never had before, and apparently now everyone in the entire department sucked at their jobs.

If Wolf's time in the Army had shown him one thing, it was that if you didn't trust the man next to you in battle, you might as well count yourself dead. As far as he was concerned, these numbers showed the department was a sinking ship.

Wolf sought Patterson's and Wilson's help finding the solution to the problem, and after a couple months of deliberation and outside counsel from Dr. Hawkwood and other experts, they came to the conclusion that leadership training across the board for managers and high-level staff was desperately needed.

The decision did not come lightly, as that would mean Wolf, Wilson, and Patterson would be among those taking classes. But if it meant the place's morale lifted, if everyone trusted each other even half as much as they did now, Wolf counted it well worth the effort.

Or, at least, that was the plan.

Wolf turned around to find a ponderous Patterson.

"What's Helms's problem?" she asked. "You showed them the peer review results, right?"

"Yeah. But ..."

"But what?"

"I might have pissed him off when I mentioned his roof repair budget was a hundred grand over, and that the construction firm he approved was suspiciously close to his family."

"You said that?" She exhaled. "I thought our plan was for you to go in with your nice face."

"He's an asshole, what can I say?"

Patterson hopped to the couch and sat heavily. "If we don't get anything approved by the council before MacLean's back, you know he's just going to take fifty-grand and upgrade his boat house up on Cold Lake."

Wolf nodded. "That's what they said. They want to get everything into the state in the next week, before MacLean gets back. Apparently we push back less than he used to."

"Really."

Wolf nodded.

"You know," Patterson said, "Margaret says he's changed. Apparently he's all about fruit and vegetable juice now. And enemas or something? She says he's calm."

Wolf had heard the rumors and the vague explanation of MacLean's recovery from the single phone conversation he'd had with the man that spring. "I'm not sure people like MacLean change. He beat advanced-stage pancreatic cancer. He'll be coming in with more cocksure swagger than ever."

"Who knows? Maybe he'll be all for this training, too?"

Wolf raised his eyebrows. "I wouldn't count on it. It would be tantamount to admitting he made a mistake with his hiring two years ago."

She exhaled. "Yeah. You're right. So...okay, tell the council we'll start pushing back on other things unless they approve it. We need that in place, it's an abomination that we're not offering more support to our—"

Wolf held up a hand. "I know, I know. Listen, I think I misspoke...they're on board with the fund, but the stipulation is that we give them an itemized list of what exactly the fund means, what's going to be included, which positions get what training. And, of course, the cost of everything itemized out 'to the last class' as Helms put it. He wants a spreadsheet."

Patterson upturned a hand. "Well, why didn't you say that? That's simple enough. We can get quotes from Hawkwood's friend who does the training. We can check with another company or two. You just set up a spreadsheet, maybe type up a page report, no problem." She snapped her fingers.

Wolf eyed the stacks of paper. Had they grown since they'd started talking?

She read his face. "When does the council need this itemized report by?"

"And the spreadsheet."

"Right. And the spreadsheet."

"By the end of today."

"Geez." She looked at the papers on his desk. "Okay. And when's Wilson coming back again?"

"Five more days."

"Five?" she asked, exasperated. "What's he doing down there in Denver, anyway?"

"His father's not doing too well."

"Oh. Oh yeah, right."

"The Denver PD offered him a job."

She raised her eyebrows. "Are you serious?"

"Assistant Chief."

"Wow."

"He turned it down." Wolf shrugged. "Maybe he'll change his mind and won't come back."

She stood with her mouth open.

"I'm kidding."

She sighed and thumbed through the papers on his desk, this time looking more carefully at individual layers in the stacks. Quickly, she began reconfiguring chunks of the papers into various piles. When she was done she held up a four-inch thick pile and flapped it at him. "Okay, listen. I'll take these to take some stress off you and to make Charlotte and her staff a lot happier. The rest of this can wait a week for Wilson." She studied the ream of paper in her hand. "Shouldn't take me more than an hour at the most."

"Thank you, Heather." Wolf wondered how long it would have taken him. Probably the same hour of work, but spread out over a dozen hours, spread over five days. "When's Lorber ready with his preliminary on Chris Oakley?"

"He's finishing it now. We're headed down to go over it with him at seven-thirty. The three men from Jackson Mine are coming. Should be enough time to debrief Lorber and be prepared for the interviews." She flapped the papers again. "And you know it's not that tough. You could set aside thirty minutes every morning, where you only do paperwork. That way it never piles up."

"I'll keep that in mind."

"I'm sure you will." She fumbled with the crutch holding the stack of paper. The other hand with the cast barely held onto the other crutch to begin with. She seemed to realize she was in a bind.

"Here, let me at least carry those."

She waved him aside. "Just open the door."

He rushed around the other side of the desk and opened it wide.

"You might want to get some ice for that head."

"I owe you one."

"You owe me more than one." She teetered out of the doorway and into the bustling squad room.

"I owe you seven."

"Hundred," she said.

Wolf grabbed his stuff and headed downstairs for the showers.

47

HEATHER PATTERSON HOBBLED down to her office, managing to avoid speaking to anyone, which was a feat given the number of deputies in the squad room. She shut the door, savoring the silence.

She dropped the paperwork on her desk on the way to her chair, eyeing the beauty of the early summer day outside through the open blinds. It was tough to appreciate with her brain focusing on the throbbing pain in her ankle.

She sat down, put her crutches on the ground along the back wall, rolled her chair into position, and gingerly put her ankle up on the windowsill.

"Ah."

The blood flowed up her leg and some discomfort evaporated, but after a short time the pressure of her skin against the sill sharpened to a knife's edge. Either the angle or the height was all wrong. She tried using the top of her desk, which wasn't right either, so she moved to the loveseat, her foot resting on the cushioned surface. *Ahhh.*

Damn it. The paperwork was still sitting on the desk.

Two sharp knocks rattled the door.

"Yeah!"

Rachette popped his head in. "You ready to go down to Lorber?"

She eyed her watch. "Already?"

"He sent an email saying he was ready. Didn't you see it?"

She sighed and got up, grabbing her crutches. A deep ache began to bloom in her ankle, and it felt like she'd just pushed her foot into a hornet's nest.

"How's it feeling?" Rachette watched her, sipping his coffee.

"Not bad."

"You're a terrible liar."

He gave her a wide berth as she hobbled through the doorway, into the hallway, and down to the elevator bank.

"Take any painkillers?" he asked.

"Nope."

"Why not? That's the best part of getting hurt."

"Getting hooked on meds?"

"Yeah."

They stepped into the elevator and Patterson went to the corner and leaned against it.

"I guess TJ hit a home run last week," Rachette said.

"Really? Oh yeah, and you were doing the training. Sorry you didn't get to see it."

Rachette smiled to himself. "Charlotte says he dribbled it off the tee about forty feet and then proceeded to run around the bases while the other kids threw the ball a hundred times."

Patterson smiled despite the ache in her foot.

"So, when are you going to get Tommy into baseball?" Rachette asked.

"He's not into it."

"It's not a matter if they're into it or not. You just put them into it."

"Is that how it works?" Patterson asked. The truth was she

and Scott had tried to play in the backyard plenty of times and the kid wasn't interested. Sometimes she wished she could be in the stands watching her son play, other times she couldn't care less. This was one of those times.

"It's how it works in my house."

"I don't doubt it," she said.

"What's that supposed to mean?"

"It means let's be quiet. My leg hurts."

"I thought you said it wasn't bad."

She said nothing.

"Why aren't you home resting?"

"Why are you still talking?" The elevator stopped and opened, and they stepped out into the cool recesses of the basement, the domain of Lorber and his forensics department.

The air chilled her to the bone, smelling deeply of embalming fluid.

Rachette pulled out a pocket tub of Vicks VapoRub and put some under his nose. He held it out.

"No thanks."

"Sicko."

The sight and smell of dead bodies didn't bother her too much when they were in the morgue. It was a different story out in the field, with varying degrees of decay, heat, and other factors.

With every step, her crutches gripped the glistening terrazzo floor with a tiny squeal. Her armpits ached from the constant pressure. She probably needed to wrap a towel around the cushioned part of each crutch with the amount of time she'd be spending on her feet for this investigation.

Turning the corner to Lorber's room, she slowed when she saw Wolf was inside already.

Rachette moved on ahead of her inside. "How's it going, gentlemen?"

"Hey Patty," Lorber said. "How's the ankle? Heard it's a bad sprain."

"It's a regular sprain. It's okay."

"Good. Glad to hear it's not another break."

She nodded at Wolf, who gave her a curt nod in return, giving her the impression he was avoiding her gaze. He looked freshly showered and his dispenser-soap scent mixed with the chemical aura of the room.

She had assumed the report and spreadsheet would have been Wolf's first priority. Apparently she was wrong.

She blinked out of her thoughts and turned to Lorber. "So, what do you have so far?"

Lorber put on his glasses, magnifying tired-looking eyes. His hair, usually worn down to the middle of his back, was wrapped on top of his head, making his medical skull cap look like a pregnant turban.

The ME approached the illuminated body on the metal table at the center of the room, wasting no time lowering the sheet to breast level.

Sasquatch had nothing on body hair compared to the man known as Chris Oakley. His chest was a black bathmat, his shoulders wearing toupees. His scalp was a matted mess, but Lorber had cleaned him of dirt and mud.

Lorber picked a pen out of his lab coat pocket and pointed under Oakley's chin. "We have an entrance wound right here, and an exit wound at the top of the head. No other injuries, other than one here on his arm, made post-mortem by one of the teeth of the front-end loader, presumably made when he was scooped up by Casey Lizotte."

Patterson leaned forward, hopping nearer to get a good look. A deep slice had opened up the man's triceps, revealing striated muscle beneath a thin layer of fat. Lorber had shaved around the clean hole piercing the top of Oakley's head.

"You can tell the entrance wound is here at the chin because of the spidering due to the gas outburst from the barrel," he said.

"Was there any GSR found on his hands?" Wolf asked.

"None."

"So no suicide," Rachette said.

"No suicide," Lorber said.

"Can you tell what caliber it was?" Patterson asked.

"Powerful enough to be a through and through, tunneling the tongue, sinus cavities, up into the brain tissue and out the top of the skull."

"They all had forty-fives, didn't they?" Patterson asked.

"That's right," Rachette said. "All Glock 21s. Must have been a special at Kmart the day they got 'em."

Lorber took off his glasses and rubbed his nose as he walked toward four plastic bags sitting on the counter. Each held one of the guns in question.

"I've swabbed the gunshot residue from his chin and we'll do a test, trying to match the signature coming out of each of these weapons. But these were all loaded with the same ammo, full to the brim—full magazines and one in the chamber, and all of them looked like they're meticulously cleaned. No carbon residue, suggesting they haven't been fired recently."

"Or somebody fired the shot through his head, then cleaned his gun and put another bullet into the magazine," Rachette said. "To make it look like it wasn't fired."

Lorber shrugged, conceding the point.

"What kind of ammo did we find on the property?" Patterson asked Rachette.

Rachette shook his head. He pulled the small notebook out of his back pocket and started flipping pages, again with that air of looking at a book he'd never seen before and someone else was responsible for the illegible chicken scratch within. He found something and pointed a stubby finger. "Here. We found boxes of forty-five 230 grain full metal jackets. Same brand—Federal Bear Silvers. Like Lorber said, looks like they all used the same ammo."

Patterson's foot throbbed, feeling like it was a water balloon about to burst. "How long is it going to be for the GSR tests?" she asked.

"That'll take some time." Lorber said, his eyelids looking even heavier now. "At least a couple days."

"What else?" Wolf asked.

"Daphne has Oakley's phone, which we found in his pants pocket," Lorber said, gesturing to a room on the other side of the hallway. He walked over and knocked on the open door.

"Yep?" Daphne answered.

"Sheriff is here with his detectives, wanting to know about the phone," Lorber said.

"How are you, Daphne?" Wolf asked, leading the group as they crowded into the office.

Daphne turned around in her chair. Her shoulder-length hair was dyed a deep bruise-purple this week and pulled back into such a tight ponytail the shine of her hair was reflected in the computer screen in front of her. "I'm great. Hey, Patty, heard about your ankle."

She turned around and clicked her mouse, apparently done with the sympathies. "We have a lot of text messages between Chris Oakley and the other miners—Scott Sexton, Eagle McBeth, and Kevin Koling. Mostly bathroom humor."

"That's important stuff," Rachette said.

Daphne cocked her head a few degrees, her hand coming off the computer mouse.

"Sorry," Rachette said. "Continue."

"Thanks. There're some more intimate texts between him

and his girlfriend, a woman he refers to as M.E., ME. A lot of scheduling sex, what I'm going to do to you next time we have sex, here's my freshly shaved sex organ."

Lorber cleared his throat. "Daphne, let's..."

"Move on? Okay. Thursday, the day before he was killed, he had an exchange with Kevin Koling." She clicked the mouse, revealing the speech bubbles of a text conversation on her screen.

Oakley: *If we don't start getting gold in the box I'm bouncing. Fuck him.*

Koling: *I don't blame you.*

Oakley: *You're not bouncing too?*

Koling: *And go back to what?'*

Oakley: *Who cares? Working at Burger King up in Jackson will pay more. Screw this.*

She clicked and another conversation popped up on screen.

"Here's another very interesting exchange. Of course, I'm not the investigator here. But take a look at this."

Spritz: *Hey bro, I saw Hammy and ME making out last night at the bar.*

Oakley *What???*

Spritz: *Yep. Just thought I'd give you a heads up.*

Oakley: *You sure?*

Spritz: *100% I wouldn't make that shit up.*

Oakley *Okay. Thanks.*

Spritz: *Yep.*

"Who's M-E?" Patterson asked.

"The phone number is registered to a woman named Mary Ellen Dimitri. It's a three-oh-three area code. Her current address is in Dredge."

"And what about Spritz?" Rachette asked.

"Not sure. It's a prepaid phone. No name associated."

Patterson looked at Rachette. "You writing this down?"

He upturned his hands. "You're usually on top of this."

She flicked her eyes to her cast, and then the other hand holding the crutch.

"Oh, yeah." Rachette pulled out his notebook again and scribbled furiously.

Daphne pulled up another set of texts. "Here's another one. Oakley's final, between him and Mary Ellen Dimitri, or ME."

Oakley: *Hey, come up and visit tonight? I'm lonely.*

ME: *I'm so tired. Long shift today.*

Oakley: *I'll pamper you. Give you a massage. The way you like it.*

ME: *Okay. Fine. I'll see you after I'm cut.*

"And that's it," Daphne said.

"Wait, so Spritz told Oakley his woman was cheating on him, and then Oakley lures her up there to come visit?"

"Looks like it to me," Daphne said.

"Anything else?" Wolf asked.

"No more messages after that. Really, nothing of any importance I can see before Thursday, but I'll put a couple weeks-worth in the full report."

"When exactly did Oakley's phone die?" Wolf asked. "Did you figure that out?"

Daphne clicked the keyboard. "The phone stopped transmitting to the towers Saturday morning at 3:38 a.m."

Patterson cleared her throat. "Are you sure that's when it stopped transmitting, or when it was turned off?"

Daphne cocked her head toward Patterson this time, her hands dropping to her lap. "I'm sure. Power drained at 7:42 a.m. Stopped transmitting four hours earlier."

"Aha. I see. Thanks."

"So, are we saying that's when he was buried?" Rachette asked. "At 3:38?"

Daphne nodded. "That's what I'm saying. If he was buried

at 3:38 a.m., he would have stopped transmitting to the towers, even though his phone was still on, until 7:42 the next morning when the battery ran down and it stopped supplying power to the antenna."

"So, that's when our killer buried him," Rachette said. "Could have been killed any time before that point, though."

Daphne shrugged. "That's your department."

Patterson's ankle started getting that pinprick feeling again. She was going to have to elevate this thing soon. Maybe she did need some painkillers.

Everyone was looking at her. She realized they had said something.

"What?"

"I asked you if any of them heard anything," Wolf said.

"About what?"

"Heard any gunshots," Rachette said. "Friday night. Saturday morning."

"No, sir. Well, honestly I don't think we've gotten around to asking them that yet. Unless Rachette has?"

Rachette shook his head. "No, ma'am."

"Let's put that on the list for the interrogations," Wolf said.

Rachette scribbled again.

"And how about a phone number for Chris Oakley's family?" Patterson asked. "I'd like to get that phone call out of the way as soon as possible."

Daphne tapped and scrolled on the phone. "I've got a Pa. P-A. That's it. Could be his dad.""

"Good enough for now," Patterson said.

Daphne read it out and Rachette wrote it down.

"So what's next?" Wolf asked.

"Well," Lorber stretched his arms overhead, his hands touching the ceiling. "If you don't mind, I'd like my team to rest a bit. It's been a long night for Daphne and the rest of the staff."

"Of course," Wolf said. "That goes for you, too."

Lorber gestured at Patterson's leg. "You should get home and rest, too. What are you doing here?"

"I'll be okay." She blushed at the unintentionally defiant snap in her voice.

Lorber nodded, smiling at her. "After a few hours rest we'll get started on the GSR match test with these weapons, see if they match with the residue on Oakley's chin."

Wolf slapped the ME on the shoulder and walked out of the room. "Let us know if anything else comes up. Rachette, Patterson, my office, please."

Wolf walked quickly down the hall, Rachette on his heels. Patterson struggled to keep up, taking long strides with the crutches. At the end of the hall, they had pushed the button and were already climbing in the elevator when she was only halfway there.

Wolf held open the elevator door and waited. Her left crutch was less stable, as she had to grab it with her cast hand, and it flipped sideways out of her grip. Just barely, she caught herself from falling over when the crutch slipped out of her armpit and slammed to the ground with a loud smack.

She stopped and backed up, having to hop to get it, then slowly lost her balance and fell onto her backside, like she'd just tried a pistol-squat and failed.

"Damn it," she said under her breath.

Wolf was quick to her side, taking the crutch and hooking a hand under her armpit. "You need to go home and rest."

She popped to her feet and snatched the crutch. "You need to worry about your own job and not me."

Wolf stared at her. She stared back, punctuating the moment with a cock of her eyebrow.

Wolf walked away toward the elevator, where Rachette still held the door open. They all rode up to the third floor in silence,

Rachette burying his nose in his phone and Wolf staring through the elevator door. When they reached the third floor, Rachette and Wolf walked on without her. She took her time, making sure all three points of contact hit the floor solidly as she followed.

Wolf stopped short, gesturing to her office door. "We'll go in here so you don't have to walk so far."

"Suit yourself," she said.

When she walked into the office Wolf and Rachette had already taken seats at her desk.

She hesitated, yearning for the soft cushions of the couch to elevate her foot.

Wolf must have read her. "Yeah, take a seat there." He twisted the chair to face the couch and Rachette followed suit.

She decided not to argue and sat down, put up her foot, and sighed as the pain, first magnified, swelling, and then ebbed slowly away as the blood pressure eased.

"I'm taking over this investigation," Wolf said.

The words hit her like a slap to the face. "Why?"

"Because you're hurt, Patterson, in case you hadn't noticed."

"I'm hurt, but it's my job to run this investigation. I'm the chief detective."

"I know that, but right now you're injured and I'm taking over. I'm the sheriff, and it's my call."

She went silent.

"Rachette, why don't you follow up on trying to get hold of Oakley's parents, okay?"

"Yes, sir." Rachette left and shut the door.

Patterson's eyes locked on the window, staring outside in defiance. When she finally flicked her eyes to Wolf she saw a gentle gaze that doused some of the fire within her.

Averting his eyes again, she sighed and scratched her forehead. Who was she kidding? She was hurt. Standing in Lorber's office for just a few minutes had almost done her in.

"Heather."

"What?"

"I was hoping you might be able to do something else for me."

She looked at him. "Okay?"

"Could you please create that spreadsheet and report for the council?"

She looked at the stack of papers she'd already taken off his desk, now conspicuously perched on her own, and the anger came back white-hot. "What am I, your secretary? What is it? The woman in the room can't fight through the pain like a man? I can't man up and get the job done, so you decide to take me off patrol and stick me behind a desk? You and Rachette have been hurt on the job before and you've continued to do your job. You didn't tap out."

"I'm not saying that. I'm not asking you to tap out."

"Damn right you're not. I'm your Chief Detective. I'm in charge of your detective squad and I'm running this investigation."

Wolf flexed and squeezed both hands a few times. "I need you to do something much more important than run this investigation."

"Ha! Your paperwork?"

"I need you to secure the future of this department." Wolf's voice rose above hers. He leaned forward and straightened to his feet. "The future of this department lies in that stupid spreadsheet and in that stupid report. And if it hasn't already been made clear, I can't do it!"

She recoiled at the volume of his voice.

"I can't even put a title on a damned spreadsheet without

messing the whole piece of shit thing up. And they need it by the end of today, or else, like you said, MacLean's going to come back in here and unravel everything we're aiming to do. Because of my incompetence."

"You're not incompetent, it's just—"

"I'm not done!"

"Ooo-kay."

"And you're not my secretary, damn it. You're the best person I've got!"

She blinked. "Okay."

Wolf walked toward the window, his hands rubbing the back of his neck.

"We've got twenty-eight deputies," he continued in a low voice, "some younger than my own son, out there carrying guns, tasked with a next to impossible job, and we've figured out that they can't trust each other. So what are we going to do about it?" He turned to Patterson. "Well, I'll tell you what I'm going to do. I'm the sheriff, at least for now, and I'm putting my best woman on the job. I'm not screwing this up as my final act in office. Okay?"

The sound was sucked out of the room as Wolf stared at her.

"Okay," she said.

"Good." He quickly straightened the chairs. "And I want you to work from home," he said. "Seriously, think about how comfortable you would be in bed right now with your foot propped on a nice soft pillow, a laptop on your lap."

She dared visualize that for only a second. Maybe a hot tea sitting next to her on the nightstand, Scott bringing her lunch in bed. "No, it's okay," she said. "Really. I'm fine here."

She silently screamed at herself, willing Wolf to make it an order for her to leave.

It almost looked like he was going to do it. He looked at her foot, her eyes again. "Okay, fine." He walked to the door and left. The door clicked shut behind him.

She stared after him, letting her mind slip back to a year ago, back to a conversation she'd had with Wolf on his front lawn. It had been during the barbecue for MacLean's going away and it looked like Wolf was about to be in office for a long time. He'd made it clear that day he didn't want the job. That he was on the lookout for somebody to train to take his place.

And then he'd looked at her strangely. Like, as in, he'd meant her.

Of course, she'd been mightily drunk that night. The drunkest in a number of years, if that next day hangover was any indication.

But she'd heard what she'd heard.

She straightened upright as a thought hit her. Was MacLean really coming back? What if he wasn't? Then what?

And how about Wilson? Was he really taking the job down in Denver? MacLean retiring and Wilson leaving would explain Wolf's current state of mind. Did he know he was going to be sheriff for the long haul and it was stressing him out? It would be just like him to keep that piece of information to himself, letting it eat away at him.

She tilted her head, the new thought physically knocking her skull sideways.

Then who was going to be Undersheriff?

Undersheriff Patterson. Now there was a training ground for sheriff if there ever was one.

She shook her head, flinging the thoughts out of her brain. None of that made any real sense. MacLean was coming back as sheriff. Wilson was coming back as undersheriff. She was moving back to detective and Wolf was moving back into his position as Chief.

The truth was Wolf was just a basket case when it came to paperwork—office work in general, if she was being honest—and it was stressing him out. And that was that.

She looked back at the mounds of paper on her desk. Dang it. She should have told Wolf to hand those over on his way out.

CHAPTER 6

WOLF WALKED into the interrogation room at 9:08 a.m., a few minutes late by design, where Eagle McBeth sat alone.

"Mr. McBeth. I'm Sheriff David Wolf, I'll be joining this interview today."

McBeth stood and shook Wolf's hand, and it was like shaking a lumpy sandpaper glove.

Rachette opened the door and came inside, sliding a cup of coffee in front of McBeth. "Here you go, sir."

"Thank you."

Rachette sat down, putting his notebook on the table in front of him.

McBeth sat comfortably, sipping his coffee. He had a chest-length beard and wore a trucker hat. His outfit said he hadn't gotten to the laundromat in the last few weeks. Mud caked one arm of his flannel, grease streaked his jeans, and his Pabst Blue Ribbon hat was thoroughly sweated through.

McBeth seemed to read Wolf's eyes and became a bit self-conscious. His hand went to his muddied sleeve, sending a few flakes onto the floor.

"Sorry," McBeth said. "Shoot. Getting dirt all over the

place. This is pretty much as clean as it gets in my wardrobe these days."

"It's okay," Wolf said with a smile.

"Got a nice shower last night, though," McBeth said.

"That's good."

As McBeth busied himself with one shirt sleeve, the other slid up his forearm, revealing an angry, circular scar climbing up his wrist and out of sight beneath the fabric. He quickly covered the exposed skin and dropped his arm to his side.

"Thanks for coming," Wolf said. "So the place was okay last night, was it?"

"Yeah. Wasn't bad."

"Good. And we appreciate you coming in today." Wolf tapped the digital recorder in the center of the table. "We'll be recording this conversation to aid our investigation."

McBeth looked between them. "I thought about bringing a lawyer."

Wolf said nothing.

"But I have nothing to hide."

Wolf nodded. "Good. Then you're doing everyone a service. Most of all, Chris."

"So what happened to him?" McBeth asked.

Wolf let the question hang for a second, trying to read the man's tone. He looked genuinely curious. "You don't know?"

"Well, no. I saw blood on the top of his head when Casey dropped him on the hopper grate. There was some on his neck, too. What was it? An accident?"

"That was from a gunshot," Wolf said. "The bullet entered just under his chin, and exited out the top of his head."

McBeth looked at Wolf. "What are you saying? Suicide?"

"There was no gunshot residue on his hands," Rachette said. "So we know he didn't shoot himself."

McBeth stared a thousand miles beyond the wall.

Rachette waved a hand in front of him. "You there?"

McBeth blinked, shaking his head. "He was murdered?"

Wolf nodded. "That's what we think."

"Who did it?"

Wolf smiled. "Good question. That's what we're trying to figure out."

McBeth took a quivering breath. "Shit. I guess I probably should have gotten a lawyer. Do I need a lawyer?"

Wolf shrugged. "That depends. Did you kill him?"

"No. Of course not."

"Then..." Wolf shrugged, as if that gesture told the man everything he needed to know. "Of course, you have the right to have an attorney present. Anything you say can and will be used against you in the courts. And we are recording this conversation right now, as we mentioned before."

Wolf held his breath, his eyes on McBeth. He seemed to really consider it now.

"I don't have anything to hide. I didn't kill him. You can ask me any question you want." He sat back with arms folded over his barrel chest. One hand stroked his beard, the non-scarred one, Wolf noted. That scar was tucked away safely in his armpit.

"You, Mr. Sexton, Mr. Koling, and Chris are from Jackson Hole, Wyoming," Wolf said. "Correct?"

"Yeah."

"And Casey Lizotte is from Dredge."

"That's right."

"Excluding Lizotte for the moment, how long have you original four been mining in Colorado?"

"This is our third season," McBeth said.

"And why down here?" Rachette said. "Why not up in Wyoming? There no gold up there?"

McBeth inhaled deeply and let it out with a sigh, as if he'd answered the question a thousand times before. "We looked for a good claim in Wyoming, Montana, and Idaho first. We couldn't find anything promising. I had an in with a family friend down here who knew of a claim. So..." He shrugged. "Just came down here. We found a little bit of gold right at the beginning. Seemed like some promising ground. We've been here ever since."

"And how is the ground treating you now?" Wolf asked.

"Not bad. I mean, not good, not at the moment. But that's just how gold mining goes. The next motherlode is under the next scoop of dirt, and then you're making good money. It just takes getting it out of the ground. We know it's there from the first season. I have faith we'll get on it again."

"Is it stressful?" Wolf asked.

McBeth scraped at a nail. "I've got a lot of bills. I'm paying for fuel and rental of all the equipment. I lease that wash plant for a ton of money. I've incurred a lot of debt over the last two years."

"Costs are high," Rachette said.

"Yeah."

"And so is the pressure to find a lot of gold, I bet."

McBeth nodded.

"Was Chris Oakley upset about the current state of the mine, and how it was being run right now, and how you guys were not finding gold?" Wolf asked.

McBeth snorted a laugh. "How did you guys know that?"

"We found some text messages on his phone between him and a friend."

"What friend?"

Wolf said nothing.

McBeth pinched the bridge of his nose. "Yeah, he was pretty pissed off. They all are. I know it. Nobody likes working for free for weeks on end, but that's how it is. I got to pay the bills. And if we want to keep running the machines, I got to pay those bills first and then pay the men next. Without machines, there is no gold."

"I understand," Wolf said. "Why don't you tell me about last Friday night. What happened with that argument you spoke of?"

McBeth looked up at the ceiling. "We were up drinking. We usually do that every Friday night. Chris was pretty upset. He'd gotten a text message from a friend down in town."

"Is this the message from Spritz we found on his phone?" Rachette asked.

"Yeah. That's it. Spritz had seen Oakley's girl, Mary Ellen Dimitri, making out with another guy in town."

"The message refers to somebody named Hammy," Rachette said. "Who's that?"

"Rick Hammes," McBeth said.

Rachette scribbled the name down. "You know him?"

"Yeah. Big dude, like big as Oakley, but scarier. Has a bunch of satanic tats all over his body. Crazy as shit. He shot at a truck full of teenagers who were making too much noise a couple years ago and served time. He just got out on parole over the winter and he's back in town...shit, you guys probably know his story."

Wolf did not know, and judging by Rachette's furious note-taking, neither did he. It was the first Wolf had ever heard the name.

"Let's go back to Chris Friday night. What happened next?" Wolf asked. "After he got the message from Spritz telling him about Rick Hammes and his girlfriend making out?"

"He was pissed. Got all worked up about it. Talking about how he was going to kick his ass. This and that."

"Hammy's ass," Rachette said.

"Right."

"When did Oakley get this text?" Wolf asked, already knowing the answer was sometime between three and four p.m.

"I don't know. After we finished for the day. Like, 3:30 or something?"

"And did Oakley ever leave the premises after getting that text?"

"No. He was just...you know, commiserating with us. Tilting back a few. He sent off a text for Mary Ellen to come visit him. And he was talking about how he was going to... confront her... about it."

"Confront her?" Rachette asked.

"Yeah."

"Meaning?"

"I really don't know. But, yeah, I was a little concerned, if that's what you're wondering. Oakley's a hothead as it is."

"So what happened?" Wolf asked, keeping him on track.

"She agreed to come up after her shift at the casino. And she showed up at like nine? Right after it turned dark. Anyway, she got there, and Oakley took her into his trailer. Me, Sexton, and Koling were like, we'd better stick close. We didn't know what Oakley was going to do. So we kind of milled around outside.

"They immediately started yelling at each other. She's feisty though, I'll tell you that. She was screaming harder than he was. Didn't take any of his shit. And then she came storming out. Got in her truck and drove out of there."

"And then what?" Wolf asked. "After she left."

"Well, he had kind of gotten shown up by Mary Ellen, you know? He had been talking smack the whole afternoon, and we got the sense he had something special in store for her or something. Not like, to hurt her or anything, at least I don't think. But, like, you know, maybe make her feel bad, I guess? Doesn't matter. Cause it backfired on him.

"So, he probably felt more than a little awkward about that.

He needed somebody to blame, you know? So he came at me. The guy likes to...liked to do that. He got pissed, said he was done with Jackson Mine if we didn't start putting gold in the box. Ripped into me a bit more, and then...well, he just walked down to the cut and started his night shift."

"After drinking?" Rachette asked with a chuckle. "I mean, after a few beers I'm ready for bed. Not a few hours behind the wheel of some heavy machinery."

"It's seven hours," McBeth said. "And he didn't have that many."

Rachette nodded. "Sorry. Continue."

"You said that Oakley ripped into me a bit more?" Wolf asked.

"Yeah." McBeth shrugged. "He was just pissed off."

Wolf nodded. "And is that the last you saw of him? When he walked off and started his night shift?"

"That's right."

Wolf sat back, taking it all in. After a beat he frowned. "So why all the time in between? Weren't you concerned the next day, Saturday, when he wasn't around? Or how about the next day? Sunday?" Wolf ticked two fingers in the air, then a third. "Heck, you guys found him Monday morning when Casey Lizotte put him on top of the wash plant. That's almost three days later. Didn't you consider filing a missing-persons report with the Dredge deputy any time before that?"

"No." McBeth unfolded his arms and held them out. "I didn't know he was missing before that."

"How's that work?" Rachette asked.

McBeth ticked his own fingers. "First of all, he usually sleeps Saturday if he's got the night shift that Friday night. Everybody does that the next day, especially if we were drinking the night before, which we're always doing Friday night. So I figured he was just sleeping it off on Saturday. When Sunday came around and he never came out of his trailer, I figured, well, then he must be just mad at me. I figured he was sulking. And then when Monday came around, I started getting a little bit concerned, I'll give you that. But before I could do anything about it, that's when Lizotte had dumped him onto the top of the wash plant."

Wolf narrowed his eyes to slits. "I think I'm missing some steps here. Casey Lizotte works with you guys, too?"

"No," McBeth said. "I mean, he did. But not anymore. I hired him over the weekend."

"Can you please explain that?"

"Well, the argument between Oakley and me was pretty heated. One of the things I had said was he can go back to Jackson Hole if he didn't like what was going on here." McBeth shrugged. "But he still started his night shift. The next day, though, it looked to me like he hadn't done very much down at the cut. I figured he might have had some time to think and decided he was done with the mine after all. Like he'd quit in the middle of the night."

Or been shot in the head, Wolf thought.

"When Saturday and Sunday went by and he still hadn't come out of his trailer I figured he was packing up in there or something. Making a statement. Me, Sexton, and Koling were out there working our butts off all weekend, getting the wash plant tweaked to catch the gold better, and he never set foot out of the trailer.

"I was pissed. I moved on because I thought he had, so Sunday afternoon I went down to Dredge and talked to Casey Lizotte. He works down at the bar in town."

"The same bar Spritz works at?" Rachette asked.

"That's right. Anyway, Casey and I are friends, and we all knew he's had some experience working at mines in Fairplay. So I told him, hey, if you need some extra money, you could work a few day shifts for us. He agreed right on the spot. Said when do I start? I said tomorrow morning would do just fine. I figured I'd send a message to Chris, you know? Get the new guy in there working the tractors, so when Chris decided to roll out of his trailer he'd see that I moved on. That I'm not the slow-moving weakass he said I was."

McBeth's face blushed. He sipped his coffee.

"So you were going to pay this man to come in as a temporary worker?" Rachette said. "But you're not paying the current workers that you're with."

"They get paid. It's different. They're co-owners of the mine. They might not get paid that much when times are tough, but anytime we're shopping for food or beer, it's my credit card that's getting zapped. They don't pay for shit. Not lodging, or eating, or nothin'."

"Then Monday morning," Wolf said, "when Chris didn't come out of his trailer, weren't you the least bit concerned?"

"Yeah. Like I said, Monday I was worried. I did start getting concerned. I asked Koling if he'd talked to him. Koling was always way closer than I was with Oakley. That's when we went and knocked on his door. When Oakley didn't answer we went inside and saw he wasn't there. Koling said he hadn't been answering his phone or texts, either.

" At that point we were like, what the hell, you know? His truck was still there. And we realized maybe he hadn't been there the whole time. It was freaky, to tell you the truth. We called Mary Ellen, and she said she hadn't spoken to him at all since Friday night. Koling called around."

"This is Monday morning you're doing all this calling around?" Wolf asked.

"Yes, sir."

"Keep going," Wolf said. "What then? Who else did you call?"

McBeth shook his head. "I don't know. Maybe just Mary Ellen, actually. Basically right at the same time, that's when Lizotte dumped his body up on the wash plant. I'm telling you it happened one, two. Just like that. That's when we called you guys. And then, man. I was sick to my stomach, thinking he was sitting dead in that dirt the whole time."

"You asked if it was suicide before," Wolf said. "He was buried in the dirt, wasn't he? Wouldn't that be a clear indication that he was killed by somebody else and then buried?"

McBeth rubbed his forehead. "I don't know. We'd moved all sorts of dirt on Saturday and Sunday. I was just thinking. Shoot. I don't know. I thought I might've moved his body or something. As much as I hated hearing Chris tell me all those things Friday night, it really lit a fire under my butt. I realized we weren't getting it done at the mine. He was right. I was being lazy. We needed to fix the plant settings and re-run some of the dirt we'd already run, because we might have missed out on a lot of gold in the box.

"Moving all the tailings, I just figured maybe I accidentally scooped up his body or something and brought it up there. Without even noticing or something." When he opened them again, his eyes glistened with tears. "I was just wondering."

They sat in silence for a beat, watching McBeth suppress sobbing. It was either a good act or the real deal. Maybe they were staring at regret disguised as grief.

"After that argument with Oakley, what did you do?" Wolf asked.

"Me?"

"Yes."

"I went to bed."

"Just like that. Straight to bed?"

"We work hard during the day. I'd had a few beers. I don't

have much trouble getting to sleep. Even after a run-in with Oakley, I guess."

"Did you hear anything later that night?"

"Well...yeah," he said with a chuckle.

"What did you hear?"

"Geez, there's so much noise that happens at night around our trailers. Whoever's working the night shift will be down on the excavator in the cut, loading the rock truck. Then they drive up the rock truck, dump out the dirt. Repeat that a few times. When they have enough to run through the plant, they fire it up and load it for a couple hours with the front-end loader. That's a lot of rock hitting steel. Then whoever's on duty repeats the process."

"And you sleep through all that racket?" Rachette asked.

"You get used to it. But I use earplugs. Every once in a while a good rock hitting the wash plant will wake me up for a second or two. But, yeah. I sleep through it."

"Did any big rock wake you up that night?" Rachette asked.

"No sir."

"No sounds at all that were anything out of the ordinary?" Wolf asked.

"I don't know."

Wolf waited for more explanation but none came. "Can you think of anybody that would have wanted to hurt Chris Oakley?" he asked.

McBeth smiled. "You mean besides me and half the people that ever met him?" He laughed without mirth, then his face went somber. "Sorry. I mean, Chris Oakley was not an easy guy to get along with. The guy was loud, obnoxious, and antagonistic, to say the least."

"How about the people in the town of Dredge?" Rachette asked. "Did he have any enemies down there?"

"Not that I know of."

"What's the bar called where Spritz and Casey Lizotte work at?" Wolf asked.

"The Picker."

"And Chris Oakley was a friend of this guy named Spritz?" Wolf asked.

"Yeah. Spritz has a bunch of dirt bikes. Oakley used to do motocross growing up, so they would hang out every once in a while. Oakley would ride with him."

Wolf sat back, pulling himself out of the quagmire of the Jackson Mine lives for a moment. He stretched his neck then dove back in. "How many guns do you have?"

"Here? At the mine?"

"Yes."

"Just the forty-five."

"And, for the record, what is that weapon?"

"A Glock 2 1."

Rachette nodded, pointing at his notebook. The same one they'd found inside Oakley's trailer.

"Listen, when are we going to be able to mine again?" McBeth asked. "This is...I mean, I get we have to figure this out. But I'm under a lot of pressure to get that mine back up and running."

"The mine will be a crime scene until we're done gathering clues," Rachette said. "There's really no telling when the case will be solved."

McBeth frowned, his gaze moving between them. "And our stay at the Edelweiss? Are you going to continue to cover that for us?"

"I can get you guys a deep discount with the hotel," Wolf said. "We have an agreement in place with the owner."

McBeth chuckled. "Yeah. How much is that a night?"

Wolf shrugged. "I'm not sure what their going rate is for a

night right now. Is there anywhere else you guys can go? A friend's place?"

"Yeah, up in Jackson."

"We'd really appreciate it if you could stick around in case we have more questions for you," Wolf said.

"Yeah, I bet." McBeth put both hands on his forehead, now exposing another ring of scar tissue, interlocked like an Olympic ring, further up his left forearm as the shirt fell down.

"What happened to your arm?" Rachette asked.

McBeth dropped his hands, putting the scar away again. "Well that's rude of you to ask like that, isn't it?"

"I'm sorry." Rachette held up his hands. "I was just curious."

"Maybe you should just mind your own business." He glared furiously at Rachette. Then he blinked, as if catching himself, and he flushed a deep red. "I don't need to be here anymore." He stood up and walked to the door. "I know enough about the law to know that. What the hell? It's locked? Open this up." He pounded on the door.

Wolf got up, pulled his key ring and opened it. "If we have any more questions—"

"—If you have more questions, you can talk to my lawyer, who I'm going to get right now." McBeth walked out through the observation room, Yates holding open the door to the squad room for him.

Rachette sat motionless, hands still up in the air. "Sorry."

Yates let the door close. "Nice work, you nosy bastard."

"Let's take five," Wolf said. "Then who's next?"

"Whoever you want. We have Koling and Sexton next door," Yates said.

"No Lizotte?"

"He called and said he couldn't make it. Had to work."

"Send in James Sexton. And then find Mary Ellen Dimitri and this Rick Hammes guy. And anything we have on him and his shooting up a truckload of teenagers. Have you heard of him?"

Yates tilted his head in thought. "It's not ringing a bell for me. Must have been taken care of by the Ashland office and it didn't filter up to us? I don't know."

"Anyway, get on the phone with Oakley's girlfriend and this Hammes guy and tell them we'll be coming to talk to them this afternoon."

Yates nodded. "Yes, sir."

CHAPTER 7

"THANK you for coming to speak with us," Wolf said, shaking James Sexton's hand. Every one of the man's fingernails was in some stage of growing back from being ripped, split, or peeled off altogether.

"You're welcome." Sexton was of average height and build, with a clean-shaven face. His lack of facial hair was in stark contrast to his fellow miners.

Sexton sat down, his clear blue eyes flicking between the camera mounted on the ceiling and the recording device on the table.

"We'll be recording this interview for our investigation," Wolf said.

"Right."

"Cup of coffee?" Rachette asked.

"No, thanks."

Wolf put on a smile, noting Sexton's eyes still on the recorder. "So where did you learn to drive a tractor like that? Formula One school or something?"

Sexton cracked a smile himself, although it was short-lived. "No. Just...had a lot of experience, I guess."

"You grew up mining?" Wolf asked.

"No. Not really. Just, used a lot of tractors up on the ranch in Wyoming."

"Oh, really?" Wolf asked. "What ranch is that?"

"Place up in Jackson. Actually, the McBeth family ranch."

Wolf nodded. "Really."

Sexton sat stone-faced.

"Right. Well, we'll visit that subject later I guess. Right now I'd like to talk about your work history at the mine. You've been working there with McBeth for three years now?"

"That's right. I'm the mechanic."

"Is that right."

"Yes sir. Among other things."

"Like what?"

"Like, everything. We all do everything. The digging, the rock trucks. Night shifts."

Wolf nodded. "I understand. And how do you feel about how the mining operation is going right now?"

Sexton shrugged.

"Could you please answer for the recording?"

"Yeah, I don't know. We're not finding much gold right now. But we did pretty good the first year. It's just a matter of time until Eagle puts us back on the gold."

Wolf nodded. "You have faith in Mr. McBeth's operation."

"Yeah. He knows what he's doing."

"So, you're not upset about not getting paid right now."

"No." Sexton shrugged. "More important things than money."

"I agree," Wolf said. "And what about Chris Oakley. Was he upset about not getting paid?"

"Yeah. He was. What's that gotta do with his death, though?"

"We're just trying to get to the bottom of what happened to him," Wolf said.

"So he was murdered?"

Wolf chose not to answer for a beat. Sexton stared at him without blinking.

"What makes you think he was murdered?" Wolf asked.

"Not sure why you'd be talking to us like this if you didn't think he was."

Wolf tilted his head. "What happened after Lizotte dumped Chris's body up on top of that wash plant? Who climbed up and looked to see who it was?"

Sexton's eyes narrowed, then blinked. "We knew it was Chris."

"Okay. But he could have been hurt. Did you go up and see if he was okay?"

"Eagle did."

"And not you, Kevin, or Casey?"

"No, sir."

"So Eagle climbed up, looked at him, and came back down to relay the information?"

"Yeah. That's right."

"What did McBeth say had happened to him?"

"He wasn't sure. He said he had blood on top of his head and on his neck."

"And you guys weren't interested in investigating any further than that?" Wolf asked. "To see for yourself?"

"Heck no."

"How about Koling? Did he go look?"

"No."

"Did you suspect it was murder?" Wolf asked.

"I didn't know what to think." Sexton's eye contact was unwavering. "So what happened to him?"

"Gunshot wound," Wolf said. "The bullet went in through his chin and out the top of his head."

"Suicide?"

Wolf shook his head. "He was found in the dirt, right? You can't shoot yourself and then bury yourself."

The eye contact wavered. "Yeah. I guess so."

"But he could have inadvertently been buried," Wolf said.

Sexton nodded.

"But we found no gunshot residue on his hands." Wolf shrugged. "So had to have been somebody else shot him."

Sexton nodded, closed his eyes, and took a deep breath.

"Were you close to Chris Oakley?" Wolf asked.

"Not really. He was close to Koling. Those two have been inseparable since high school. I never really got along with him."

"Why don't you tell me about Friday night," Wolf said. "From that afternoon, when you guys were done with work for the day, up until whenever you saw Oakley last, could you please tell us exactly what happened?"

Sexton crossed his arms over his chest and began his recounting of events. He touched on all the same points that McBeth had: the text message from Spritz about Mary Ellen and Rick Hammes, Mary Ellen coming up to the mine, the argument between her and Oakley, ending with Oakley and McBeth getting into a heated argument.

Sexton's version of events was so similar to McBeth's it could have been rehearsed over a few beers in one of the rooms at the Edelweiss. Or maybe it was just the truth. So far it was tough reading the Jackson Mine's mechanic.

"At any point did Eagle McBeth threaten Oakley during that argument?" Wolf asked.

"No, sir. If anything, it was the opposite way around. Oakley doesn't go through a day without threatening one of us."

"Does he ever harm you?" Rachette asked.

"No. Not really."

"How about anybody from town?"

Sexton looked up, thinking about it. "No. He was pretty good ever since we came down to Dredge. He used to get in fights all the time up in Jackson, though."

"You told us Oakley went down to the cut to start his night-shift after the argument," Wolf said.

"That's right."

"And what did you do?"

Sexton shrugged. "Went to bed. I was beat."

"And did you hear or see anything after that?" Wolf asked. "Anybody coming down into the mine?"

Sexton stared at the table, lost in thought.

"Mr. Sexton?"

"No, I didn't see or hear anybody coming down into the mine. I mean, there's always so much noise. Could have been somebody came in and I wouldn't have noticed. If there's not a lot of noise at night, then something's wrong. Then I get woken up to fix things. Noise means peace and quiet for me."

"But you didn't see anything out of the ordinary, is what the sheriff is asking," Rachette said.

"No, sir."

"And then the next day?" Wolf asked. "Tell me about your Saturday."

"Woke up. Made some coffee. Went outside."

"What time?"

"Like, seven."

"And then what did you do?"

"Saw Eagle was already up, over at the plant looking at the riffles. The place where the plant catches the gold. That's when he launched into his idea to fix the wash plant. And then we started our weekend of trying to turn around our operation. I could tell Eagle was pretty shaken up about the argument the night before. He seemed...subdued, but determined."

"So, what did you do?" Wolf asked. "What was this plan of his?"

"We changed out the riffles to a bigger set. Changed the drop angle of the chute. Dialed back the water pressure."

"And that all took place at the wash plant?" Wolf asked.

"Yeah."

"So who did that work?"

"Me."

"Just you."

"Yes, sir."

"And what did McBeth do?"

"He got to work bringing up the dirt from the cut."

"And what, exactly, is the cut?" Wolf asked.

"Where we get the pay, the paydirt. Where we take the overburden off the top, so we can get down to the ground that holds the gold. We cut into the ground to get to the pay. The cut."

"Ah. Thanks. I get it now. And Eagle was the first to go down there Saturday?"

Sexton shrugged. "Yeah. The only one to go down there Saturday."

Wolf nodded. Rachette wrote some notes.

They sat in silence for a beat.

Sexton looked like he wanted to say something.

"What is it?" Wolf asked.

"I'm just thinking about how you asked if I heard a noise that night."

"Yeah?" Rachette said. "And?"

"And I just keep thinking that...well...I'm pretty sure I would have heard a gunshot. With all that noise going on, I still think a gunshot would have woke me up. It would have been out of the ordinary. But, not a gun with a silencer on it. I'm not sure if I would have heard that."

"Okay," Wolf said, unsure what the man was driving at. "What makes you bring that up?"

"Because Chris had a gun with a silencer."

Wolf and Rachette looked at one another.

"It was a whole project that him and Koling did last year. They converted a solvent trap into one. I helped them with the threading."

Rachette continued writing, keeping his eyes on the page.

"You didn't find it in his trailer?" Sexton looked between them.

"How many guns did Chris Oakley have?" Wolf asked.

"Two Glock 21s. One with a factory barrel, and the other he swapped out with a threaded barrel."

Rachette folded his arms. "How many guns do you have?"

"Just the one."

"Name it, please," Rachette said.

"Glock 21."

"And Koling?" Rachette said.

"Same thing. Glock 21."

"And McBeth?"

"Glock 21. Same thing."

Rachette leaned forward. "And that's all the guns. No more suppressed models? No more hunting rifles, or AR-15s?"

"No, sir."

They sat in silence for a while. The man looked like his pulse was low. Like if he closed his eyes he would have been asleep.

Wolf pushed his chair back. "Thank you for coming in to talk to us, Mr. Sexton. We'd appreciate it if you'd stay accessible and not leave town, in case we have more questions." Wolf nodded toward Rachette, who pulled out a card and handed it over. "And if you think of anything else important, please don't hesitate to give Detective Rachette a call. His cell number's on that card right there."

Wolf opened the door and let him pass through.

When Sexton had exited the observation room, Yates joined their huddle, arms crossed in front of him. "Why didn't McBeth mention this suppressed weapon when you asked him about hearing noises Friday night?"

Wolf shrugged. "That's a good question."

"I called Mary Ellen Dimitri," Yates said. "She didn't answer her cell number, so I called the Motherlode Casino, where she works in the cocktail lounge. They say she didn't show up to work today."

Wolf cocked an eyebrow. "And Hammy?"

"No answer on his cell phone, either. And here's an interesting fact. Parole work papers have him employed at the same Motherlode Casino. Supposedly in the restaurant."

"The same casino Mary Ellen Dimitri works at?" Rachette asked.

"Yep."

"You said supposedly," Wolf said. "Why does he supposedly work in the restaurant?"

"Turns out he hasn't been working there for the last two weeks. He quit."

Wolf led them out of the observation room and into the hallway.

The big miner named Koling sat on one of the chairs in the hallway leading to the squad room. He was looking up at Sexton, talking in a hushed tone. They both stopped talking at the sight of Wolf, Rachette, and Yates.

Wolf checked his watch. It was only 11:05 but it felt like the afternoon with all the talking they'd been doing.

"Let's get this over with, I'm hungry as shit," Rachette said, succinctly voicing Wolf's next thought.

"Mr. Koling," Wolf said. "We're ready to talk to you now."

The man stood up, towering over Sexton. He fist-bumped his fellow miner and walked towards them.

As the big man walked past into the observation room, the tang of alcohol ingested the night before streamed in his wake. "In here?"

"Yes, sir. Rachette, if you would escort Mr. Koling in, please? Would you like some coffee, Mr. Koling?" Wolf asked.

"Yes, please."

"Rough one last night?" Rachette asked.

Koling looked down at Rachette. "We just found my best friend lying dead on the wash plant yesterday. So yeah. You could say that."

"I'm sorry about your friend," Rachette said, doing the best impression of sympathy Wolf had ever seen as he walked the big man into the interrogation room.

Wolf turned to Yates. "I want you to get on the phone with Deputy Piper Cain. Have her get eyes on Mary Ellen Dimitri, and if she can, Rick Hammes. But I want to be clear," Wolf raised his eyebrows to hammer home the point. "I don't want her engaging either of them."

CHAPTER 8

Piper Cain knelt down next to the bathtub, averting her eyes to anything below the waist on her father's naked form. "Okay, Dad. Are you ready?"

"I'm cold."

"I know, that's why we have to get you out." She stood and put her hands under his arms. "Let's go. Up."

Her father was tall, and even though he'd deteriorated with age, his large frame still carried some of the muscles from his heyday in the Summit County Sheriff's Department, where he'd frequented the exercise gym six days a week.

"Geez, help me." She grunted, her hands slipping on the soapy film under his armpits. "I'm going to drop you! Stand up!"

Her father shrugged his shoulders, making it harder. Sometimes she wondered if he was doing it on purpose.

"Stand!" She stepped her bare foot inside the tub, reassured that the grip tape on the base would give her good purchase. But there was a thin film of soap there, too, enough to shoot her and her father's feet out from under both of them with one wrong move.

"I'm standing," her father said with ultimate disdain. One foot got under him, then the other.

They both shook as she flexed everything and heaved her father's weight upright.

Damn it, they needed to install one of those bathtubs with a door. Or at least a handrail. This was the last straw, she was going to order one online, no matter the cost, and install it herself. That is, if they both survived this ordeal.

He yelped. "Your nails are digging into my skin!"

Good, she thought. Maybe that would prod him to use his own muscles.

"Okay. Turn slow." She kept both hands on him.

They clenched hands, and it was now that she felt the weakness inside her father. He used to have a bear's bite grip, and now it was a puppy's nibble.

"Are you ready to step out?" she asked.

"Yes."

She braced herself. The towels on the floor were in position, it was now or never, when the momentum was going their way.

"Okay, step."

Her father teetered, raised a foot, then dropped it down immediately. "It's too hard."

She had gone all her life never hearing her father say that, and now it seemed it was his mantra.

"Come on! One! Two! Three!"

He raised his foot, slowly put it over the edge of the tub, and put it on the towel.

"Good."

Her phone rang on the bathroom counter. It vibrated and chimed the Naked Gun theme song, which she had put on there to indicate phone calls forwarded from her on-duty phone.

"It's my day off," she said under her breath.

"What?"

"Nothing. Okay, step the other leg over."

"What's that racket? Is that your phone?"

"Forget about it. Just step your other leg over." Her legs were shaking now. Even with all the yoga and hiking up the mountains surrounding the Dredge Valley, there was only so much she could take. "Come on!"

Her father leaned forward and raised his back foot.

The phone stopped, and then the song repeated.

His back foot returned to the water. His momentum hadn't quite made it to his forward foot.

"One more—"

Just then her father's rear foot slipped and his body went down. She held her breath as a knocking noise echoed off the vaulted ceiling.

"Ah! My knee!"

"Shit." She doubled her efforts, wrapping her arms around her naked father's waist.

With a loud grunt she heaved him back upright before he went all the way down with her landing on top of him. The next few seconds were a blur as she gritted her teeth, flexing every fiber of muscle in her body to the tearing point. Like those stories of mothers lifting cars off of their trapped babies with the aid of adrenaline, she helped get her father out of the bathroom, onto the soft padding of the carpet of the hallway, into his bedroom, and onto the edge of his bed.

She collapsed against the wall and sat down, forearms on her knees.

Inside the bathroom the phone dinged, indicating a voicemail.

"Is that one of your boyfriends calling?"

She frowned, looking up at her father. Even given all the trials and tribulations due to the onset of her father's dementia, that was a strange comment. He sat, shoulders hunched, his hair plastered to his forehead.

"Boyfriends?" she asked.

"Your mother and I don't want you seeing that boy anymore," he said.

"What boy?" She was genuinely curious. Where was he? When was he?

"Jonathan."

A spark of electricity sparked through her at the thought of Jonathan. In her mind she was back at Summit County High, her afternoons spent hiking the trails in the woods, alone with him, her body intertwined with the only boy she'd ever truly loved.

"Me and Jonathan don't date anymore, Dad. Haven't for almost twenty years."

The confusion on his face was heartbreaking, so she closed her eyes and raised her chin to the sky. "I need help," she said.

"With what?" her father answered.

She stood up and went to the bathroom, plucked her phone from the counter and walked down the hallway to the living room. Sunlight speared in the windows from the east, illuminating the spacious house her father had spent his golden years building. Outside the panoramic windows the Dredge Valley spread out in spectacular glory, but it may as well have been a brick wall.

Her chest was heaving, and she sucked in a breath to try and calm herself.

Her brother smiled from a picture frame on the end table next to her.

She made a fist and struck it as hard as she could, sending it flying across the room. It smacked the wood floor and the glass shattered into a thousand pieces.

"Are you okay?" her father asked from the other room.

"Yeah."

This was what she was now. A caretaker for her father. A cop who'd veered a one-eighty degree turn off her career path for this second-string bench-warming position in the middle of the woods in nowhere, Colorado.

Why had her father just mentioned Jonathan? Was this a sick joke, pulling that memory out of the cloud of his mind and shoving it in her face, reminding her that to top it all off, she was alone in this, devoid of anything close to resembling romance in her life?

"Shit." She looked at the glass sparkling on the floor and went to the kitchen to get a broom, quickly sweeping it up.

When she was done, she went back to her father's room, surprised to see he was fully dressed, pulling a sweater over his head.

"You're dressed."

"Yeah," he said, turning toward her with a smile that contained all the light in his eyes.

She smiled back. "Good."

"Why wouldn't I be dressed? I'm a grown man."

She shook her head. "No reason."

She walked back to the living room, pushing the marvel of her father's condition out of her mind. She pressed the voice-mail button on her phone and put it to her ear.

"Hi, this is Detective Yates over here at Headquarters in Rocky Points. I have a request from Sheriff Wolf for you. He wants you to, quote, 'get eyes on Mary Ellen Dimitri and Rick Hammes if you can. It's in connection to the murder up at the mine yesterday. Anyway, I was hoping to get hold of you...'"

Yates talked some more and read off some addresses, and Piper wrote them down on a piece of paper in the kitchen.

Sheriff Wolf had a request, and he wants her to *get eyes on*

Mary Ellen Dimitri and Rick Hammes? What did that even mean—get eyes on them?

She hovered her finger over the button to call Yates back, thinking about Wolf.

When Piper had moved down from Bozeman she had originally been hired by Sheriff MacLean. After a few months in the forgotten outer reaches of the county, she had decided to relocate with her father to somewhere with more social interaction, with more support available should they need it. Five months ago, back in February, she had applied for the two deputy job openings over at the Rocky Points headquarters. She had heard absolutely nothing in response. Which was strange. Sheriff Clegg up in Gallatin County had given her a shining letter of recommendation. Her history was spotless, and she was a damn good deputy if she said so herself.

When she had followed up with a call to the Rocky Points receptionist, she'd been told she would be considered by the sheriff himself and contacted either way within the month. That was five months ago.

As far as she was concerned, Wolf had forgotten about her back then. And now he's specifically requesting her to do something? Now he's calling her, by name, to go *get eyes* on someone? What did that even mean?

Situations are what you make of it. Her mother's words echoed in her head.

She watched her father enter the kitchen and pour himself a bowl of cereal. He picked up the remote control off the coffee table, turned on the TV, and sat back in his favorite chair, munching his Kix cereal.

"What am I supposed to make of this situation, Mom?" she asked herself.

"What?" her dad said.

"Nothing."

Maybe this was her opportunity to involve herself. Her in. Back in February she'd allowed herself to dream while her resume was being vetted. She had driven into Rocky Points and seen the thriving Main Street economy. The walking paths. The parks. The trails. The ski mountain.

She could see herself living among it all. Right now Piper had the help of her mother's former best friend, Stacy Armistead. Stacy did a good job helping with her father here in Dredge, but she had her own problems, her own life with three grandkids and a son who needed help raising them. As far as professional help beyond Stacy, there was none available here in Dredge, at least not of the caliber Piper sought for her father.

With a full deputy salary and benefits down in Rocky Points, she could afford professional care during the day while she was at work.

And what about work? Just like back in Bozeman, she'd be rubbing elbows with dozens of other men and women. Skiing in the winter. Mountain biking in the summer. Friends. Bars. Restaurants. Maybe even a romantic life.

"Yates here."

She looked down at her phone, realizing she'd accidentally pushed the call button. She put it to her ear.

"Hi. This is Deputy Cain, you just left me a voicemail."

"Oh yes, hi Deputy Cain. Detective Yates, we met yesterday."

"Right, I remember," she lied, trying to put a face to the name and coming up blank. "Listen, I got your voicemail, I just wanted to make sure I heard that correctly. You want me to find Mary Ellen Dimitri and Rick Hammes?" She read off the addresses.

"That's correct. And, like I said, you're not to engage either of them."

"Okay. What's going on?"

"They're people of interest in the Chris Oakley murder yesterday."

"Rick Hammes is already on my list," she said. "With his parole I mean. I'm aware of him." She chuckled. "And I'm glad you're telling me not to engage him. I'm not sure I'd feel comfortable writing him a speeding ticket. But I'll give his house a drive-by, and see if I can't find Mary Ellen Dimitri as well."

"Great. Keep me posted on this number. This is my cell."

She hung up, feeling invigorated. She was working with actual people, on an actual case. With people from headquarters.

Her father laughed at the television.

Shit.

She dialed Stacy's number and it went straight to voicemail after a ring, like she'd been screening the call.

Of course, Piper couldn't really afford the help anyway.

"Hey, Dad. How about you go on a ride with me?"

"Where?" He howled with laughter at the episode of "Leave it to Beaver."

"I have to go to work." She stood between him and the television. "Come on."

He looked up at her, utter confusion on his face again.

She blinked. "It's me. Your daughter, Piper. I'm a cop, and I have to go to work. Now get up, you're coming with me."

"No I'm not," he said, leaning back in his chair. He looked past her to the TV. "I'm not going anywhere. There's a marathon of "Gunsmoke" on after this with all the best Burt Reynolds episodes. I'm staying right here."

Piper closed her eyes and exhaled slowly. Then she walked out the front door and onto the wraparound porch. She leaned her body over the railing, getting the right angle to see a sliver of the neighbors' house down the road. Both vehicles were parked out front.

She went back inside, quickly changed into her uniform, put on her duty belt, and went back into the family room.

Her father had a beer sitting next to him now, but other than that, he hadn't moved a muscle. Burt Reynolds had his shirt off.

"You going to be okay if I leave you for an hour or two?"

Her father ignored her, or didn't hear. She stepped in between him and the TV again. "I'm going to work for a bit. I'll be back, okay? I'm going to get Ethel and Jerry to check in on you."

Her father raised his beer. "Okay, Honey Bear."

He used to call her mother that.

"Okay."

Before guilt froze her completely, she walked outside, down the porch steps and got in the Jeep Cherokee. She drove down the pine-forested drive and hung a right onto the county road toward Ethel and Jerry Clark's house.

With the engine running, Piper ran to the front door. After two sets of knocks Ethel moved aside a lace curtain and pressed her face to the glass.

"Hi," Piper said, waving.

Ethel smiled and opened the door. "Hi, Piper. What are you doing here?"

"Is that Piper?" Jerry called from inside. The man loved Piper, and never missed an opportunity to talk to her. Piper hoped that boded well for her now.

"Yes, it's Piper. Come to the door if you want to talk to her, you lazy bum."

"Hi, Piper." Jerry peeked around his wife, his arms out for a hug.

Piper allowed herself to be pulled into his arms, and then Ethel's.

"Uh, listen. I have to go to work for a couple hours. My dad is pretty adamant about not coming, and to be honest, it would help if he was not there. I'm wondering if you two could check on him while I'm gone?"

Jerry put both hands on his hips. "Heck yeah. You got it. Anything for you."

"And your father," Ethel said. "We'd be happy to. I'm going into town in an hour. I'll stop by on the way in. And then I can swing by again on the way back. And if you're still not back by then, Jerry will go over and check on him after that. How about you just let us know when you're back and we'll stop going over."

Piper nodded and smiled with a wash of gratitude as she watched these two selfless individuals heed the call of duty. "Great. Thank you."

"No problem-o," Jerry said with a wave of his hand.

She waved back as she climbed into the Jeep.

CHAPTER 9

"HE BURNED HIM WITH A CIGARETTE?" Wolf asked.

Kevin Koling had just finished recounting his version of events from Friday. Just like the two miners before him, he touched on the same points—the text message from Spritz, Chris being upset about Rick Hammes and his girlfriend, Mary Ellen's visit, their argument spilling outside, Mary Dimitri leaving, and then Oakley and McBeth getting into an argument of their own. Only he'd added one detail the other two men hadn't.

"Yeah, got him in a headlock, put his cigarette out on his chest. Well, the chest of his jacket actually. Not, like, his actual skin or anything."

"Still a bit much though," Rachette said.

Koling shrugged. "That was Chris for you."

"And then what?" Wolf asked. "After the cigarette burning episode?"

"Well that was it," Koling said. "I pulled him off, Jimmy pulled Eagle back. That's when Chris went out to start his shift."

Rachette wrote in his notebook. "You're calling James, the mechanic, Jimmy?"

"Yeah. Sorry. James. Jimmy. We call him Jimmy."

"And then what did you do?" Wolf asked.

"I went to bed."

"Did you hear anything out of the ordinary later that night?" Wolf asked.

"Nah." Koling wrung his baseball mitt-sized hands in his lap and shook his head. "We usually get after it on Friday nights, and I'm one to enjoy my drinks. I slept pretty hard."

"Have you heard about how Chris was killed?" Wolf asked.

"I just talked to James on the way out. He says you guys think he was shot in the head, and that somebody else did it. Wasn't suicide."

"That's right," Wolf said.

"And he mentioned you guys think it might have been he was shot with his suppressed G21."

Wolf and Rachette eyed each other.

"Is it true?" Koling asked.

Wolf decided to leave the question unanswered. "You exchanged a lot of text messages with Chris, didn't you."

"He was my best friend." The big man's eyes welled up, but the tears didn't flow.

"We gather he was very upset with McBeth, is that correct?"

"Yeah, sure. I mean, he was more upset about the mine."

"But he was holding McBeth responsible, right?" Wolf asked.

"I don't know. I guess."

"That's what those texts look like. He said to you, quote: *If we don't start getting gold in the box I'm bouncing. Fuck him*'."

"Yeah, I guess that's right. So...what?"

"I'm just trying to establish the relationship between Mr. McBeth and Mr. Oakley," Wolf said. "Would you say it was antagonistic?"

"Relationships with Chris Oakley were always antagonistic." Koling smiled, looking proud of his deceased friend.

"Except for with you," Wolf said.

"That's right. We never fought."

"Never?"

"Not once. Well, not since kindergarten, when I whooped his ass." Koling smiled again, but this time a tear fell down his cheek. He wiped it quick, then closed his eyes and let a stream flow down his face.

Rachette ducked out of the room and returned with a box of tissues.

When Koling blew his nose, it sounded like a bear caught in a trap. They waited in silence until the wave of emotion passed.

"Ah. Sorry," Koling said, twirling his finger for them to continue.

"It's no problem," Wolf said. "When your best friend was not coming out of his trailer for the next couple of days after that night shift Friday night, were you concerned?"

Koling nodded. "I was. I mean, not on Saturday, whoever has the Friday overnight always sleeps the whole next day. But when he didn't come out Sunday, I texted him to see what was going on. When he didn't answer I was like, what the hell? I went into his trailer to check on him, saw he wasn't there."

"You actually went inside the trailer?"

"Yes."

"Okay, so he wasn't there," Wolf said. "And then what?"

"I was confused. His truck was there. At that point I assumed he must have been with Mary Ellen. I figured she came in and got him while we were in town earlier. You know. They were making up."

"When did you go into town?" Wolf asked.

"Sunday, lunch time. McBeth wanted to hire on Lizotte so we went to The Picker to have lunch. When I came back that's when I went to Chris's trailer. I wanted to talk to him about what McBeth was doing, you know. That he was serious. And he was pushing Oakley out."

"And then Monday comes around," Wolf said.

"Yeah, Monday morning I was wondering what the hell was going on. I was very concerned at that point. So, I called Mary Ellen and she told me she hadn't seen him at all over the week-end, not since Friday. As soon as I hung up with her I called you guys right away."

"Did you have any inkling of what might have happened to him?" Wolf asked.

"That he'd been shot in the head?"

"Yes."

"No. Not at all."

"Do you know of anyone who might have wanted to hurt him?"

Koling crossed a leg, his bass boat of a foot bouncing on his knee. "I don't know, I mean, maybe Rick Hammes? The guy was screwing his girl. The guy shot up a truckload of teenagers a couple years ago. Seems like an Rick Hammes type of thing to me, doesn't it?"

"Did you hear anything out of the ordinary Friday night? Like a gunshot?"

"No."

"Tell us about this silenced weapon of Chris's," Wolf said.

"It's a G21 with a solvent trap converted into a suppressor. Tough to buy a silencer, so Chris made his own."

"Where does Chris keep this silenced Glock 21?" Rachette asked.

"In his drawer with his other one. Top drawer of his dresser." Koling answered without hesitation. After a few seconds he narrowed his eyes. "We all knew that. We all know where we keep each other's guns."

"We didn't find the silenced gun there," Rachette said. "We found another Glock 21 without a silencer."

"Yeah. He has another one."

"Are you sure that's where he keeps the silenced weapon, too?"

"Yeah. I'm sure. Like I said, we all know."

"You guys talk about that, huh?" Rachette asked.

Koling's foot dropped off his knee. "What the hell is this? Are you saying I have something to ..." He moved his mouth around, sucking in a hissing breath through his nose, like rage was a thrashing monster trying to escape through his lips. "Are you saying I did this?"

"No, we're not," Wolf said. "We're just saying it stands to reason that somebody got hold of that silenced gun and shot him."

"And we can't find that gun," Rachette said.

Koling stared through the room.

"Would Rick Hammes have known where to get that gun?" Wolf asked. "He doesn't live there with you guys. Isn't as familiar with your weapons or where they're kept. Or is he?"

Koling's eyes remained fixed for a few seconds more, then he stood up. "I'm not answering anymore of your questions without a lawyer."

He walked to the door and jiggled the handle.

Yates was ready this time and twisted the knob from the other side. Before the door was open Koling pushed his way out, then left through the observation room out into the hall.

Rachette swiveled in his chair. "Well? What's next?"

"Now we need to talk to Rick Hammes and Mary Ellen Dimitri," Wolf said.

"So, up to Dredge?" Rachette asked.

"Yeah."

"I spoke to Deputy Cain." Yates eyed his watch. "She should be calling me any time now with their status."

"How about Oakley's family?" Wolf asked Rachette.

Rachette shrugged. "I called the number for *Pa* we found in his phone. It's definitely his father, according to my records search. But I can't get hold of him. The voicemail said his mailbox is full. I've got the Teton County SD helping out. They're supposed to call me with news."

Wolf nodded. "I need to make a call to the sheriff up there also."

"And then what?" Rachette asked.

"And then we have a long drive ahead of us," Wolf said, walking out the door and down the hall. "It's time to head up to Dredge."

CHAPTER 10

DEPUTY PIPER CAIN drove the Jeep Grand Cherokee away from her father's house, out of the forest and into the wide-open valley floor towards Dredge, which sat a few miles away. From here the view of the landscape was even more spectacular than up at her father's house. The three walls of mountains enclosing the fortress-like valley were in full view, filling the windshield and mirrors. Up at Dad's the view was much the same but surrounded by the occasional lodgepole pine obstructing the majesty beyond.

Ahead, the town of Dredge sparkled in the afternoon sunlight. The history of the place was a variation of a well-worn tale in the Rocky Mountains. Back in the late eighteen hundreds a handful of men had found gold in the river running through the center of the valley. They'd struck it rich, and word had gotten out. Even these thirteen-thousand-foot fortress walls couldn't hold that piece of information secret for long.

One man from Denver with deep pockets named Victor Hanfield decided to come up and get in on the action. He had built himself a Dredge to extract the gold from the river, but at industrial levels. According to Piper's father's account, Hanfield succeeded mightily, buying up more claims, pushing other small-timers, which was everyone else, out before they could compete.

He built a hotel. He built a casino. He built a theater. Over the next few decades he took his hoard of gold and built the town. More people came. And the town flourished for a short time. They named the town Dredge, after Hanfield's machine that made it all possible.

But then Hanfield died, and after that the town went into a steep decline. Nobody could seem to find the gold like the famed man from Denver with a Dredge.

Now the town was a step or two above a ghost town, with only a population of 1,300 people in peak summer season. Hanfield's Dredge was a battered, weathered, shell, lying on the shores of the river just off Main Street. The casino in town had been converted to a warehouse sometime in the mid-1950s. The hotel was still a hotel, but nothing anybody wanted to stay at. The theater had shut down at the turn of the century.

Now a new resurgence was trying to take hold. A megacorporation had moved in, building a monstrous casino on the southern edge of town, trying to pull people into the valley like Hanfield had all those years ago. As far as Piper could see, the corporation had made a poor investment. But, then again, she was no businesswoman.

She was a cop. And with that thought, she looked toward the other side of the valley, where a lone vehicle kicked up dirt on the road that she knew led up to the mine.

Wind came in through her open window, buffeting the side of her face, pushing against the car so hard she had to hold the wheel tight. The scent of grass and crystal-clear air filled the cab. She tapped the wheel with both thumbs, even though no music came out of her radio. The combination of her assignment and brisk air had her humming.

She flicked her eyes back to that dirt road that led to the mine. Rick Hammes lived on that road, too, just outside of town. Hammes was one bad cookie and she didn't relish the thought of *getting eyes* on him. It would definitely be a drive-by, she decided. And she would be driving fast. The guy had already proven he had a penchant for shooting up cars, and she'd hate to be next.

Once she reached Dredge, she decided to hang a right on Main Street and stop at Mary Ellen Dimitri's first.

The noise lessened as she drove off the dirt and up onto the freshly laid pavement of the state highway. She passed The Motherlode Casino on the left, the colossal rectangular building covered in an earth-toned stucco erected ten years ago that was trying to rekindle Mr. Hanfield's magic. She was glad her father wasn't with her now. He would have said, "It's a damn shame they littered this valley with that monstrosity." He would have thought he was being clever saying it, and not just repeating the same thing he'd been saying for the last ten years.

Piper came out of her thoughts and made a right on Poppy Lane, easing off of Main onto potholed dirt. A plume of dust kicked up behind her, billowing past the front of her car and into the windows. She coughed and rolled up the windows as she slowed at the corner of Third and Poppy.

Mary Ellen Dimitri's house stood on the corner. It was identical to the others on the street, boxy and small, one of many two-bedroom houses built sometime in the early 1900s. She parked along the side of the house and got out.

In between wind gusts the sun warmed her skin. The faint scent of bar food from somewhere in town rode on the breeze, making her mouth water. She had eaten only a snack for lunch before she left. She could eat later.

She walked around the side of the house to the front porch,

swishing her feet through long, unkempt grass that she suspected had yet to see a lawnmower this year.

Stepping up onto the concrete slab in front of the door, she pressed the glowing doorbell. As she backed off the porch, the image of Chris Oakley's dead body sprawled across that monster machine the day before flashed in her mind. She put her palm on her holstered Glock and stood alert, waiting for Mary Ellen Dimitri to show herself at the door or one of the windows.

Thirty seconds went by with no answer, so she walked up, this time knocking heartily on the front door. She put her ear close, hearing nothing. Then she put her ear directly on the warmed surface. Still nothing.

Two windows at the front of the house flanked the front door. She went to the edge of the porch and leaned over the metal railing to get a good look inside the left one. She stumbled forward as the iron railing gave way from the side of the house. Sucking in a sharp breath she grabbed behind her, barely catching the edge of the brick surrounding the front door before she toppled into the bushes. She straightened on the porch and the metal bounced back with a squeak.

Muttering quietly to herself, she walked off the porch and surveyed the house.

Deciding the shrubs in front of the left window were less overgrown, she ducked to the side and went in for a closer look. As she leaned in, she was jabbed by a tiny thorn. A bead of blood appeared on her arm. Stuck halfway in, she decided to press on. She unholstered her gun and used it to push more needle-covered branches, careful to keep the gun pointed at the ground.

After a few seconds of maneuvering through the shrubs she was at the window, her back pressed into the side of the house. She squatted, noting her legs were shaking a bit, but felt strong.

Her religious workout regimen and yoga at least five-times-a-week had paid off.

She rose slowly, her face close to the dirty glass. Her eyes gradually adjusted to where she could see the darkened room inside. A desk stood against the far wall, covered in unopened mail, magazines, and local newspapers still in their plastic bags. Apparently not a fan of reading.

Piper put her eye close to the window and looked the other way. A hallway led from the front door into a kitchen, where a table held another pile of unopened envelopes. Was she stealing mail from the neighbors?

The overhead light above the kitchen table was illuminated, though it appeared dim compared to the sunlight coming through the sliding glass door behind it.

Piper held her breath, thinking she might have heard a sound. Even over the din of the rushing wind, she was certain she'd heard a cry. Was Mary Ellen hurt inside?

She could feel her heart pumping, her breathing quickening.

Suddenly there was a flash of movement in front of her, a mass of red hair lurching up from below.

The needle-covered branches poked through her shirt and sports bra beneath as she backed up and ducked out of sight. Her ponytail covered her face, caught on the bush. When she pulled it away, the branch swiped across her cheek.

"Dang it," she said out loud, because she realized then what she had seen. And heard.

Rising, she saw the cat on the other side of the glass, licking its paw, unfazed by her presence.

"Scared the crap out of me, you little..." Piper eyed the cat's tongue as it lapped along the rim of its mouth, then the back of a curled paw. Then she noticed the bright red substance clotting the cat's fur. "What the hell?"

CHAPTER 11

WOLF's SUV skidded on the dirt as he turned off the paved road of Dredge's Main Street onto the side street called Poppy Lane.

He flicked the dashboard switch and the blaring siren went silent. Ahead, Deputy Cain's Jeep Cherokee was parked a few blocks up and he saw her leaning against it, rising at the sight of his approach.

The plume of dust kicking off the back of his vehicle reached her first, engulfing her in a cloud that she ducked to avoid.

He parked and got out. "Sorry about that. You okay?"

She waved her hand, and when the dust blew away he saw her face was covered in streaks of blood.

"Are you hurt?"

"Heads up." She turned away and covered herself again with an arm.

Wolf turned around in time to get hit square in the face with Rachette's vehicle dust.

Wolf assumed the defensive position, holding his breath. Once the maelstrom passed he brushed himself off.

"You're bleeding," Yates said, running up.

"You okay?" Rachette pushed up next to Yates. "What happened?"

Deputy Cain put up a hand and stepped back. "I'm okay, I'm okay. I was looking in the front window and got scratched by a thorn bush." She upturned her hands. "I'm okay."

Wolf stretched to see over the fence into the back yard. The rear windows came into view and he thought he saw the curtains move.

"Yeah, come here and take a look," Piper said, walking past him to the fence.

"Wait, I saw movement."

She ignored him, putting her hands on the top of the wooden slats and hoisting herself into a half-pullup to see. He followed, only having to get on his toes.

The wind blew Cain's ponytail straight towards him, along with her floral scent. He noticed she held the position, there in a half-pullup, her face not showing any strain.

"I went to the front door," she said. "I rang it, then knocked. No answer."

Rachette jumped up next to Deputy Cain, grunting with exertion.

"I went to the window to look in and saw a cat covered in blood. That's the movement you're seeing in there." She nodded her head. "You see that?"

Wolf did. Thin, light-colored drapes covered a wide rear window. At the center point where they met there was blood spatter on the fabric and drops that had run down the glass.

"I hopped the fence after I called you guys and looked inside," she said. "It's her. Mary Ellen Dimitri."

"Did you touch anything?"

"No, sir." She lowered herself down and swatted away the splinters from her uniform shirt and jeans. "I mean, I did check the back door and the back window." She pulled a pair of purple latex gloves from her rear pocket. "But I did glove up. Sir."

"Were they open?" Wolf asked.

"No, sir. The front right window is open, though."

"You didn't go in, did you?" Rachette asked.

"No. Of course not."

Wolf walked to the front of the house, through long grass and swaying wildflowers.

A neighbor down the street had come outside and was eyeing them.

"Check with that neighbor and see if she saw anything," Wolf said.

"I'm on it." Yates marched down the dirt road.

"That window there, on the right." Wolf looked at Deputy Cain.

She shrugged. "You guys took a while to get here. I was curious. I'm sorry."

"It's no problem."

"Unless you screwed up some fingerprints on that back door handle," Rachette said.

"I never touched the handle. I pulled from the back of the door. When it didn't budge I stopped."

Rachette eyed her skeptically.

"I may be out here in Hicksville but I have some experience under my belt."

"You think?"

"Yeah. I do."

"I said it's no problem," Wolf said.

He grabbed gloves and a jacket from his SUV. Putting both on, he went back to the front of the house and ducked into the bushes, putting up his jacket-covered arm to ward off the tiny thorns.

"That's cheating," Rachette said. "You're supposed to lead with your face, right, Cain?"

She said nothing.

"What? I'm kidding. We'll get along just fine."

"You think?" she said.

Wolf smiled to himself as he reached the window and pushed up with both hands against the glass. It slid easily with a creaky spring sound, letting out the unmistakable scent of death that hit Wolf's nostrils like a punch.

He ducked away and turned his head. Through the branches he saw Cain's eyes watching him.

"You smell it too?" she asked.

"Smell what?" Rachette asked. "Ah, shit. Never mind. Yeah."

"Be right back," Wolf said, hopping up and into the house. His belt buckle caught on the windowsill and threw him off balance, and with a crash he fell, his elbow knocking hard against the wood floor.

"You okay?" Rachette asked.

Wolf put a thumbs up out the window. Trying to look nonchalant as he stood, he ignored the pain firing down his arm.

Stacked cardboard boxes filled a small front room. To his left was the entryway. He walked past the front door to another anterior room, where he scanned a pile of junk mail, magazines, and old newspapers on an antique desk. Bloody paw prints marked the sill of the other front window.

The floor creaked as he walked down the hallway to the kitchen table, and another pile of mail. He took his time in the kitchen, delaying the sight of what he knew waited for him if he turned left.

A collection letter. Coupons. Dirty dishes. An unmade pack of mac and cheese on the counter.

The smell was getting unbearable. He needed to get this over with, so he blanked his mind and looked.

Mary Ellen Dimitri sat in the darkened family room, in the middle of the couch, her head back, opaque eyes open and staring through the ceiling above her.

Her cat perched on the top of the couch behind her, licking the wound on top of Mary Ellen's head.

"Get off of there!" Wolf stomped his foot. The cat jumped off, zipped across the room, and disappeared out of sight at the back of the house.

Wolf's eyes returned to Mary Ellen Dimitri. A red hole pierced her chin, from which a stream of dried red led down into her tank top.

His entire body started with shock as he noticed she was moving. With mute horror he watched as she tilted sideways with impossible slowness and stopped after a few degrees. His breathing returned as he realized the cat must have jostled her when it jumped.

His radio scratched. "What do you got in there?"

He plucked it from his belt and pressed the button. "Mary Ellen Dimitri dead on her couch. Call Lorber."

"You got it," Rachette said.

"I'm going to clear the rest of the house."

Wolf put the radio back on his belt, pausing to study the scene in front of him.

In front of Mary was a coffee table, on top of which stood two tall cans of those fruity alcoholic seltzers, two remote controls, a cell phone, and a brimming ash tray. Both cans were opened and marked with lipstick. A fabric lounge chair was positioned next to the couch, and between them sat an end table. Two beer bottles stood at attention on the table.

Ignoring Mary's body for the moment, Wolf walked over and saw there was no lipstick on the bottles.

111

The ashtray was filled with white filters, sucked down to the same level before being smashed out, all slathered in the same shade of lipstick. Two brown filters of a different brand stood out, smoked down the filter's edge. No lipstick.

Wolf looked at Mary's phone screen and saw numerous fingerprint smudges. He knew he should leave it untouched for Lorber's team, but curiosity won out. He nudged the phone, getting no response, then tilted it with two gloved fingers. The screen came alive, indicating twenty-three percent charge on the battery and five missed text messages.

The cat appeared behind him, the hair on its back standing on end, ears laid back. When Wolf turned around the feline went to the sliding glass door and stood expectantly.

Wolf inhaled another breath saturated with death.

"Good idea," he said, following the cat to the door. He flicked open the lock and slid it open.

The cat squeezed out, running into the backyard, hopping the fence and disappearing into the dirt back alley.

Wolf stuck his head out, pushed all the air out of his lungs, and sucked in a breath of mouthwash-clean air.

"Everything okay?" Rachette called from the fence. Deputy Cain's face floated next to his.

"I'll be out in a minute."

Wolf pulled another lungful of the good stuff and went back inside, shutting the door behind him. Quickly now, he went into the back hallway where two small bedrooms flanked the bathroom.

He poked his head inside each room, seeing nothing of interest at first. Mary Dimitri was not a stickler for order and hygiene, he decided. Just like she rarely opened her mail, she rarely folded clothes, or hung them on hangers. Her entire wardrobe seemed to be laid out on the bed in some stage of a laundry routine. The bathroom counter was completely covered in beauty products and makeup.

With every passing minute he felt the stench coating his skin and the inside of his lungs. Worst of all, he was starting to get used to it. With that thought he made his way for the front door, and out into the world of the living.

CHAPTER 12

"You HAVE to be kidding me right now." The voice scratched through into Rachette's ear.

"Sorry, sir. Not kidding. She's DOA inside her house. We need the forensic team back up here ASAP."

Lorber made a noise and started a stream of cuss words on the other side. Rachette felt a grain of chew between his teeth and picked it out with his fingernail, spitting it on the ground.

A few paces away, Deputy Cain leaned up against the plank fence with her eyes closed, head turned towards the sun. She looked distressed. She looked good. Damn it, what was his problem? He was married, happily married, with two kids.

"Are you listening to me?" Lorber's voice came through the earpiece.

"Sorry, Yates was saying something...what was that, sir?"

"I asked how many people have entered the scene."

"Just Wolf. He's inside right now."

"All right. Nobody else goes in."

"Of course." Lorber clicked off and Rachette put the phone back in his pocket.

Cain was now squatting down, both palms pressed against

her forehead like she was in anguish and she was trying to hold it inside of her head or something.

Yates was standing at a distance, holding guard position against the neighbors who had begun to funnel out of their houses and congregate nearby. Eyeing her again, Rachette felt bad for ribbing her earlier. He'd been insensitive, as Charlotte would have put it.

"You okay?" he asked her.

"Yeah, I'm fine." She said, keeping her hands pressed against her forehead. Her eyes were screwed shut.

He went over and laid a hand on her shoulder, squeezed it gently. "It's okay," he said. "Dead bodies are not something you see every day."

She popped her hands from her forehead and looked at his hand, then up at him. For a moment he kept it there, frozen, feeling the warmth of her shirt and the bone and firm muscle of her shoulder underneath.

And then he pulled it away.

He suddenly felt like he'd done something terribly wrong. He felt his face go red and he stood up and turned his back to her. What the hell was he doing, grabbing her shoulder like that? He'd seen that reaction plenty of times. If he was in a bar right now he'd be dodging a drink flying into his face. Shit.

Yates was looking at him, his eyebrows knitted together.

Rachette flipped him the finger and turned back around. He had to put water on this fire before it flamed out of control. "Hey, listen, sorry. I didn't mean to..." He didn't know what to say.

She stood up, looking like she was feigning confusion. "Didn't mean to what?"

"Nothing. Sorry, I just... I'm married, you know. I have two kids."

"Good for you."

He nodded, deciding she sounded genuine. No condescension detected. She was cool after all. "Yeah," Rachette said. "Her name is Charlotte Munford. You ever met her?"

"No, I haven't."

"Right. Yeah, you're up here. I just wondered if you had been in headquarters down in Rocky Points. Maybe you might have met her there. She's a deputy." Mercifully, his phone vibrated in his pocket and he pulled it out. "Got to take this."

Seeing it was Nelson, he turned around and took the call. "What's up?"

"Hey, where the hell are we going? Where's this house?" Rachette looked down the dirt road and saw Nelson's vehicle speed past, and then go out of sight.

"I just saw you drive past, turn around, stop. Take a right on Poppy, head east, you'll see us." He hung up.

"That was Deputy Nelson. He's heading down from the mine," he said to Cain. She ignored him and continued pacing, her arms crossed over her chest. Rachette tried to act nonchalant, like nothing awkward had happened between them. Maybe nothing had. Maybe he needed to chill out. Something about this woman got him all riled up. He crossed his own arms.

He could use a dip. Maybe that was it. That was the most repulsive thing that he could possibly do with a woman present. At least that's what Charlotte had told him a thousand times. And that was a good way to show that he didn't really care what Deputy Cain thought. He packed the Copenhagen, popped open the lid and put one between his lip and gum.

Deputy Cain seemed not to notice, looking instead toward the front of the house as Wolf walked across the lawn.

"Lorber's on his way," Rachette said. "What did you find?"

"Looks like a single gunshot wound," Wolf said. "Same injury as Chris Oakley up at the mine."

"Same guy," Rachette said.

Wolf nodded. "Looks like it." Wolf looked at Deputy Cain. "You okay?"

Deputy Cain nodded. "Yes, sir."

Nelson's vehicle rumbled down the dirt road, tires popping gravel as it came to a sliding halt behind Wolf's SUV. Deputy Nelson and a young new deputy, John Chavez, stepped out.

Chavez was wide-eyed and so was Nelson, both chock full of adrenaline by the looks of it.

"Yates!" Wolf waved him over.

Yates came over and joined the huddle. "What's up?"

Wolf pointed at Chavez, Nelson, and Cain. "You three stay here, we're going to see Rick Hammes."

"I'll go with you," Cain said, raising her chin when he looked down at her.

Rachette smirked to himself. She had some guts, he'd give her that.

"From what I'm gathering, this Hammes guy is dangerous," Wolf said. "He shot at a car—"

"—a truckload of teenagers. Yeah, I know. I've been keeping an eye on him for the last year per MacLean's orders. Sir, I trained with SWAT up in Bozeman. I've seen action before. Besides, I know the roads around here like the back of my hand. You'll probably not want to go into his place full-bore with everyone rolling up and spooking him. I know exactly where his house is. Where we can stop early and walk in from a distance."

She stopped talking and held unflinching eye-contact with Wolf.

Her eyes were the color of the darkest rainforest wood, and just as hard, Rachette thought.

Wolf stared at her for a beat, then nodded. "Okay. You're coming with us."

She nodded, the tough façade cracking a bit as she noticed for the first time Rachette and the others looking at her.

"You two stay here," Wolf said, pointing at Nelson and Chavez. "Keep those neighbors away, and I don't have to tell you to stay out of the house. Let's go."

"I'm driving," Rachette said to Yates.

Cain's Jeep slowed and turned on the unmarked county road that Wolf recognized as the same one they'd used to get to the mine the previous morning. Wolf followed close in his own SUV with Rachette and Yates behind him.

Here the forest was dense and tall, covering the flat land of the valley floor. The road followed a straight path for a mile or so then veered toward the western wall of mountains toward a steep valley, where the mine lay another few miles up and over a knife-edged peak.

Wolf tried to see exactly where the mine was, remembering the view he'd been given from up there of the Dredge Valley. But as he slipped into Deputy Cain's trail of dust he brought his thoughts back to the moment at hand.

How, when, why, or what did he know her from? His mind kept turning circles trying to come up with the answer. Every moment he spent with this woman he had the feeling of déjà vu, like they'd crossed paths before. Why did he keep mulling this over? Because she was startlingly attractive? Probably.

"It's coming up here on the right," Piper's voice came through the radio.

He pulled the radio and pressed the transmit button. "Copy that."

Her brake lights bloomed through the dust and all three vehicles pulled over. Wolf stepped out into even cooler air than before. Clouds blocked the sun, threatening rain.

Deputy Cain closed her car door and joined him in the shade. "He lives just right up there," she said, pointing down the road to a clearing in the trees. "On the right side." To the left stood a second property, set back and just inside the line of pines on the other side of the clearing.

"Who lives there?" Wolf asked.

She shrugged. "I'm not sure."

A dog's bark filtered through the trees.

"He has a huge pit bull," Cain said.

"Is it nice?" Rachette asked.

"I've never stuck my hand in the fence to see," she said.

The dog was now interspersing growls between barks.

"I'm going to go out on a limb and say hell no," Yates said.

"Let's go." Wolf led the way, hugging the right side of the road.

Hammes's metal chain link fence came into view first, followed by the front of his house. The dog barked even more intensely, putting its giant paws up on top of the chained-shut gate.

"Hey, buddy," Rachette said, making kissing noises as they walked up.

The dog bared its teeth and barked, spitting saliva. Then it squatted down and did its business. After two seconds it kicked some dirt backwards and began barking again.

"Yeah, that thing's a full-blown menace," Rachette said.

The dog dropped back and paced inside a well-worn groove on the other side of the fence. The yard behind it looked like it was once grass but was now almost completely dug up. Plastic toys, all chewed to shreds, littered the space.

A cracked concrete path led from the chained gate to the front door. The house was a squat one-story, its blue paint shedding in large flakes. Like most other places in town, it appeared to have been built at least half a century ago.

Though there was no proper front porch, Rick Hammes had set out a mangled couch and two wire chairs on the dirt. A stump placed in the middle, littered with beer bottles and an overflowing ashtray, served as a table.

Wolf squinted, studying the bottles, and put his hand on the butt of his gun.

"What is it?" Rachette asked.

"Those beer bottles are the same brand that were inside Mary Dimitri's house." Wolf recognized the labels.

"No vehicle parked outside," Yates said, nodding in the direction of the twin-rut driveway with a detached shed at its end. "That shed doesn't look big enough fit one, either. I don't think he's home."

"What does he drive?" Wolf asked.

Cain spoke up. "A beat-up Dodge pickup."

"Color?"

"Gray."

A pathway led from the shed to a house side door, which was on the outside of the fence and unguarded by Cujo.

"Sheriff's department!" he yelled, knocking on the door.

The others fanned out behind him. He flicked a glance to Cain, noting she looked rock solid under the pressure. She ignored him, stepping sideways to get a view to the back of the house.

"What do you see?" he asked.

"A back door," she said. "Closed. Two windows. I see no movement inside the windows."

Wolf knocked again. Again, no answer.

"Do you have his phone number?" he asked Rachette.

Rachette pulled out his notebook and read off the number. Wolf dialed it and listened to the trill in his ear. He had to step away from the dog in order to hear, but nobody answered anyway.

"You've reached Rick Hammes, fuck you," the outgoing message said. He shut off the phone and put it in his pocket.

"Sir." Deputy Cain pointed and nodded toward the rear of the house.

Wolf and Yates could see her pointing beyond the back of the house, to the neighboring place down the road. A man was outside, watching the action. He raised a hand and waved.

They waved back, and then the man started down the road toward them. They walked to meet him halfway.

The neighbor was dressed in old jeans and a red and black checked flannel dirtied with food stains down its front. He wore a trucker hat sideways on his head, shading the sun from his eyes. A look more utilitarian than stylish.

"You guys looking for Rick?"

"Yes, sir," Wolf said. "Do you know where he is?"

"Must still be up in Aspen...or Vail? Somewhere doing some construction work or something. I've been tasked to feed that demon monster of a dog every day for him while he's gone."

The man stopped and stared at the dog with squinted eyes. "He'll bark like that for a good half-hour now that you guys came by. He does the same thing to me. I just fill up the bowl and scoot it underneath the fence. Try to not get my arm chewed off in the process. First time I did it he stole the bowl. It's still in that yard, lost forever as far as I'm concerned. Rick owes me four bucks for that when he gets home. But I figured out a great way to do it." He smiled, revealing castle-turret teeth.

When the man said nothing more, Wolf said, "Yeah? What's that?"

"I took an old broom handle and drilled a hole in it. Screwed an old bowl of mine onto the end. Now I just fill it up with food, push it under, pull it back. Hah!" The man clapped with delight. When he laughed it sounded like an engine failing to turn over. His eyes landed on Deputy Cain. "Well, hello. Who's this?"

"When did Mr. Hammes leave?" Wolf asked.

The man cocked his head and pulled up his pants high on his hips. "Heck must've been...what's today?"

"Tuesday," Rachette said.

"Then it was a week ago. He left last Tuesday. No, Wednesday."

"And you're not sure if it was Aspen or Vail?" Wolf asked.

The man thought. "Vail. Definitely Vail. Because he mentioned Edwards, too. You know, the town down the highway from Vail? Got that real expensive hoity-toity ski resort there. Beaver Creek. I used to ski there before they had all the ritzy places that cost ten-grand a night, or whatever it is." He looked at Cain. "I used to be a ski patroller back in my day for Rocky Points."

Wolf cleared his throat. "Are you sure he's been gone since last Tuesday or Wednesday? Did he come back at any time?"

"You know, funny you should ask that. The dog barks if a squirrel farts, you know what I'm saying? But he really goes off if somebody comes over. That's what brought me out to look and see what you guys were doing. Anyway, I heard the dog barking like this last night. I was in bed and it woke me up. I was going to come see what was going on, but he stopped before I got my shoes on. Only person in the world that can get that thing to shut up is Rick. He said he was coming back today or tomorrow, so I figured he might have been back."

"Did you see anybody?" Wolf asked. "Did you come out and look?"

"Nah. Once the dog shut up I went back to sleep. Besides, I can't see my wiener from my face at night. Probably for the better." He looked at Rachette and laughed heartily again.

Rachette gave him a thumbs up.

"Did you hear anybody?" Wolf asked. "A vehicle?"

"Nah."

The man eyed Deputy Cain again, looking like he was going to say something.

"We appreciate you speaking with us, sir." Wolf pulled a card from his back pocket and handed it over. "Could you please give me a call if you see or hear Rick Hammes come home again?"

"Yeah, sure. You got it, Sheriff...David Wolf?"

"That's right." Wolf shook his hand. "And I'm sorry I didn't ask you your name."

"I'm Ned. Ned Larson. Say, you related to Dan Wolf? Sheriff from way back?"

Wolf nodded. "That was my father."

"He was a good man."

"Yes, sir. He was, thanks for saying. And if you could give me a call I'd appreciate it."

"Right. You got it." The man turned to Piper Cain and winked.

She pulled Rachette's move and gave Ned a thumbs up.

They parted with the neighbor and walked back toward house. The dog had stopped barking as it squatted down and relieved itself once again.

"Got the shits, buddy?" Rachette asked.

Wolf averted his eyes as they walked past, because clearly Rachette was right on the money.

Yates put his phone to his ear, plugging the other with a finger as the barking started back up. After a brief conversation he hung up and turned to them. "That was Lorber. They're almost at Mary Dimitri's."

CHAPTER 13

WOLF'S FEET hurt from standing for over an hour in front of Mary Ellen Dimitri's house. He rolled his neck, sneaking a glance toward the group of deputies talking near the side fence. He could have joined them, but while the deputies let off some steam, he felt obligated to maintain a vigil against the growing number of neighbors gathering on the street. They kept their distance, but Wolf had already turned away one overly curious man.

Deputy Cain was laughing heartily as Yates told a story, and Wolf wondered if she was interested in the detective. She was probably closer to Yates's age than his. She seemed to be in her mid-thirties, but she had that ageless quality about her. She must have eaten incredibly healthy.

On his next inhale Wolf felt his own gut push against his belt. Over the last year his activity level had definitely dropped. He was going to get back into the gym as soon as this case was over.

"Stop staring."

Wolf started and turned to see Lorber standing next to him, somehow appearing from the thin Colorado air.

"What did you find in there?" Wolf asked, ignoring the smirk on Lorber's lips.

When Lorber's grin disappeared the exhaustion shone through again. "I'm setting time of death at twenty-four to forty-eight hours. I'll be able to get more specific once I get her on the slab and cut into her."

Lorber had a way with objectifying the dead like no other. Wolf had once decided this was the man's defense mechanism that allowed him to do the job.

Another smattering of raindrops fell from the sky and Wolf zipped his jacket a few inches to his chin. Behind the clouds the sun was dropping lower in the sky, and with it the temperature.

"Daphne will crack into the phone," Lorber said, "but I agree with you: it's an older model so it shouldn't be able to hold a charge very long. It was sitting at about nineteen-percent power when we bagged it. I'm leaning more towards she was killed last night. We'll get an outgoing text or call. We'll probably be able to pinpoint time of death by that alone. Nobody goes more than a second without messing with those devices anymore, and especially nobody from her generation." He flipped a hand at the group of deputies. "See?" he said, as Rachette answered a call.

Wolf said nothing. It was best to refrain from engaging the demon that took over when Lorber was low on sleep and food.

Two forensic technicians pushed Mary Dimitri's bagged body out on a gurney and wheeled her to Lorber's van.

"If Hammes's prints are on that bottle," Lorber said, "they'll show up immediately in the databases. I'll get that going when we get back to the lab."

"Have you talked to Daphne lately?" Wolf asked. "She's still up at the mine, right?"

"She is, and I have not."

"Okay, thanks. Keep me posted." Wolf turned to join the deputies at the side yard.

Rachette paced past him, his cell pressed to his ear. "... just have that one dude pitch. What's his name? Jepson? Jefferson?... oh yeah...I know...I'll be there next week, though...make sure to tell him to keep his right shoulder level when he's swinging..."

Yates, Nelson, Chavez, and Cain stood silently, watching Mary Dimitri's body being loaded.

"Any news from Lorber?" Yates asked.

"Nothing yet."

Rachette walked up to them, pocketing his phone. "What did I miss?"

"Who was that?" Wolf asked.

"Charlotte."

Wolf looked at his watch—6:15. "TJ has a baseball game tonight. Is that what you two were talking about?"

"Yeah."

"You missed last week's game, too, because of training."

Rachette nodded. "Yeah. Well, cop first, right?"

Wolf felt the other eyes on him. He felt Deputy Cain's eyes on him. "Why don't you head back and catch your son's game."

"No, sir, it's okay."

"That's an order. Yates, you head back with him. Nelson and Chavez, you two stay here."

"What are you going to do?" Yates asked.

"I'm heading to the casino to find out when Mary Dimitri was last seen at work and who she might have been with."

"You sure you don't need help?" Rachette asked.

Wolf shook his head. "No. Go." He looked at Deputy Cain. "Thanks for your help today. You can head home, too."

"I'll go with you," she said.

He wanted to say no, almost said it, but then nodded. "Yeah. Okay, thanks."

The other men were staring at them in silence.

He waved a hand. "Get out of here."

As Wolf walked to his SUV, Cain asked, "Should I ride with you?"

"Uh, yeah sure."

She started toward his SUV when Wolf shouted "Wait!" He ran past her and opened the door, scooping all the trash—fast food bags, wadded-up napkins, and three stray French fries—into one bag, and put it in the rear.

When he got behind the wheel she was already seated in the passenger seat. He was acutely aware of her scent battling it out with the smell of old food and months of general use.

She lowered the sun visor and looked in the mirror, touching the numerous bandages on her face.

He fired up the engine and cracked the windows. "Sorry about the..." He let the sentence trail into nothing.

"The what?"

"The smell of my car."

She smiled. "I've smelled worse. My ride's not the cleanest either."

"I had my head inside of it yesterday. But I appreciate the lie."

Wolf turned the SUV around and headed toward Dredge's Main Street.

"Left here," she said, then checked her cell phone and put it in her pocket again. Her hands patted out a beat on her leg.

"You sure you don't need to go home?"

"No. I'm fine."

He nodded, letting silence take over for a bit.

"How long have you lived in Rocky Points?" she asked.

"All my life. I was born in the county hospital."

"Oh, wow."

"What about you?" Wolf asked. "Where are you from?"

"Summit County. My father was a deputy with the sheriff's department. We lived in Breckenridge." She pointed out the window to the north, where a wall of mountains separated them from her childhood home.

"You said you worked up in Bozeman?"

"I was with the Gallatin Sheriff's Department for nine years."

"Nine years. Wow. So, what brought you here?" he asked.

"My father's not doing too well, and my mother passed away a few years ago."

"Oh. I'm sorry to hear that. What's wrong with him?"

"Dementia. Alzheimer's."

He thought about his own mother down in Denver, also battling the early stages of dementia.

"You left your job in Bozeman to take care of him?"

She stared out the window. "Yeah."

Silence enveloped the cab for the next block, until Wolf said, "That's noble of you. You must love him very much."

She said nothing in response, but took a deep breath, and Wolf heard tension in the exhale.

"You probably want to turn here," she said. "And park on that side there."

"Do they ever use this many parking spots?" Wolf asked, as they coasted through an asphalt lot the size of a football field. "Doesn't seem like they would get this many visitors from Denver. It's nowhere near I-70."

"Not that I've ever seen," she said. "Right here, in front of that entrance. The casino and lounge is through there."

Wolf parked and they got out. He stretched his back, studying the casino ahead. As he'd noted before on the drive in, it was brown stucco, accented with huge lodgepole pines framing the entrances and banks of glass windows reflecting the surrounding mountains.

"Here we are," Cain said. "The Motherlode Casino."

"After you," he said.

Piper Cain could feel the sheriff's eyes on her as she led the way through the parking lot toward the casino. The wind was relentless, whipping her hair into a frenzy behind her. It was going to take forever to get the knots out after the day's events. Beneath their bandages, the scrapes on her cheeks were starting to itch fiercely, but she willed herself not to touch them.

She pulled out her phone and quickly looked at the screen. Still no messages or missed calls. She was assuming no news was good news, and she hoped she was right. Pretty soon she was going to have to wrap up this field day with Sheriff Wolf and get back to her father.

But not yet. The more time she could spend with these people—the sheriff being the most important of them all—the better.

The wind died down when they got to the automatic doors of the casino. In the glass reflection, she saw her hair swirling like smoke coming off a doused ember, so she quickly redid her ponytail. She could swear she saw Sheriff Wolf eyeing her backside as she bent to tie back her hair. When she straightened and looked at him, his attention was somewhere else completely.

She watched as he continued through the casino doors. She had to admit she didn't mind watching that cute rear end of his, either.

Or maybe you've been seeing things and you need to get a grip.

She passed through the doors and into a jackpot bell to her senses. Smoke choked the air, invading her lungs. Bells, whistles, screeches, whines, cartoon barking, and all manner of digital sounds, both from this planet and fictional ones, flooded her ears. People of all shapes, colors, and sizes sat on stools, feeding their money into the machines in front of them.

It was so disorienting she had to slow down to find Wolf. It didn't take much, he was a good head taller than anybody else in the place, except for a security pit boss who was standing next to him now, pointing in the direction of the lounge.

She followed him into a sunken area filled with cocktail tables doubling as electronic poker money ingesting machines. Only a few of the tables were occupied. Two middle-aged men stared at her, smirking and talking to one another. She felt her facial skin flushing under the bandages. She got the overwhelming urge to go to them and give them a closer look, maybe a smack upside the skull, but she ignored them instead.

When a cocktail waitress wearing high heels and short shorts walked by, Wolf stopped her and spoke into her ear.

"What was that, honey?" she asked.

"Does Mary Ellen Dimitri work here?"

The woman's face soured. "Well, she should be working here. In fact, she should be working right under this tray, but I'm covering for her ass because she never showed up tonight."

Wolf's head swiveled. "Can you please point me to her boss?"

The woman tipped her chin toward the corner of the lounge, where a neon pink flamingo glowed on the wall above a bar. "See that guy with the blue shirt on? That's Jed. He's our boss." She looked at Piper and then back to Wolf, something clicking in her brain. "What are you two doing in here, anyway, asking about Mary Ellen?"

Wolf said nothing. "Thank you, ma'am. We're going to go talk to your boss now."

"Wait a minute. What happened to Mary Ellen? Is something wrong? Is that why she's not answering her phone?"

A drink slid off of the tray, crashed to the floor, and then five more drinks followed, splashing all three of them in the legs with liquid and shattered glass.

Piper backed up, feeling the liquid seep through to her shins and into her socks and shoes. She watched in mute fascination as Wolf, even more soaked than she was, act as if nothing out of the ordinary had happened. He simply bent over, put the tray on the ground, and began putting the glasses back on top. Then he plucked the sharp shards of glass off the carpet, putting them on top of the tray. Before she realized she was standing there like a doofus doing nothing, it was all over.

The woman picked up the tray in both hands, holding it to her belly.

Wolf nodded toward the bar. "Back there, you said?"

She nodded, saying nothing.

"Thank you, ma'am."

Wolf led the way again, Piper following closely. The way he dove into action like that, and pretty much every other Wolf interaction she'd seen today, suggested this man was thoughtful and kind.

So how did her resume get overlooked without a single word? It must have been a disconnect somewhere in the department that Wolf was unaware of. He would have mentioned something by now if he'd remembered her. But that woman, the receptionist and dispatcher named Tammy, had told her the sheriff would get back to her personally. That she'd personally delivered her resume to his desk.

Maybe she was lying. Maybe he was lying.

Whatever was happening, it all started from the top and trickled down. She'd seen men acting like perfect gentleman until the going got tough, and it was tough to straight up tell somebody they didn't get the job, or that they were fired. She suspected Sheriff David Wolf had somebody who did his dirty work for him. Maybe Tammy was tasked to do his dirty work but she was too scared to go through with it. Two cowards ducking and jumping over responsibility, passing it back and forth, like a shitty game of dodge ball.

Wolf arrived at the bar and leaned on an elbow. "Are you okay?" he asked her.

"What? Good. I'm fine."

He studied her for a second, then turned to the passing bartender. "Excuse me, sir?"

The bartender, a skin and bones man with thinning hair, avoided eye contact as he picked up a soda gun and filled a glass with dark liquid. "Yes, sir. What can I help you with?"

"I'm Sheriff Wolf, this is Deputy Cain. We'd like to speak to you in private, please, about one of your employees."

"I'm a little busy right now. It's the rush."

The man re-holstered the soda gun and walk to the far end of the bar, placing the soda on a tray and then filling a beer in one fluid motion. With expert precision, he angled the glass, filled it with urine-yellow liquid topped with no head and placed it on the tray, spilling some in the process. He picked up a piece of paper, read it impatiently, and dove into a stack of cocktail glasses, filled them with ice and poured two cocktails.

She eyed Wolf, wondering what his play would be. The sheriff seemed unfazed. Had he moved since they'd gotten there? His eyes tracked the bartender.

"The rush," she said.

Wolf said nothing.

The bartender walked past, not looking at them. He filled up another soda. "Look, I'm one server short today. What's going on?"

"That's who we're here to talk about. Mary Ellen Dimitri."

The bartender's eyes flicked to Wolf's, then narrowed. "What about her?"

"When did she last work?"

"I'd have to check the schedule." The man gathered some tiny pizzas out of a toaster oven and put them on a plate. Piper's mouth watered at the sight and smell of the casino lounge fare, which meant she was beyond hungry. It had been so long since she'd eaten.

The waitress from before appeared behind the counter in front of Wolf and Piper. She slid the broken glass into the trashcan.

"What the hell happened?" the bartender asked.

"I dropped the tray."

"Shit. You're killing me, Janine!"

"Something's wrong with Mary Ellen!" Janine shouted.

The bartender turned around, looking at them as if noticing them for the first time. "What's wrong with her?"

"I think something happened," Janine said.

"What happened?"

"Ask them," Janine said with a quivering voice. "Can't be nothing good. She didn't show up tonight. She's not answering her phone or texts. She always shows up, Jed. You know that." She looked at Wolf and Piper. "Tell us."

The bartender came over, lowering his rag onto the bar counter. "Okay, you have my attention."

Wolf looked sideways at a man sitting belly-up to the bar. He was staring at them, a forkful of food hovering over his plate.

They walked down the bar the opposite direction. "I'm afraid we have bad news. We found Mary Ellen dead in her home this afternoon."

"Oh my God," Janine said. "I knew something was wrong. I knew it. I knew..." She stopped talking and began crying.

The bartender put an arm around her and glared at Wolf. "Why didn't you say that in the first place?"

Wolf straightened, then turn towards Piper and leaned his other elbow on the bar. His knee brushed her leg and she held it there, letting him move first, which he did, but only after a few moments. For the first time, Wolf's non-descript masculine scent cut through the smoke and food. Probably a budget shampoo or bar soap from Walmart mixed with a generic fabric softener and a splash of aftershave. Whatever it was she decided it smelled okay on him.

The bartender waved them further down to the end of the bar and then met them at an opening. "Okay, what the hell is going on? What happened?"

"Sorry we can't discuss any of the details just yet, not while we're investigating."

"Investigating? What does that mean? Was she...murdered or something?" he whispered the last part of the sentence.

Wolf said nothing for a while, then nodded. "It looks that way, yes."

Janine made a face that would have made a D-list horror actor proud. "Who killed her? Was it Rick?"

"Are you talking about Rick Hammes?" Wolf asked.

"Yes."

"Why would you ask that?"

She started shaking her head. "I told her what she was doing was stupid. She was screwing him on the side. Shit. Chris was killed, too."

"We really need to know when Mary Ellen was working last," Wolf said.

The bartender nodded and pulled a clipboard off a hook on the back wall. He flipped up a sheet of paper and tapped his finger. "Says here she was first cut yesterday."

"First cut?" Wolf asked.

"Yeah. The first of the waitresses to get to go home."

"And what time was that?"

"It's usually seven."

"Usually?"

"I wasn't here. Janine, what time was first cut last night?"

"Yeah. It was like, seven," Janine said.

"You're sure?"

"Yes. Seven. It was seven. Monday night. It's always seven, unless its football season. It was seven."

Wolf nodded. "I'm sorry to give you guys this news. I know it's hard."

Piper cleared her throat. "Why were you asking about Rick, Janine?"

Janine looked over at Piper as if she'd just materialized. "Like I said, she was hooking up with him. We've all heard about Chris's death up at the mine. Shit, Mary Ellen was crying about it last night at work. That's why we let her go at first cut. I was just...I've been thinking maybe Chris's death had something to do with Rick. I mean, Rick's a real scary guy. I was telling her she was playing with fire with him. She's always hooking up with the wrong guy." She put a hand over her mouth and started crying again.

Piper's phone vibrated repeatedly in her pocket, like she was getting a call, but she ignored it. This was not the time. Damn it. She needed to get back to her father. She'd already pressed her luck by at least three hours by her count.

She reached down into her pocket and pressed the call end button.

Almost immediately the phone vibrated again, and then another time. Another call.

She turned, slipping it discreetly out of her jeans and saw it was Jerry Slavens, her father's neighbor. Again she pressed the call end button and pocketed her phone.

"... but they went to The Picker all the time. I think she went there after work. You'd have to check with them..." Janine was really talking now.

The phone vibrated three times fast, indicating a voicemail.

She pulled out her phone and read the transcribed message, and her heart almost exploded, it began beating so fast. "Shit."

"What is it?" Wolf asked.

"I...I have to..." she shook her head. "I have to go, sir. I have to go right now."

CHAPTER 14

WOLF WATCHED Deputy Cain's fingers dig into her thighs, her blunt nails pushing into the denim fabric of her jeans. She gripped her phone with white knuckles in her other hand.

"Is there anything I can do to help?" Wolf asked.

"You could maybe drive a little faster."

Wolf hit the lights and siren and pushed the accelerator.

"Where am I going?"

"Back to my Jeep," she said.

"No, I'll just take you straight where you need to go. Forget the Jeep."

"No!"

He turned to her.

"No. It's...look it's not that big a deal. But I need to have my own car and deal with this on my own." She forced a smile. "Really. Thanks, though."

They sat in silence, listening to the roaring engine. It wasn't long before he had to jam the brakes, though. What little traffic there was on the Main Street of downtown Dredge was pedestrian.

"Just hang a right here and go the back roads the last couple blocks."

Wolf followed her orders, a minute later coming up on her Jeep, still parked on the side of Mary Ellen Dimitri's house. He pulled up to her driver's door and stopped.

She was out of his vehicle before he'd come to a complete halt, and then into her Jeep in a flash. She started up, cranked the wheel, and spit dirt as she accelerated around him and back the way they'd come.

Two deputies sitting inside a cruiser parked along the street stared out the windows in muted awe.

Wolf gave a thumbs up, sitting with the engine idling. What could possibly have spooked her so bad? It had to be something to do with her father.

He slammed the accelerator, fishtailing a one-eighty degree turn and following the stream of dust.

He followed down Main, speeding back through town, past the casino, and out a dirt county road that shot left up the eastern side of the valley floor. The engine howled as he passed a row of cows munching grass along a barbed wire fence. When he reached a dirt straightaway he pressed the accelerator harder, the vibration of the cab humming.

The sun had dropped behind the mountains in his rearview and the dust trail clung low to the ground over the road. He sneezed and coughed, feeling like he'd inhaled pepper, as the dust billowed through his vents. He hung back a bit, confident he wouldn't lose her now that he'd caught her trail.

Five minutes later the road broke into a wall of trees, the light dipping even more.

A short while later the trees opened up and he passed a sprawling yard that stretched up to a modern house surrounded by a white wraparound porch. His headlights illuminated the dust trail leading straight ahead, so he followed. A bend came up quick and he let off the gas.

Halfway through the turn he jammed the brakes and slid to a stop. Ahead, Deputy Cain's vehicle was stopped and angled at forty-five degrees, her headlights illuminating a form shrouded in dust in the middle of the road.

Wolf stepped out into the choking air and shut his door.

"Who's that?" a male's voice came from the center of the road.

Deputy Cain stood at the edge of her headlight stream, ignoring Wolf's arrival as she approached the man with both hands up, palms facing him.

"He's a friend," she said. "Dad, please. Put down the gun."

The dust rolled into the trees, revealing her father, naked save a pair of white briefs and sandals. He was tall and gaunt, ghostly white in the blazing lights, and he was holding a shotgun.

Wolf put his hand on his own gun, but saw Deputy Cain shaking her head, her eyes wide and pleading for him to stand back.

Wolf put his own hands up, showing her. But when he looked back at her father, his heart lurched, because the double-barrel was pointed straight at him.

"I said who's that?"

"Dad, that's my boss. That's the sheriff."

Her father lowered the gun and put a hand up over his eyes to peer at him. "I can't see him."

A house stood on Wolf's left, tucked inside the trees. Two elderly people were peering out the window, ducking low.

"Forget him. Listen, Dad, what are you doing? Why do you have a shotgun?"

Her father seemed preoccupied with something on the ground now.

Wolf stepped quietly to the side, coming up on Cain's nine o'clock and into the edge of the headlight cone.

Her father pointed his shotgun at the dirt, tucking the stock into his armpit. Wolf tensed, every fiber in his being wanting to pull his Glock and start yelling, but her father aimed toward the other side of the road. Anything ricocheting would have hit the trees opposite the elderly couples' house. Wolf opted to stay silent, giving the situation to Cain.

The silence seemed to intensify before the expected blast, but it never came. Instead, her father lowered the gun and looked up at his daughter like he'd just awakened from a deep sleep.

"Honey, what are you doing here?"

Cain's chest heaved as she clenched her mouth shut, then took a breath. "Dad, please come here."

Her father's face slowly turned to Wolf. The shotgun, still aimed at the ground, followed. "Ah, Jonathan," he said, "You're looking dapper tonight. Come. Come on in, boy."

That was different.

"You're looking very nice." He held the shotgun in the crook of his arm. "Tell me. Where are you taking my daughter tonight?"

Wolf cleared his throat. "Um...I'm..."

"Speak up, boy. You gotta have confidence. Didn't your father ever teach you that?"

Wolf looked at Cain, getting no ideas from her, he cleared his throat again.

"You're not just going to go to the dance, are you? Surely you're going to take my daughter out to dinner. Show her a good time on the town first, right?"

"Yes," Wolf said. "We're going to the steakhouse, sir."

"Which one? Buck's or Green Acres?"

"Buck's, sir."

Her father's face lit. "Fancy. How are you paying for that? Do you work?"

"Yes, sir."

"Where at?"

Wolf looked at Deputy Cain. She stared back, resignation in her eyes.

Wolf remembered how she'd grown up in Summit County. The man was obviously living sometime in the past. "I'm on the ski patrol...in Breckenridge."

"A little young for that, aren't you?"

"Yes," Wolf said, offering no more explanation.

Her father looked at him skeptically, then smiled. "What else? Just dinner?

"No, sir. There is a community play at the Playhouse...it's an improv night that I'm taking her to." Wolf drew on a high school memory of his and Sarah's senior prom.

Her father laughed heartily. "I've seen the improv show there before. It's funny. You guys will love it." His face darkened and he gripped the shotgun, broke open the barrel just enough to check the shells inside, and show them, then snapped it shut again. "Then you'll have her home by 11, right?"

"Yes, sir."

"If you harm my girl in any way..." He pointed a finger at Wolf.

"I would never harm your daughter, sir."

"Good." He looked at Piper, back at Wolf. "Do you like her, son?"

Wolf hesitated.

"I asked you a question."

"Yes, sir."

"Yes, sir, what?"

"Yes, sir. I like your daughter."

"Look at her," he beamed at Cain. She looked down at the ground.

"She looks beautiful, doesn't she?"

"Yes," Wolf said, this time not hesitating.

Cain looked up at him. Tears streaked down her face.

"She does look beautiful," he added.

Her eyes flicked back to the ground.

"Well, you two have a good time. Come give me a kiss, honey."

Cain went over, took the gun from his hands and hugged him. She held out the shotgun behind her and Wolf eased up quickly, took it from her, and backed away, cracking open the barrel and expelling the shells.

Wolf went to the back of his SUV, popped open the back and put the shotgun inside. He grabbed a thermal blanket, shut the hatch and went back. He handed over the blanket to Cain, who took it and wrapped it around the shoulders of her father before steering him into the passenger seat.

"Thank you," her father said. "I'm cold."

Wolf watched in silence as she shut the door, walked back to the driver's side, got in, and drove away the way they had come in.

"Everything okay?" A light flicked on the neighbors' front porch.

"You tell me," Wolf said. "Are you two all right?"

"We'll be fine." The light flicked off and the front door closed as they went back inside.

Wolf stared at the darkened house for a second, watching the two people inside settling down in front of a television.

He got back in his SUV and turned around. Slowly, he eased down the road, coming up on the next house with the sprawling lawn and wraparound porch.

At the top of the driveway near the side of the home, Cain's Jeep lights blossomed red, and then went black.

He pulled over at the mouth of the driveway, rolled down his window, and watched her escort her father up the side steps, onto the porch, and into the house.

She left the front door wide open, letting the light spill out in a long dagger across the lawn, reaching the road in front of Wolf. He put it in park, turned off the engine, put his elbow out into the cool air, watching through the house windows as she walked her father into a back hallway and out of sight.

She came out into the hallway again, ducked into another room, flicked on a light. After a second the light flicked off and she appeared briefly before disappearing again.

He felt a twinge of guilt looking in on their life. He was unwelcome guest. Had he just helped or almost blown a situation completely out of control? Staring at the still wide-open front door, he remembered her words before. *I need to take care of this myself.*

Just then Cain came outside, shutting the door behind her. She waved at him and ran down the steps, jogged across the lawn and crunched her way down the dirt driveway to his window.

She put both hands on the edge of the door either side of his elbow. She was slightly out of breath. Her eyes glimmered like pools of oil in the shadow of her face.

"Everything okay?" he asked, shifting back into park.

She said nothing.

"Sorry. Stupid question."

"I left him here alone," she said.

"Oh," Wolf said. He wasn't sure what else to say.

They stood in silence for a beat. She stared past the hood of his car into the trees, looking like she wanted to say something.

"Listen," he said. "I'm sorry about—"

He stopped talking, because at that moment she grabbed his arm and squeezed. Her hand was warm and soft. Firm but gentle. It lingered there, and then when she pulled it away it was almost a caress.

"Thanks for your help," she said.

He opened his mouth to respond, but she turned and ran back up the driveway and across the lawn.

He watched her go, hypnotized by her quick, fluid strides. She climbed the steps two at a time, ducked back inside, flicked off the light, and shut the door, sending the front lawn into darkness again.

Wolf shook his head and fired up the engine. He shifted into drive, and when he started coasting down the road he said, "You're welcome."

CHAPTER 15

PATTERSON GOT out of the elevator on the third floor and hobbled down the hall to the spacious office she would call her own for a few more weeks. Pretty soon she would be back in the squad room sitting in that desk across from Rachette with all the sights, smells, and sounds that came with.

She pulled the blinds up all the way, letting the view to the west fill her vision. At 6:15 a.m. the sun had not yet risen above the peaks that caged in the eastern half of the Chautauqua Valley, but the land outside was brightening into full beauty.

She loved this time of the morning, before the swing shift started, when the bustle of the nighttime deputies clashing with the daytime starters riled the building into a frenzy of activity. This was her time.

She set down her stuff, grabbed her crutches, and went out into the squad room for a coffee. Wolf's glass-enclosed office was dark, the blinds pulled tight, and she wondered if he was sleeping inside again.

"Hey there." A voice called from the squad room.

Charlotte Munford-Rachette stood up from her desk and stretched her arms overhead. "How's your ankle feeling?"

"You scared me." Patterson hobbled over. "It's feeling better this morning. But not by much, I guess."

Charlotte's eyes were half-closed and bloodshot. Her normally vibrant smile was subdued.

Patterson looked at the stack of paperwork on Charlotte's desk. "What are you doing?"

Charlotte suppressed a yawn. "I'm just trying to catch up."

Patterson sighed, seeing the familiar pile of paperwork that had been on her desk yesterday. "I talked to Wolf yesterday about those," she said. "He and Wilson miscommunicated. They won't come in this late anymore. I'll make sure of it."

Charlotte nodded. "Thanks. To be honest, it's not that bad being out of the house bright and early for a change. I'll let the nanny change the peed sheets for a change."

"Oh no. Rachette?" Patterson used his last name, knowing Charlotte had started referring to her own husband by his last name to avoid confusion with their son, Tom.

Charlotte laughed. "No, he hasn't peed anywhere interesting in a few years. The plant is doing much better."

They chatted some about the efficacy of overnight diapers, until Charlotte picked up a sheet of paper from her desk. "You want to know something interesting I just saw?"

Patterson looked over her shoulder. "Sluice-Byron County Pension Fund contribution to stop..." her voice faded as she read the name printed on the sheet.

William James MacLean.

"What does this mean?" Charlotte asked. "They want to stop paying contributions to his pension? Now? When he's about to be reinstated?" She slapped the paper down. When she turned around her eyes were alight with mischief. "Or, are we seeing the first evidence he's really retiring? That he's not coming back?"

Patterson blinked. Holy cow. Maybe her harebrained idea

yesterday wasn't so crazy. Maybe she was about to be Undersheriff after all. Her breathing tensed. How did she feel about this? What did this mean?

She checked herself. *Just wait a minute.* This was crazy. She had to be wrong.

"I don't think he's coming back," Charlotte said.

"I don't know."

"But why stop contributing to his pension, then?" Charlotte pecked her finger on the paper. "And look at the date? It's the date he's supposed to return."

Patterson shook her head. "Listen, that's not what I've heard. You know him, he's pretty financially savvy. He's making some play that's beyond our comprehension."

"I think he's retiring."

"Please don't start that rumor."

Charlotte straightened and backed away. "Geez. Yeah. I wasn't going to, I was just..."

"Just what?"

"Nothing. Yeah. You're right. It's weird, but we have no clue what it means. We'll know in a couple weeks." Charlotte got busy checking paperwork again.

Heather watched her, thinking about telling Charlotte to refrain from telling her husband. She thought about reminding her that people like Rachette spread rumors through the county building faster than viruses spread sickness. But she knew that no matter what she said it was too late. This was going to be dinner conversation tonight at the Munford-Rachette household.

"Please tell Tom to not tell anybody," Heather said. "Not until we know more."

Charlotte put on a short-lived appalled face, then shrugged. "I'll tell him to shut up about it."

"I'm sure that will work. See you later," Patterson said, crutching to Wolf's office.

She popped open the unlocked door and ducked inside.

Wolf's sleeping bag wasn't on the floor.

She stood in the silence, thinking about that sheet of pension paper she'd just looked at. She was inclined to think Charlotte was right, although she'd never handled any HR matters so she didn't know what to think.

Patterson looked around the office. The space was surrounded by people depending on you, looking through the windows to see what you were doing. Judging. Criticizing. The glass walls of this office bore the load of the rest of the building. If they cracked, a lot of people would be crushed.

She could help Wolf do it, though. With both of them holding up these walls, this place would be rock solid. Things wouldn't slip through the cracks the way they were now. There would be no cracks.

Wilson was good, but she would be better. Was that egotistical? No, it was just fact.

Wolf's desk was clean, devoid of paperwork for once, the shiny oak reflecting the slivers of light streaming through the blinds.

She backed out and shut the door, and then stopped at Charlotte's desk one more time.

"Not to start any more rumors or anything," Patterson said.

Charlotte looked around at the empty room. "Yes?"

"But have you heard anything about Wilson leaving?"

Charlotte nodded. "Yeah. He's been looking at that job down in Denver. Assistant Chief of Police or something, right?"

"Yeah. But there's no official word on that?" She gestured to her desk. "No official human resources paperwork coming through?"

Charlotte shook her head. "No. Why?"

Patterson turned and left before the conversation turned into uncharted territory. "I'll see you later."

Patterson went back to her office and pulled another chair over behind her desk to prop her foot on, groaning as the pressure and pain released.

For the next thirty minutes she sipped her coffee and worked quietly, while echoing voices grew to a crescendo as seven o'clock neared.

Two sharp knocks rapped on her door and Wolf ducked his head inside. "Good morning."

He stepped in and sat down. "I saw that spreadsheet and report. It looked really good. I just sent it off to Margaret."

She set down her pen. "You did? I wanted to go over that with you before you sent it."

He shrugged. "Why? It was perfect. No reason to. Seriously. Good job."

"Well, I just wanted to know if you wanted to make any changes."

"Do you think there needed to be changes made to it?"

She shook her head. "No."

Wolf smiled. "That's why I sent it off. Really, it was great. I knew you were perfect for the job."

She nodded, eyeing him. He was in a better mood than she'd seen in a long time. Maybe it was the load of the report off his back.

"What?" Wolf asked.

"Nothing."

"Did you talk to Hammes's parole officer yesterday?" Wolf asked.

She pushed a manila folder forward. "There's his file."

As Wolf opened it up, Rachette barreled through the door, knocking as he entered. "Hey, what's going on in here?"

"Hammes's parole file," Wolf said, flipping pages.

Rachette stopped behind him, looking over his shoulder. "Yates is down with Lorber, checking on the prints off those beer bottles and Mary Dimitri's autopsy."

"Good," Wolf said. He tapped his finger on the sheet in front of him. "There's nothing in here about Rick Hammes working at a construction company in Aspen or Vail."

"Did you talk to his boss at the casino?" Rachette asked. "I was hoping maybe he quit amicably. Maybe told somebody where he went next."

Patterson looked at Wolf. The sheriff kept his head down.

"Sir?"

"Yeah."

"Did you talk to Hammes's boss at the casino restaurant?"

Wolf flipped a page. "Uh. No. I actually didn't get around to it."

Rachette frowned, looking at Patterson. Patterson shrugged.

"I thought you and Cain went to the casino," Rachette said.

"We did. We talked to Mary Dimitri's boss, though. We found out she was working until seven P.M. Monday night. She left alone. So she was killed Monday night, or early Tuesday morning."

"We have to track down Rick Hammes," Patterson said. "And... why, exactly, didn't you talk to his former boss at the casino restaurant?"

Wolf sat back, finally looking up at her. "Deputy Cain's father had...an episode. I had to go help her with it. When it was over, it was late. I was tired. I came home. I slept. I'll go back up today and finish the interviews." Wolf dug back into the file.

Rachette popped his eyebrows and mouthed the words, *Deputy Cain.*

Wolf turned around. "What?"

"Nothing, sir. Yates is down talking to Lorber."

"You already said that."

"I did. Yes, I did."

Yates came into the office, knocking. "I was just down talking to Lorber."

"So we've heard," Patterson said. She put her foot up on the chair, savoring deflation of pain out of her ankle again. "What did he have?"

Yates held up a piece of paper in his hand and fluttered it. "He found prints on the two beer bottles matching Hammes."

"Okay," Rachette said. "Now we're getting somewhere."

Yates read from the paper. "The bullet hole in the top of her skull was the same size as the one through the top of Chris Oakley's head. Same stippling on her chin. As Detective Rachette and I ascertained yesterday, none of Mary Dimitri's neighbors heard any gunshots Monday night, or the night before."

"The Sheriff just told us he spoke to Mary Ellen's boss at the casino," Patterson said. "She was working Monday night until seven p.m. So, she would have been shot Monday night, or early Tuesday morning."

Yates nodded, pointing at the paper. "Lorber's report puts the time of death around midnight, Monday night."

Yates put the sheet of paper on Patterson's desk, still holding another couple of sheets in his other hand.

"What's that?" she asked.

"The warrant you were going to ask me to get for Hammes's arrest." He slapped it on the desk.

"And?"

"The search warrant for his house."

Wolf scooped them up. "Let's go."

The three men walked out of the room at full speed, leaving a swirl of their aftershave and, in Rachette's case, cheap cologne, in their wake.

With a sigh she got up, the blood thumping back into her

foot, hammering down with an explosion of pain with each hop as she went to her door and closed it. Once back to her desk she sat again, put her foot up, and gripped her computer mouse.

She clicked over to her email and saw a new one from Margaret Hitchens, her aunt and mayor of the town of Rocky Points. It was a reply from an original email from Wolf to Margaret including the report and spreadsheet. The County Treasurer, Leo Helms, and the other members of the county council budget committee, Mike Barrish, and Jack Herschel, were CC'd along with Patterson.

She clicked it open.

Excellent work Heather and David! I've already spoken to everyone and we like it. Looks like we will be able to move forward with this. We'll stay in touch if we need anything else, but really this is above and beyond. Excellent job.

Patterson stared at the words, pride welling up inside her.

She had to admit. She could get used to this.

CHAPTER 16

THE ROAD to Dredge looked different under a morning sky devoid of clouds. Wolf cracked the window to test the air and was rewarded with a chill swirl to the face.

He rolled it back up and sipped his coffee, checking the rearview. Rachette and Yates, followed close behind, rounding the bend behind him.

His thoughts returned back, for the what seemed like the thousandth time, to Deputy Cain squeezing his arm the night before. Not in a very long time had a touch sent so much electricity flowing through his body. The way she'd held the sustained pressure, and swirled her fingers as she let go.

And then there was that brushing of their legs in the casino at the bar. That had been something, hadn't it? At first it had been a clear mistake, but not pulling her leg away was no error. Of course, he'd kept his leg still, too. It had been like a mini game of chicken, and for a few moments neither of them had backed down.

Or it had been two innocent, incidental contacts with Deputy Piper Cain. My God, he had to get ahold of himself. He rolled down the window again, this time all the way, dousing any heat coming off his body with a roiling blast of frigid air.

He took the wheel with both hands and let the air clear his head for a full few minutes.

As he came around a bend the valley opened up. Aspens shimmered along the river, the sunlight poking through, and he could detect the scent of the river. Another good day to be out on the job and not behind the desk if there ever was one. With MacLean's triumphant return from his battle with cancer he was bound to have many more of these days.

His phone vibrated in the center console, bringing him back to the present.

He picked it up and saw a missed call from a phone number he didn't recognize. There was a voicemail, so he pressed the button and put it to his ear, rolling up the window so he could hear.

"Hey, it's Ned. He's back. Out petting his dog right now. You said call, so I called."

Wolf frowned and lowered the phone, momentarily confused by what he'd just heard. And then he remembered Ned Larson had been the neighbor and he was talking about Rick Hammes.

Wolf slowed to a stop on the side of the road, hoping he was still inside one of the rare eddies of cell reception in this area and dialed the number back.

"Mr. Larson? This is Sheriff Wolf. You just called me?"

Wolf lowered his window and held up a finger to an approaching Rachette, who had stepped out of his own car and was walking up. "I'm just making sure I heard your message correctly, sir. Did you say Rick Hammes is back at his house?"

"Yes, sir. He already came over and yelled at me. Bastard thinks I fed his dog steak. I know about the damn dog not being able to digest meat, and I didn't feed him no T-bone. I told him he's lucky I fed him at all. Well, I didn't tell him that. The man's scary as hell. Don't—"

"Sir," Wolf interrupted him. "Is he still there now?"

Rachette narrowed his eyes, waiting for Wolf's answer.

"Yes, sir."

Wolf nodded for Rachette's benefit.

"Looks like's he's settling in," Ned said. "He never said anything to me about leaving again. I tell you I'm not going to watch his dog again if—"

"Sir," Wolf stopped the man's rant again. "I have to go. Thank you very much for the call. I appreciate it."

Wolf hung up. "He's there. Who do we have up there at Mary Dimitri's?"

"Chavez," Rachette said. "He stayed the night."

"Who's at the mine?"

Rachette shrugged.

Wolf thought about it. "Okay. Get Chavez over there, I'll figure out who was at the mine and have them head over there, too. But tell Chavez not to engage," Wolf pointed at Rachette, "and make that clear to him. He's just there to make sure Hammes doesn't leave."

"And if he does leave?"

"Then tell Chavez to follow him. At a distance."

"What about Cain?" Rachette asked. "I'd trust her on the job more than Chavez. He's a good guy and all, but he's green as they come."

Wolf nodded. "I'll call Cain. She might not be available, so get Chavez, go."

Looking through his phone contacts, Wolf realized he didn't have Deputy Cain's phone number. He dialed Tammy.

"Yes, sir. What do you need?" she said in a sing-song voice.

"Tammy, who do we have up at the mine right now?"

"Deputy Nelson."

Wolf filled her in. "Can you call Nelson and tell him to make his way down to Hammes's house?"

"Will do."

"Anything else?"

"Yes. Do you have a phone number for Deputy Piper Cain, the satellite unit up in Dredge?"

"That cute girl who came in to apply this winter. Sure do."

"Yeah. Wait, what?"

"I have the number. Just a second."

"No, the part about applying. What did you say?"

"Yeah. She came into the department this winter with her resume."

"Oh." Wolf's world rearranged, memories of Deputy Cain coming out of the recesses of his mind, shuffling, forming a full picture.

He'd looked at her resume as it came across his desk. That's why she looked familiar.

He thought of the way she'd been acting yesterday, how when he'd asked about her past she'd looked at him with that unreadable expression. This winter he'd hired Deputy Chavez by recommendation from Wilson, who knew him through a friend of a friend, but Wolf had put the next hire on hold when the storm had hit—a seven day onslaught of snow not seen in five decades that had shut down the entire town, even the ski resort, crippling the ski lifts.

Wolf had meant the pause in hiring to last a week, but it had stretched to two, then a whole month. Once again he'd been playing catch-up and the storm's aftermath only made getting back to normal harder.

Those are excuses, he told himself, using a voice that sounded a lot like his father's.

"Hello? You there?"

"Sorry, yeah. Can you please patch me through to her cell?"

"Yep. I'm patching it." A few seconds later, there was a crackle and then it began to ring in his ear. She picked up quickly.

"Deputy Cain here."

"Deputy Cain, this is Sheriff Wolf."

"Oh, hello. How are you?"

"I'm good. Um...how's your father doing?"

"He's doing well. He got a good rest last night and seems to be doing better. Thanks for asking."

"Right. Actually, I'm not calling for that. I mean, I'm glad he's doing well, but listen, are you able to leave your house?"

"Yes. I'm already out on duty. I have regular help that comes to stay with my father when I'm at work. Yesterday was just different. It was..."

"It was what?"

"It was my day off."

"Oh. I didn't know that. Well... Listen, Rick Hammes is back in town. I just got a call from his neighbor. I've got Deputy Chavez en route. I'd like a little bit more experience backing him up. If you could please go there right now, that would help."

"Yes, sir. I'm close already."

"We should be there in about twenty minutes," he said. "We'll see you there. Do not engage. I repeat: Do not engage. We have reason to believe he's probably armed, and we already know he's dangerous."

"Yes, sir."

Wolf shifted into drive and pushed the accelerator.

Deputy Piper Cain lowered her phone, her adrenaline spiking her heart rate. She clicked off the gas pump, cutting short the Jeep's fill-up, and waited for the receipt to spit out of the machine.

Why did she just tell him it had been her day off yesterday? Because she didn't want him to think she was a monster for leaving her father unattended at home. But it had come out like she was looking for a pat on the back for working above and beyond her duties. She wasn't.

She hung a left out onto Main street and sped up to fifty miles per hour, driving through a red light and a four-way stop on the way through downtown, past the road to Mary Dimitri's house, the casino, and toward the county road to Hammes's house.

The dashboard clock read 8:05. Her still-wet hair was pulled up into a ponytail, and now sweat was beading on her forehead from the adrenaline. A nice wakeup call if there ever was one.

When she reached the dirt county road, she pressed the gas harder, flying across the base of the valley. When she hit seventy miles per hour, she decided that was a little too fast and let off the gas.

She needed to calm down, but images of Rick Hammes flashing through her mind were making it tough, with that big, muscular body, satanic tattoos crawling all over his skin, and his long hair always pulled into twin braids, like he was trying to look like a horned animal.

Wolf had said he was sending Chavez over there. She remembered meeting that deputy yesterday, all the while wondering why they'd hired him and not her. The kid was no more than twenty years old and had the eyes of a trapped deer. She just hoped the kid had gotten the same orders as she did and was keeping his distance.

Rick Hammes picked up the longest of the already smoked cigarette butts from his ashtray and lit it, sucking on it until he hit the filter. His lungs burned, but he kept it in as long as he could, savoring the slight nicotine buzz. He picked through the tray, looking for more signs of tobacco, but found nothing.

Dex whined, cowering onto his cushion in the front room.

"What are you complaining about?"

Dex put his chin down and looked up at him.

He should have stopped and got some smokes on the way back this morning, but he thought he had at least a couple more packs in his stash. One of the reasons he bought cigarettes in bulk was so he wouldn't run out. Damn it. The trips north had screwed up his schedule.

His body ached from the early drive and he was ravenously hungry. At least he wasn't hung over. He'd been smart last night to cap it at three beers.

Waiting for the pan to warm up so he could make his six-egg omelet, he took off his shirt and stretched his arms overhead, feeling his muscles stretch and his joints pop. He bent over at the waist with straight legs, placing both hands on the carpet with ease.

"You seeing this, Dex? Both hands flat."

Dex yawned.

Hammes straightened and looked himself in the full-length mirror. The Sigil of Baphomet tattooed on his chest was a bit asymmetrical now since his pecs had grown a few inches in all directions. That was one good thing prison had given him—another thirty pounds of pure muscle. He was a veritable god now.

The squeaking of brakes drew his attention to the front of the house.

Dex got up, growling and whining at the window.

"What is it, Dex?"

Hammes looked outside and saw nothing. Probably Larson driving in or something.

But he hadn't heard that old bastard's loud as shit truck, so who was it? Hammes pulled up the blinds all the way and leaned into the window, looking both directions.

"What the hell?" A vehicle was parked across the street, way down the road to the left, just where the bend came into view. Even though the truck was in shadow he could see the light bar mounted on the roof and a round logo on the side. "What's a pig doing up there, Dex?"

Dex whined in response.

He couldn't see inside through the glare on the vehicle's windshield.

"What's going on around here?"

Dex whined again.

He'd heard from Mary about her boyfriend getting killed up at the mine. In fact, she'd even had the audacity to ask if he'd done it.

Hell no. Like he was itching to get back in prison or something.

The strange thing was, when he'd rolled through town this morning, he'd swung by Mary's house but hadn't stopped, because there was a cop parked out front and an X of crime scene tape stretched across her front door.

So what the hell was going on? She wasn't answering her phone this morning either. Or any of his texts.

Staring at this cop, some things clicked into place. Come to think of it, that was the same cop car he'd seen outside her house. Same logo. Same model SUV. Same cop.

Did they think he had something to do with that asshole's murder up at the mine? Mary must have been feeding the pigs information. And the reason her house was sealed up? Maybe she was giving them DNA evidence or something. One of his used condoms from last week or something. Damn, he'd left a toothbrush over there.

"What's going on?" he asked Dex again.

Mary had spoken about how much of an asshole Oakley was. She'd even requested Rick rough him up to teach him a lesson. Maybe Mary had decided to teach Oakley a lesson herself, killing him. And then what? Now she was telling the cops he did it?

Was that it?

It was outrageous, but a surge of certainty flowed through him. "She's playin' me to the cops, Dex."

Dex lowered his head and made another gagging noise. "Get back outside with that."

He opened the front door and pushed Dex out and watched him retch again onto the front lawn. At least it wasn't coming out of his backside anymore. It was going to take a while for the rain to clean the front yard after what that dog had done.

He stepped outside and picked up the steak bone lying in the dirt. And then that old bastard feeding his dog this shit?

He dropped the bone in the metal bowl sitting by the door. Everyone was out to get him.

Up the road another vehicle pulled up. He didn't see it, but he heard the crackle of tires, another squeal of brakes, and a car door thumping shut. He backed inside, shut the door, and looked out the window again.

It was that hot chick with the badge that he'd seen around town walking across the road, looking toward his house.

"What the fuck." He started pacing furiously. The walls pressed in on him. The ceiling seemed to shrink a few feet. His skin prickled with sweat. That helpless, trapped feeling set his heart racing. It was like that first year in jail all over again. It was happening. They were gonna put him back in.

"The hell they are," he said, marching to his room. He reached into his nightstand, knocking over a beer bottle onto the carpet, and pulled out the nine mil.

.   .   .

Piper parked along the right side of the road and hopped out, heading for the passenger side of SBCSD vehicle and knocked on the window.

"Chavez, right?"

"Yeah. Hey. Cain, right?"

"Yep. So, how's it going?"

His eyes darted between her and out the windshield toward Hammes's house. "I just got here. I haven't seen anything yet."

"Why are you parked in plain sight of the house and not on the other side?" she asked.

His eyes flashed. "Because I need line of sight. That's why."

She softened her face, nodding. "Okay. Yeah, sorry, makes sense. But this guy was put in jail three years ago for shooting at a vehicle. I'm not sure how he got out, but I'm not one to believe he's reformed all that much. We don't want to start anything. He's not going to take too kindly to cops staking out his house if he sees us."

Chavez upturned a hand in response.

"So why don't you back it up, park behind my vehicle on the other side of the road, out of sight, and we'll wait for the sheriff there."

"Okay, yeah." His eyes darted toward the house, then he jolted in his seat. "Shit, there he is."

She looked and saw Rick Hammes marching down his pathway from his front door to his gate. He was shirtless, his tattooed skin rippling with muscles that flexed into striated rocks as he hopped the fence, landed deftly on the other side, and continued toward them at a full speed-walk up the road.

"What the hell is he doing?" Chavez said, popping open his door and getting out.

They walked to the front of Chavez's vehicle and, standing next to one another, put their hands on their weapons.

"Now calm down," she said, seeing Chavez's hand flicking open and closed.

Hammes continued up the shoulder of the road, looking left and right into the forest, pointedly ignoring their presence as he closed in fast.

"Okay, stop right there, please," she said, hearing a bit of a wobble in her voice as it came out.

Hammes put both hands up over his head and skidded to a stop. "Oh! Hello officers! Why, what are you doing here?" He took a step forward, putting his arms out at his sides. His eyes were popped wide. Veins bulged through his inked skin, which was stretched impossibly tight over his rhinoceros muscles.

"I'm just trying to go for a nice nature walk. And it looks like you apparently have a problem with that? Because you both have your hands on your guns, and you're parked here because you're watching me. What's that about?"

"Sir," she said, searching for the words, but Hammes threw her off as he took another step forward. His pectorals bounced like water balloons before contracting into river rocks.

He was a good twenty paces away, but she felt the heat rising with each step the man took.

"Just stay right where you are," Chavez said, pulling his gun and holding it pointed at the ground.

"Whoa, pig! The fuck are you doing?" Hammes came to a stop and put his arms at his side again.

The dog began barking down the road, sounding even more vicious than the previous day. Seemingly fueled by concern for its master, the pit bull turned into a monster.

Chavez flicked a glance toward Piper. "What do we do?" he asked under his breath.

Piper stepped forward, keeping one hand gripping her gun

and holding up the other. "Sir, we're here waiting for our sheriff. That's why we're parked here."

"For what? Why are you watching me?"

"We were coming to talk to you."

"About what? What's Mary saying I did?"

Cain shook her head, momentarily confused by the question.

"What's she telling you?" Hammes asked. "Well? Come on, you want to talk, I'm right here. Talk away. Why are you pigs watching me? What's that bitch saying? You think I'm going back to jail, you got another thing coming."

"Sir. Please go back to your house and we'll come talk to you when we're ready. We're not here to bring you to jail. We're just here to talk." Piper was pretty sure she was lying and it sounded like it to her own ears.

Hammes stared at her, shaking his head slowly.

Wolf had said he was to be considered armed and dangerous, and not to engage him. Too late. They had engaged. So what now? She thought back to her academy training. She needed to talk, make him calm.

Down the road there was a metallic ping and a sharp barking noise as the dog rolled over the top of the fence and landed heavily on its side.

Slowly, looking at first to be stunned, it got to its feet. And then it began running toward them at full speed, saliva-laced growls coming out of its mouth.

"Whoa! Dex! Heel!" Hammes turned around, crouching into intercept position.

The dog kept coming full speed, swerving to the other side of the road for a straight shot at her and Chavez.

Hammes side-stepped to block but it only darted back to the other side.

"He has a gun," Chavez said.

Piper had seen it—a pistol tucked into the rear of his pants showed against the small of his back. "Drop your weapon!" she yelled, pulling her piece from her holster.

"Drop your weapon now!" Chavez said, aiming his gun at Hammes.

But Hammes ignored them, still concerned with his dog charging at full speed. "Stop, Dex! Come here, boy! Heel!"

"Get your dog under control!" Chavez said with rising panic.

"Heel!"

But the dog ignored his master, juking at the last second and slipping between his legs. Now through the obstacle, Dex, and his saliva-flinging jaws, looked to be coming right at Piper.

Shit.

Chavez fired. The dog spun wildly, a loud squeal coming out of its mouth as it landed in the dirt.

"No!" Hammes screamed.

Piper had no time to be stunned. Hammes was reaching into his waistband.

"You piece of shit!" Hammes pulled the gun into plain sight.

Time slowed to a stop. Piper felt the tension of the trigger against her finger as she aimed.

But Chavez beat her to it, shooting again, hitting Hammes in his center mass. Hammes's gun clattered to the ground as he doubled over, blood spurting through his hands as they clenched onto his abdomen, and he landed like a sack of sand next to his dog.

She veered her aim and just barely stopped herself from firing.

Chavez took a step forward.

"Stop!" she yelled. "Cease fire!"

Chavez lowered his weapon and let out a primal grunt.

And then there was only the high-pitched ring in her ears and the tangy scent of gunpowder choking her throat.

"Shit," she said. She gingerly put her hand on Chavez's shoulder and stepped in front of him. The young deputy promptly vomited onto the road. Rick Hammes writhed on the ground, his eyes glued to his dog. "Dex!"

The dog whimpered, biting at its hind leg where it had been shot.

She went to Hammes's gun and kicked it to the ditch on the side of the road. Then she pulled her radio and called for an ambulance.

CHAPTER 17

WOLF CLIMBED out of his SUV far from the flashing lights of the ambulance parked in the center of the road ahead. He walked along the shoulder, Yates and Rachette stepping next to him, all of them silent as they took in the aftermath of the action they had just missed.

Insects buzzed in the pine trees. It was hot, the air still. Ahead, Deputy Nelson knelt down next to a tree at the edge of the woods. As they grew near, Wolf saw Deputy Chavez sitting down against the trunk, both palms pressed against his eyes as he listened to Nelson talking softly, patting him on the shoulder.

Yates went to them while Wolf and Rachette continued on.

Deputy Cain stood near the EMTs crouched over a shirtless, tattooed man strapped to a stretcher. Rick Hammes.

A pickup truck was parked next to the ambulance bearing the logo of a company by the name of DVS, the words Dredge Veterinary Services beneath it. Two men and a woman were huddled up in the truck bed.

"It's okay, boy," the woman murmured.

A dog barked, growled, then whined.

"Give him two more CCs. That should do it." The woman stood and nodded at Wolf.

"You need any help?" he asked, walking up to the edge of the truck bed. The dog was on its side, strapped to a miniature stretcher. Bandages wrapped his hind leg. His eyes were half-open, and his lips sagged open to reveal teeth.

"The bullet grazed him," the woman said. "I've already cleaned the wound, but I have to take him into the office to sew him up. He'll be fine." She looked over at the EMTs huddled over Rick Hammes in the middle of the road. "Not sure about him, though."

Wolf backed away and looked toward Deputy Cain, who stood a few paces from the action, staring down at Rick Hammes.

"A little help here," one of the EMTs said, turning to Wolf. "He's heavy, may as well have the extra hands."

Wolf walked over and grabbed the handles on one side of the spine board. Deputy Cain rushed to the other side, but Rachette was already there. "I got it."

"One, two, three," the EMT said, as they lifted up.

"Is he … dead?" Rachette asked, looking down.

Hammes's eyes were closed, mouth open and streaming drool. With all the ink painting the man's skin, it was difficult to tell where the tattoos ended and the blood began.

"Not dead, though his vitals are weak," the EMT said. "Okay, easy now. He's lost a lot of blood," the EMT continued as they set him inside the ambulance. "The surgeons will have their work cut out for them."

Wolf and Rachette turned toward Cain, who had moved to a patch of shade on the side of the road.

"How are you doing?" Rachette asked.

The look she gave Rachette said she had no response for that question.

When Yates came up and joined them, Wolf said, "Why don't you two head down to the house and begin the search. I'll be right there."

Rachette and Yates walked down the road, leaving Wolf with Cain.

"What happened?" he asked.

She told him.

"Where's his weapon?" Wolf asked.

"I bagged it and gave it to Nelson. It was a Beretta M9, nine-millimeter."

He nodded. Clearly not the .45 Glock 21 equipped with a silencer his two detectives were down at the house looking for.

"If Chavez hadn't shot the dog," she said. "I would have. I was just about to. And he shot Hammes first. I was just about to do that, too. I feel like ..." She closed her eyes and shook her head.

"What?"

"I feel like I failed."

"Why?"

"I don't know. I guess, like I put it all on Chavez. I didn't react fast enough, and now that rookie has to live with shooting a man and his dog." She looked toward the young deputy, who was still sitting in the trees. Nelson remained standing watch next to him.

Wolf put a hand on her shoulder, and Cain looked down at her hands. They were covered in blood.

"Can we get something over here to wipe her hands with, please?" Wolf asked a passing EMT.

The man returned with a towel, a water bottle, and a container of antibacterial wipes.

"Thanks." Wolf took them, and then he took one of her hands, poured some water on it, and gently wiped away the dried blood. It was caked under her nails and into the cracks and crevices of her hands, but he managed to get most of it.

When he couldn't get any more without scrubbing too hard, and after realizing that she probably could have been doing this herself to far better effect, he looked up and saw that she was staring at him. "There. I'll, uh, let you finish."

"Thanks," she said.

He nodded. "You didn't fail. And there's sure as hell no winning in the situation I put you in. I jumped the gun. I should have had you two stay where you were and let us take care of it."

Her eyes flashed, and then she looked into the forest. "I'm sorry I said anything. I'm just fine doing my duty, sir. I'm not looking to be coddled."

"I know. And don't be sorry for telling me what you're feeling. I'm glad you did."

She said nothing, her gaze locked on the woods.

He gave her the wipes and looked toward Hammes's house. Yates was already over the fence and at the front door, his purple-gloved hand probing something on the doorjamb as he disappeared inside the house.

"I'd better head down there," Wolf said.

"Right," she said.

"We'll have to get an official report from you, of course."

"Of course."

Wolf walked over and knelt down next to Deputy Chavez. "How are you doing?"

His eyes flicked to Wolf. "Not very good, sir."

Wolf nodded. "Shooting somebody is tough business."

"And a dog."

Wolf nodded again. "And a dog. I know you're feeling some pain and doubt. That's what happens. You're going to think about this day for the rest of your life, I'm not going to kid you about that," he said. "But you'll get through it. You acted quickly. You protected yourself and your fellow deputy. You did good. He had a gun. He's shot at innocent civilians before. If you wouldn't have shot, it would have been you or Deputy Cain out there on the road right now."

Chavez nodded, closing his eyes.

Wolf patted his shoulder. "They say the dog's going to be okay."

Chavez kept his eyes closed, tilting his head away from Wolf slightly.

"Deputy Nelson will take you back," he said, standing up.

Wolf walked down to the house, feeling a knot forming in his neck. He rolled his head in a circle, gripping his shoulder with one hand.

"What are you searching for?" Cain asked, walking up next to him. She acted as if nothing had just happened, marching in step with him down the road, her eyes forward, her chin tall.

"We have a search warrant."

"Did you tie him to Mary Dimitri's death?"

"Yes. We found his fingerprints on two beer bottles inside her house yesterday. Dr. Lorber confirmed the match this morning."

"So you're looking for a weapon," she said. "But it's not the Beretta up there."

"Correct." He told her about the .45 caliber Glock with sound suppressor that was supposedly missing from Chris Oakley's trailer at the mine.

"And you think Hammes took it and shot Chris Oakley with it?"

"That's the idea," he said. "And Mary Dimitri."

They walked down the road to the front gate in silence. The neighbor, Ned Larson, was outside his own fence line, watching them.

"You don't need to be here," Wolf said to her.

"He was yelling at us," she said.

"Who?"

"Hammes. Before the dog jumped the fence and all hell broke loose. He was saying," she shook her head in thought, "he was asking what Mary told us he did. I keep thinking about that. He said, 'what is Mary telling you I did?' Like we were in the process of talking to her or something."

Wolf narrowed his eyes. "Like he didn't know she was already dead, you're saying?"

"Yeah. Exactly. It was just...he talked about her in the present tense, like he was completely in the dark, if you ask me."

Wolf let that information settle. "Okay. Thanks for letting me know."

They walked up the dirt driveway to the side door. At the top of the drive sat a Dodge 4x4 truck, its rear bumper bent into a V from a collision.

"I'll be out here," Cain said, as Wolf gloved up and entered the open side door of Hammes's house.

He stopped inside, assessing the kitchen he'd just walked into. Three ripped vinyl chairs surrounded a tiny table. Two dog bowls sat on the floor near his feet. A dozen eggs sat on the counter, along with a bowl and a fork. A pan sat on the burner.

"The burner was on, but I turned it off," Rachette said from the next room.

Next to the eggs stood at least a dozen empty brown beer bottles matching those they had found in Mary Ellen Dimitri's house. The place smelled of beer, stale cigarette smoke, and rotting food.

Wolf joined Rachette in the living room. Framed drawings and paintings of different satanic symbolism pulled his eyes to the walls.

"Guy is devout," Rachette said. "A devout freak."

Wolf scanned the rest of the place. Hammes's belongings

were scattered about, seemingly at random: a dirty ashtray, more beer bottles, a remote control fought for space on the table; stacks of vinyl records, a laptop computer bag, a pair of dirty boots encrusted with flecks of concrete and mud, and a duffle bag lay discarded on the carpet.

"You looked in the duffel bag yet?"

"Not yet," Rachette said. "I was heading to the bedroom."

"Go ahead. I'll take this." Wolf bent over and unzipped the worn canvas bag. Inside was an array of dirty clothes: jeans muddied at the knees and crusted at the hems with the same color dirt that was on the boots, dirty socks and t-shirts, and a yellow reflective vest.

"Work clothes," Wolf said. "Construction work clothes. Where's Yates?"

"He's outside," Rachette's voice came from down a hallway.

Wolf checked the pockets of the jeans, finding a single crumpled receipt for a twelve-pack of beer purchased at a liquor store in Eagle, Colorado on Thursday, June 24th. The night before Chris Oakley's murder up at the mine.

"Nothing in this first bedroom," Rachette called out. "Checked all the drawers. Personally, I'm doubting we'll find anything. If he had any sense, that is. You don't hold onto the weapon after shooting two people. I'd go dump it in an old mine, a river, or a lake if I were him." Rachette's voice receded deeper into the house. "Maybe that's why he was gone when we came over yesterday. He was out dumping evidence."

"Hey!" Yates' voice came from somewhere at the front of the house. "Out here!" He waved from the open front door. "Over here. I found it."

"Found what?" Rachette asked, coming around the corner.

Wolf walked out, following Yates around the corner of the house to a stack of firewood piled waist high against the siding.

"Look. Right there."

Cain stood up against the other side of the fence, leaning on her elbows, her eyes wide with anticipation as she watched the action.

"What are we talking about?" Wolf didn't have to wonder for long. Following Yates' pointing finger, he spotted the matte black finish of a handgun shoved into the gaps in the firewood logs, barrel-first.

Wolf reached in carefully and pulled the weapon out. Like some sort of magic trick the gun kept coming, because about five inches of sound suppressor was screwed onto the end of the barrel.

He dangled it between thumb and forefinger, reading the stamps in the slide. "Glock twenty-one. Forty-five caliber."

Rachette opened an evidence bag. "I'd say that's our gun."

"That was easy," Yates said.

Wolf lowered the gun into the bag and met Cain's eyes. She turned away, looking into the trees and taking a breath, as if wrestling with the recent memories still rattling in her mind.

"I stand corrected," Rachette said. "The guy is a dumbass after all."

CHAPTER 18

"MY ASS HURTS," Rachette said, landing hard on Wolf's office couch. "Too much driving. Too much standing. Too much everything."

Wolf sat heavily onto his desk chair, feeling much the same.

It had been a long day. After finding the silenced Glock 21 in Hammes's woodpile, they'd spent the rest of the morning going through his house with a fine-toothed comb, then returned to Mary Ellen Dimitri's to walk the crime scene once more. After that it was back up to the Jackson Mine to walk those grounds.

A team of crime scene techs at the mine had nothing new after searching for two straight days with their K9 units and metal detectors. The claim covered over a hundred acres. Finding evidence, K9s or not, was proving to be a tough task.

Patterson creaked into the office on her crutches and shooed Rachette to slide over on the couch. "Your butt hurts? Boo-hoo," she said, sitting and propping her leg up.

"How's the ankle, Patty?" Yates asked, next to come inside.

"It's fine."

Wolf saw she was lying. She had that permanent crease in

her forehead that showed up whenever she was agitated. That, and she had been avoiding eye contact with everyone since they'd walked into the building.

District Attorney Sawyer White strolled in with his deputy Dan Wethering in tow. White was in his late forties, in good physical shape, and wore a crisp blue suit with a cream-colored shirt and a pink tie. His numerous rings and Rolex sparkled under the overhead lights.

Deputy DA Dan Wethering, younger than White by a decade, dressed in stark contrast to his boss, wearing a pair of khakis and a simple button up shirt. He nodded a greeting at everyone in turn and stood at attention in the corner. Wethering had nine children at home, all of them adopted from an orphanage in Denver.

Wolf nodded back, wondering again just how the man did it. Suddenly Wolf's sore backside and fatigue felt like less of an issue.

"You people have been busy the last few days," White said, taking one of the seats in front of Wolf. Yates took up a standing position next to Wethering, against the windows.

"Is the party in here?" Lorber walked into the office next, rapping on the door. Daphne came up behind him and stopped dead in the entryway. "Wow, standing room only."

"Come on in," Wolf said, "grab a piece of carpet."

Thunder rumbled outside, shaking the building. Another afternoon storm had rolled down from the north and was spitting rain against the window outside. Although it was only five o'clock, it was very dark.

"Did you talk to McBeth's lawyer today?" White asked Wolf.

Wolf shook his head. "We've been out in no-cell-service territory all day."

"Well, I did. He's demanding we release the crime scene

and let the miners get back to work, and he's using some credible threats. Seems the guy is pretty connected with Senator Ponsfeld."

"Seems McBeth has some money, then," Rachette said.

Wolf looked at Lorber.

Lorber shrugged. "We've had K9 units and my forensic team searching that place for clues for two days now. We've probably sifted through more dirt than those miners have. Looks like we've found all we can for now."

Wolf nodded. "I'll release it."

"Okay," White said, splaying his hands, "of course if you need to get in there for anything else, we can get a warrant. Now, onto today's exploits. I think I'm up to speed on everything that occurred, just check me if I'm wrong, please. We started with your search and arrest warrant for Rick Hammes. He finally showed up at his house, pulled a gun on our deputies and got shot, and then you found a forty-five caliber with—"

"—Not just any forty-five caliber," Rachette said. "The forty-five caliber with a do-it-yourself silencer made from a solvent trap that our miners up at Jackson mine told us Chris Oakley kept in his trailer."

White twisted and looked at Rachette. "Right. Sorry."

"No problem."

"Good," White said, turning back to Wolf. "All of this is looking like a slam-dunk against Rick Hammes so far. What else?" He looked at Lorber.

Lorber shook his head. "We had been looking into Mary Dimitri's cell phone. Now we have Rick Hammes's. Looking at the two together is interesting."

"How so?" Wolf asked.

Lorber dropped a manila folder on Wolf's desk and flipped it open. "There are a number of texts between Hammes and

Mary Dimitri on his phone that we didn't find on Mary's. She must have deleted them."

"So she wouldn't get caught by her boyfriend," Yates said.

"Maybe," Lorber said. "There's also more sexting. Pictures of body parts, but more tattoos this time. Interestingly, she calls Rick Hammes at 11:05 p.m. on Friday night, the 10th."

"The night of Oakley's murder," Rachette said.

"Correct. Phone call lasted twenty-one minutes and fifteen seconds. A significant conversation, by the looks of it." Lorber paused for effect. "The other interesting thing we found was one of her text exchanges with Hammes. This was Monday night—that was the night after we were called to the mine and Chris Oakley's dead body, mind you."

Lorber looked at White and Wethering, making sure they were on the same page with the timeline of events.

"She specifically asks Hammes, 'Did you do it?' And he responds, 'Do what?' She responds, 'Did you kill Chris?'" Lorber flipped the page. "He responds, 'Fuck no.' And then they don't talk anymore."

The room went silent.

"Just to state the obvious here," Rachette said, "that does not sound like they're in collaboration on Chris Oakley's murder."

"He could be lying about doing it," Yates said. "It's not exactly something you'd want to put in writing."

"True."

"Has Hammes really been working in Vail?" White asked. "Is there any truth to that?"

"I looked into his financials today." Patterson opened the folder on her lap and picked out her own paperwork. "I couldn't find any transactions for the last...well, he never uses a credit or debit card, let's just say that. He only uses an ATM every once in a while, but he did once last Tuesday, when he withdrew one hundred dollars from an ATM at a Circle-Q convenience store in Eagle, Colorado."

"Vail area," Rachette said. "Wolf found a receipt in his dirty pants, too. From a liquor store in Eagle, dated last Thursday the 24th, the night before the murder."

"That's something," Patterson said. "Otherwise, the ATM transaction is all I can find tying him to the Vail area. He holds a bank account at Peak National in downtown Dredge, but there are no recent debit transactions from that account or any other in his name, not since he got out of jail on February 18th. Again, the only thing I'm seeing are ATM withdrawals over the last few months."

Patterson flipped the page. "I also spoke to his former employer up at the casino today, since you guys got sidetracked. Hammes used to wash dishes at the Motherlode Casino Restaurant and up and quit two weeks ago. He never told his parole officer so I found nothing there on where he went."

"Who's his parole officer?" Wolf asked.

"Shante Laroque," White said.

"And why isn't she here right now?"

"Besides the lack of room in your office?" White asked. "She had a hearing. Couldn't make it."

"What's she saying about Hammes?" Wolf asked.

White looked to his assistant. Wethering cleared his throat. "She's saying he never missed a meeting. Passed all his drug tests so far." He shrugged. "He never told her about a Vail job."

"Okay," Wolf said. "What else?"

Patterson continued. "According to his former boss at the casino restaurant, word was travelling through the servers and staff that he was going to work construction up in Vail or the Vail area. That's as specific as he could get."

"Let's talk motive for Hammes. What is it? He was screwing Mary and wanted her for himself?"

"More exact," Wolf said, "Mary Dimitri was dating Chris Oakley and seeing Hammes on the side. According to Mary's coworker at the cocktail lounge, she'd begun seeing him a month ago. Secretly, behind Oakley's back."

"And we have the text message from a guy named Spritz last Friday sent to Oakley," Yates said, "telling Oakley the about his girlfriend's infidelity."

"That's good motive for Oakley to kill Hammes," Rachette said, "not really the other way around. Not good motive for Hammes to kill Oakley."

"Let's stop right there a second," Patterson said. "How about this Spritz guy? Have you guys gone to the bar and grill where this guy works yet? Because the temp worker who dumped Oakley's body onto the wash plant works there, too. Casey Lizotte. Spritz and Lizotte. Who are they?"

All eyes landed on Wolf, who shook his head.

"Not yet," Rachette said. "We've been a bit busy."

She made a note in her notebook. "Just asking. It's called The Picker Bar and Grill. I'll tack that onto our to-do list."

"The Picker?" Rachette scoffed. "What's that about? Oh wait, I get it now, like a big piece of gold you pick out of the ground. Not like a booger or anything."

The room went silent.

"Sorry," Rachette waved toward Yates. "Continue. You were talking about what happened? Hammes's motive playing out or something?"

Yates cleared his throat. "I was saying Oakley got the text message about Hammes hooking up with his lady. Later that night Oakley was killed. The news of Hammes and Mary getting together behind Oakley's back and Oakley's death seems obviously connected. That seems to point to Hammes as our guy."

"How's Hammes doing, anyway?" White asked, looking at

Wolf. "We gonna be able to talk to him? Or..." he finished his sentence with a slashing motion across his neck.

"He's in surgery right now," Wolf said. "We'll know more later."

"Let's hope he lives," White said.

"And talks," Rachette said.

"And what about the dog?" Daphne asked. "Is he going to be okay?"

Wolf nodded. "He's fine. Bullet grazed his hind leg. He'll have a hefty limp, but he'll be okay."

Daphne deflated. "Good."

"So what are we saying happened?" Rachette asked. "Mary Dimitri comes up to the mine that night. She gets into an argument with Oakley and then drives away. Lorber said she called Hammes that night at eleven-ish. Maybe after the argument at the mine she goes home and calls Hammes, sweet talks him for twenty minutes, tells him to go kill Chris.

"Hammes says, okay, anything for you, baby. He comes sneaking into the mine, breaks into Oakley's trailer, takes the Glock with the silencer..." Rachette stopped. "Here's a question —how does Hammes know where to find the silenced weapon?"

"Mary Dimitri knew," Yates said. "She tells him where to get it. She knows the exact drawer from spending so much time with Oakley."

They sat listening to the rumble of another thunder outside.

"Okay, fair enough," Rachette said. "And then he...what? Goes home that night? His neighbor reported him showing up Tuesday night. Not Friday night. He never said anything about the weekend."

"So he goes back up to Vail," White said.

"So he comes down from Vail to do the deed," Rachette said. "In the middle of the night, he drives two hours, gets there in the middle of the morning, shoots him, drives back up to Vail."

"Another two hours," Wolf said.

"That's a hell of a lot of driving," Rachette said.

"And then," Yates said raising a finger, "Monday he gets the text message from Mary that says, 'Did you kill Chris?' And that pisses him off. He sees that Mary's trying to play it off like she had nothing to do with the killing after she spent twenty minutes convincing him to do it Friday night on the phone. So he comes back down into town Monday night, goes and has a couple beers at Mary's, shoots her dead. Then he goes home. The neighbor, Ned Larson, hears the dog. Hammes takes Oakley's gun, shoves it in his woodpile, and then heads back to Vail."

"Why does he shove the gun into his woodpile?" White asked.

"Because he's a moron," Rachette said.

They sat listening to the rain on the window.

Wolf laid his palms on top of his desk. "Deputy Cain told me that when Rick Hammes confronted them on the road, he asked the question, 'What is Mary saying I did?'"

"So?" White shrugged.

"He used the present tense about Mary. He seemed to think Mary was still alive and talking to the cops about him. Deputy Cain said he sounded genuinely confused, or off-base, as to why they were there."

White scoffed. "This was all right before a raging pit bull and her satanic tattooed master came at her? She remembers the exact words that were said? Come on, Wolf. We know how memory works under pressure. What else do we have?"

Wolf turned to Lorber. "Did you find prints on our wood-pile-gun?"

Lorber shook his head. "There are no prints on that gun."

"And what about the rounds?"

"Partials belonging to Chris Oakley."

White upturned his hands. "If it isn't Hammes, who did it?"

"Maybe somebody much closer," Wolf said. "Somebody in a trailer next to Oakley's up at that mine. Somebody who knew exactly where that gun was. Someone who doesn't have to drive halfway across Colorado, down into a mine, in the middle of the morning hours, to do it."

"And their motivation?" White asked.

Wolf shrugged. "A blow-out argument. Maybe Oakley had crossed a line."

"With McBeth, you're saying," White said.

"Or one of the others."

"Or all of them," Patterson said.

Silence dropped on the room again.

"So, they sneak from their own trailer into Oakley's," Rachette said, "take the gun from his drawer, go out into the night, find him in a tractor or something. Wave him over. Shoot him. Bury him. And then they go and shoot Mary Dimitri a couple days later. But, if it was about the argument, about gold or whatever, why kill her, too?"

"To make it look like Rick Hammes did it," Wolf said.

Rachette nodded. "And they plant the gun at Rick's house so we'll find it." He shrugged. "Like I said, there's no reason to keep that gun around after you shoot two people with it. And out in the wood pile? Come on."

"They knew Hammes was screwing around with Oakley," Wolf said. "They had a good person to frame."

"It's a sloppy frame job when you really look at it," Rachette said. "All we have to do is prove Rick Hammes was up in Vail during that murder and he's off the hook."

"We'll get Hammes's cell phone GPS records in twenty-four to forty-eight hours," Lorber said. "That might help us."

"That will prove where his phone was," White said. "Not where he's been. We've come up against that before. You have to prove Hammes was in Vail, and that the miners did it." His eyes slid to Lorber again. "But you found nothing up at the mine, correct?"

Lorber shook his head. "We checked drains in all those trailers for blood, checked each miner's clothing for gunshot residue and blood spatter. Carpets in the trailers. Boots. We've come up with nothing."

Lorber gestured to Daphne Pinnefield.

"K9 units got a hit on some dirt with blood on it," she said. "In one of the mounds next to the wash plant, and on the scoop of the front-end loader that put his body up on the hopper. We've swept with metal detectors and come up with a wheelbarrow's worth of casings. They shoot a lot. The ammo found in each trailer was the same. All partially filled boxes. In other words, we're getting nothing from the ammo or shell casings."

"As far as the clothing goes," Wolf said, "they could have ditched what they were wearing after they shot him. Anywhere in a hole somewhere."

"Or a river or lake," Rachette said.

"We need to figure out where Hammes was working in Vail," Patterson said, repeating what was becoming a mantra. "We find that, we can ask them if he was there last Friday night. We can see if he was there Monday night."

White raised his gold pen in the air in affirmation.

"On that note..."

All eyes went to Patterson. She pulled out another piece of paper. "I did some digging into what construction projects are happening in the Vail, Avon, Eagle, and Edwards area right now," she said. She flipped to another page, looking skeptical. "There are lots of them. A few large commercial projects, and over two dozen private homes."

"It's one of the larger commercial projects," Wolf said. "There was the reflective vest in his duffel bag. His jeans had dried concrete on the cuffs, as did his boots. And the ATM transaction was in Eagle, according to the receipt I found in his pocket."

Patterson shook her head, looking at the paper. "There are no commercial projects going on in Eagle right now. The big commercial projects are happening in Vail Village and Edwards."

Wethering cleared his throat. "I have a brother in the oil industry up there. They put up a lot of workers in those cheap motels in Eagle and Wolcott." He shrugged. "Maybe a large company doing the projects in Vail Village and Edwards are housing their workers there. It would explain the Eagle trans-actions."

White smiled and nodded. "See this guy? Told you he was good."

Wolf nodded. "We'll go check it out."

"Now?" Rachette asked, leaning toward Patterson and rubbing his backside.

"No. We'll go first thing tomorrow morning."

The meeting broke up and people streamed out of the office. Patterson took her time getting up.

"Patty," Wolf said, "can I talk to you?"

She stopped. "What's up?"

He closed the manila folder on his desk that Lorber had left and crossed his legs. "Do you remember coming across Deputy Cain's resume this year? She...apparently applied, and I somehow didn't see it."

"Yes."

"Really?"

"Yeah. I saw it today," she said. "I was speaking to Charlotte earlier, and she was telling me about how you and Wilson have been dragging your feet on a few things. I hope you don't mind, but after that I finished your stack of paperwork," she gestured to the empty wire basket on his desk.

"Oh, yeah. Wow. Thanks."

"I went into your file cabinet to make sure there were no more forms that hadn't been filed since there seemed to be a few missing from May and June."

"There did?"

"Yes. But I figured it out. Don't worry." She walked to the filling cabinet, opened the top drawer, pulled a file, and slapped it on his desk. "Deputy Cain."

Wolf opened it and was greeted by a photo of Deputy Piper Cain's smiling face paperclipped to an application. Although it was a generic work photo from Gallatin County Sheriff's Department, she looked good in the picture.

A handwritten letter, signed by the sheriff of Gallatin County in Bozeman, Montana, was paperclipped to the back. Wolf skimmed it, coming across words like *exemplary* and *remarkable*. According to the letter she was a hard worker, a team player, a self-starter, and tough.

"It's a good letter of recommendation," Patterson said.

Wolf looked up and nodded. He closed the file. " Thanks. I hired Deputy Chavez as a favor to Wilson. We...I, never hired another one."

Wolf turned in his chair, facing the window. He'd had more time to mull over the time period around the winter storm. That storm had also been when MacLean had called him, touting his recovery from advanced pancreatic cancer and his intention to return to Rocky Points and the sheriff's position. Wolf had rarely felt such elation in his life as he had during that conversation, and though he was ashamed to admit it now, it wasn't because of MacLean's improved health. That had been the moment Wolf had decided to leave these millions of things that didn't involve the detective squad and Wolf's previous world to MacLean on his return.

He looked underneath Deputy Cain's resume and saw two other candidates, both with less than half the experience and qualifications she had.

A wave of guilt washed over him as he thought about Cain's predicament in Dredge, living with her father up there in the middle of the woods.

"I'm a pretty out of touch sheriff this time around, huh?"

Wolf swiveled back to see an empty office.

"Yes," he answered himself. "You are."

He pulled out his cell phone and scrolled to recent numbers, pausing at Piper Cain's in his outgoing calls from earlier today. Maybe a good sheriff would call his deputy to check in on her after a day of action like that. Then again, maybe a creepy sheriff would have done that.

He scrolled deep into the unused recesses of his contacts for another number. He found it and stared. *Dennis Muller.*

The last time he'd seen his deceased ex-wife's father was at the hospital when Cassidy had given birth to Ryan. Wolf knew Sarah's parents saw Jack, Cassidy, and Ryan regularly, visiting Carbondale to see their great-grandson, but Wolf had not seen or spoken to the Mullers more than a few times since Sarah's funeral.

Wolf got the sense that they blamed him for her death, although they'd never said as much outright.

Wolf decided that was a topic for another therapy session with Hawkwood and dialed the number.

"Hello?"

"Hey Dennis, it's David."

"Yes, hi Dave! How are you?"

They stuttered through some small talk, covering all the bases: Jack and Cassidy, his wife, Angela and her new hobbies,

Dennis and his retirement from the construction business and his lack of hobbies.

"I actually wanted to talk to you about that...the construction, that is." Wolf explained the situation with Rick Hammes, and how they were trying to track him down.

"There's a big project happening in Edwards right now," Dennis said. "The biggest, by far. They're creating a pedestrian zone, next to the new Riverwalk section of town. Putting in a hundred thousand square feet of mixed use, a park, and diverting the river for a water park. They have a huge budget on this thing.

"Of course, those workers can't afford to live in a place like Edwards, Vail, Avon, or Beaver Creek, so, yeah, they put them up in the motels down in Wolcott and Eagle. Sometimes three or four to a room, depending on the worker's tolerance for such a thing."

"Are there any other projects around you can think of that might fit the bill?" Wolf asked. "Maybe in Vail or Avon?"

"No. Nothing nearly as labor-intensive as what they're doing up in Edwards. If your guy dropped his job to come up here and work because they needed help, you want to start in Edwards. Anyway, I'll make some calls tomorrow morning, but for now I'd start there."

"You know the construction company?"

"Sterling Star Commercial," he said without hesitation. "I know the owner well. Here's his phone number. Tell him I sent you."

They finished their conversation a few minutes later with a promise from Wolf to have dinner at their house in Vail one evening soon, a promise that had been made at least three times before in as many years.

He hung up and turned back to his desk. With a flick of his thumb he opened the file in front of him and stared at Piper

Cain's picture. Her eyes were different in this photo than in real life. Brighter. Happier.

He read her vital statistics. She was five foot six. One hundred and fifteen pounds. Brown eyes, although he would have described them as black, they were so dark. Like obsidian inlaid marbles. Thirty-eight years old. He would have been almost learning to drive when she was born.

He thought of the way she'd pulled herself up on that fence again. Her lithe body. The way she'd touched his arm. The way she'd been looking at him when he'd cleaned off her hands earlier that day.

"If you hire her you can't date her."

He closed the file and stood up, feeling heat on his face. "I thought you left."

"I did." Patterson came inside. "And I also told you I'd be right back."

"Oh."

"Yeah. You were pretty zoned out."

"Sorry." He rolled his neck.

"Being sheriff used to be different," she said. "There used to be a lot less stuff to handle when we were in the other building."

He said nothing.

"Lots of administrative duties. Not exactly your strong suit."

He stared at her. "That hurts."

"Not as much as watching you try and do a spreadsheet."

He smiled.

"I just want you to know," she said, standing straight. "I'm willing to help, you know. Whatever you need. I'll be there to do it. I'm up for the challenge."

He nodded, wondering why the speech all of a sudden.

"How are you doing, Patty?" he asked. "How's your foot? You have to go home and rest. Seriously."

He nodded at her hand, and to another manila folder dangling from it. "What's that?"

"Those are three pieces of paper for you to sign, which gives me and Charlotte the power to streamline some of the procedures in the squad room, taking you out of the equation completely."

Wolf took it while she stared expectantly.

With a sigh he put the folder down on his desk, fished a pen out of the cup, and signed the three documents. "There," he said, handing it over.

She grabbed the folder. "Paperwork done in record time. Women like a decisive man of action. Cain would be impressed."

"It's time for you to go home."

CHAPTER 19

"Two more miles until the exit," Rachette said from the passenger seat of Wolf's SUV.

Wolf bit into his second breakfast sandwich, savoring the egg and bacon taste, washing it down with orange juice.

Outside the SUV's windows, the pine-covered forests of the Vail Valley gave way to lower flat-topped hills to the west, covered in a carpet of green grass and turquoise sage.

Wolf's voicemail dinged and he saw he'd missed a call from the Jackson Hole area code. He put it to his ear and listened.

"This is Sheriff Domino from Teton County SD. I got your earlier message. Sorry I missed your call. Tag. You're it."

"Who was that?" Rachette asked.

"Sheriff Domino from Teton County."

"Any new information there?"

"Not yet. Still haven't talked to him. Did you get hold of Oakley's parents yet?" Wolf asked.

"Nope. The Teton SD is having trouble locating them. I get the feeling they're not the caring type."

"That's depressing."

They rolled over a dip in the I-70 interstate highway and

Wolf felt the fat on his gut jiggle. He rolled up the sandwich and handed it to Rachette. "I'm done."

"You're done?" Rachette looked inside the wrapper. "I'll take it."

"Take it, then."

Wolf watched out of the corner of his eye as Rachette ingested the sandwich like a horse eats an apple. They passed a sign for Edwards, one mile ahead.

"You trying to lose weight or something?"

Wolf frowned. "Why? Do I need to?"

"You could drop ten or fifteen. You've been getting bigger over the last six months or so."

Wolf took his foot off the gas and coasted down the off ramp. "I'm glad you came with me this morning."

"Eh. Some of us gain weight as we get older. Join the club. It's about time you put on some L-Bs."

After following a maze of cones, they circled the town for a few minutes, passing two erected cranes, a dozen big machines, and a squadron of hard hat-wearing construction workers milling around the steel skeletons of buildings and carved-out ground.

Wolf noted a group of men pouring concrete for a sidewalk wearing the same reflective vest he had found in Hammes's duffel bag. Of course, a construction vest was a construction vest and everyone had one on, here at this site and probably a thousand more across the country. Not at all that unique.

"Over there," Rachette said, pointing toward two white trailers sitting in a dirt parking lot choked with pickup trucks. "Looks like the hub to me."

Wolf turned and rolled past white pickup trucks emblazoned with a star logo that said Sterling Star Construction.

"Hey, would you look at that?" Rachette said, pointing out

the window as they rolled past a Jeep Grand Cherokee with *Sluice-Byron County* stenciled on the side.

"That's Cain's vehicle," Rachette said.

Wolf's pulse rose. "Huh," he said.

"Are we supposed to meet her here?"

"No."

"Then what the hell's she doing here?"

Wolf parked next to a truck and they got out into air shaking with the rumble of tractors. A chill breeze carried the scent of diesel fumes.

Wolf led the way through the parking lot, eyeing the empty interior of Cain's vehicle as they passed on their way to two double-wide trailers.

They stepped up a flight of flimsy stairs into the first trailer, whose door was propped open.

Inside Cain had her back to them, pushing her phone screen toward a woman seated at a desk.

The woman was in her sixties and pulled down a pair of glasses from her nest of hair onto her nose. "Nope. I don't recognize him, sorry."

Wolf cleared his throat and Cain turned around. She did a slight double take and straightened, putting the phone in her pocket.

"Hello, sir." Her face reddened.

"What are you doing here?" Rachette asked.

"What have you found out?" Wolf asked, staving off a confrontation in front of the civilian.

Rachette stood down, realizing this was not the time or place.

"I...was just asking Mrs. Cranlin here if she could tell me if Rick Hammes worked here. When his name didn't come up in the system I showed her a picture. She doesn't recognize him."

"Cranson," the woman said. "My name's Cranson."

"Oh, right. Sorry."

"Is that right about Mr. Hammes?" Wolf asked Mrs. Cranson.

She gestured to the computer. "I don't have him in the system."

"Is that normal?" Wolf asked. "To not have your laborers in the system?"

"We have both employees and independent contractors," she said. "The employees are in the system, but we also outsource some of our labor with another firm from Grand Junction called Logiwork Services. I could give you their phone number. They have their own system that sometimes doesn't sync up with ours." She dug into a drawer, apparently searching for the number.

"No thanks," Wolf said. "No need to trouble yourself."

Mrs. Cranson stopped, raising the glasses to her head.

"Who's the best person to show this picture to?" Wolf asked. "Can you point us to a supervisor? A manager?"

"Yes, that's a good idea. You could go across the street and talk to the supervisor. He'll be the one with the red hard hat."

Wolf nodded and then looked at Deputy Cain. She stood with her back rigid, avoiding eye contact.

"Thank you."

"Wait a minute," Mrs. Cranson said. "You'll need hardhats and an escort."

She stood up and went to a closet, producing three hardhats for them. While they donned their headgear she got back on the phone and made a call in a hushed voice.

"...they want to talk to some workers...I don't know... I don't know. Bye." She smiled. "Somebody will be here in a few minutes. You can go outside to wait if you like."

Wolf led the way outside and was greeted by two corporate-looking men wearing button up shirts, jeans, and white hard hats. Both of them carried rolled up plans in their fists.

"Something I can do for you officers?" said the shorter of the two men.

"Deputies," the other man said.

"Oh, yes. Sorry about that. Sluice-Byron County, I see now. Can we help you?"

"We're looking for a worker named Rick Hammes." Wolf said. "Shirley up there said he wasn't in the system so we'd like to ask around."

"Right." The shorter of the men took charge. "He must be with Logiwork then. This way."

They walked across the street. Once to the other side the man whistled and a supervisor walked toward them.

After a round of introductions, Wolf produced his phone with a picture of Rick Hammes on screen. "Do you recognize this man?"

The guy looked at it and nodded slowly. "Yeah. Don't know his name, but yeah." He pointed toward a group of workers in the midst of pouring fresh concrete. "He's over there."

"Thanks." Hammes was currently in the hospital sixty miles south fighting for his life, but Wolf let it go and walked over to the concrete workers, Rachette, Cain, and the two corporate men still in tow.

A group of hard-looking men stood with trowels and large brooms, smoothing out the gray concoction that poured out of chute at the rotating back of a concrete truck. A couple of them noted the approach of law enforcement and nodded in their direction.

They wore the reflective vest. All of their pants and boots were crusted with concrete.

Wolf walked to the nearest worker, a tall man with tattoos

peeking through deeply tanned skin, and flashed his picture of Hammes again. "Do you recognize this man?"

The man raised his sunglasses. "Yeah. Why?"

"Can you tell me his name?"

"How come?"

"We just want to make sure he works here," Rachette said.

The worker dropped his sunglasses back on his nose. "His name's Rick. Hammy or something."

"Hammes," another worker standing next to him with a shovel corrected him. "Rick Hammes."

Wolf turned to the man with the shovel. He had bright red hair that flowed out from under his hard hat, and he looked no older than twenty-five. He ambled over, grabbing his baggy jeans by a thick belt and giving them a hike.

"You know Rick?" Wolf asked.

"Yeah."

"What's your name?"

The man's eyes bounced between the cops in front of him.

"Answer the question, son," the corporate man who'd walked them over said.

Wolf turned to him. "I think we're all good here. We've found who we came here to talk to. You two can leave us if you don't mind."

"Yeah, okay. But if you're arresting him I need to know. I'll have to cover any losses for the day."

"Arresting me?" asked Red Hair.

"No," Wolf put up his hands. "Nobody's getting arrested. We just need to ask some questions."

They stood watching as the corporate men left and crossed the street again.

"Your name?" Wolf asked again.

"Wayne."

"Wayne. Nice to meet you Wayne." Wolf introduced himself, Rachette and Cain.

Wayne's eyes raked Cain up and down. "What's going on with Rick?"

"He's been shot."

That ripped Wayne's attention back to Wolf. "Shot?"

The tall worker behind Wayne overheard and relayed the information to the others.

"I'm afraid so," Wolf said.

"Is he dead?" Wayne asked.

"No. He's in the hospital down in Sluice-Byron County. He underwent surgery last night. The doctors say there's a good chance he'll be okay. They said the surgery went well."

"Whatever. Guy's a prick."

"Ah." Wolf nodded. "How do you know him?"

"He's my roommate down at the hotel."

"Down in Eagle?" Wolf offered.

"Yeah. I got paired up with him. He snores like a pig. Mean all the time. Threatens me. Talks about being in jail. Have you seen his tattoos? Scary guy. A real dick."

"So, you didn't know him before," Wolf said.

"No. The agency put us up together."

"When is the last time you saw him?" Wolf asked

"He left yesterday morning before the sun came up. He took the day off. Said he had to go home to check on his dog, get some new clothes and stuff, and come back up."

"And how about last Friday night?" Wolf asked.

"What about it?" Wayne asked.

"Was he in the hotel room with you?"

Wayne shrugged. "Yeah. Like, with me? What are you asking?"

"No, I mean, did he ever leave on Friday night? Maybe, around midnight or even later than that?"

Wayne shook his head. "No. We were all up drinking still at midnight. Friday night we were out getting it done in town."

"What does 'getting it done' mean?" Rachette asked.

"I don't know. Having a few beers. Trying to get laid. Getting it done."

The other workers behind Wayne slowly went back to work, keeping an ear cocked toward them as they smoothed a fresh batch of concrete.

"How late were you out that night?" Wolf asked.

"We closed down the bar over here. So, like one-thirty? Must have been."

"And then what after that?" Wolf asked.

"We caught a ride back to the hotel, you know, with the phone app?" Wayne shrugged.

"And then what?"

"And then we went to sleep. And then we got up five hours later to come back up here. Frickin' hung over as shit."

"You guys work on the weekends?"

"Yeah. Work never stops here. We do Saturdays. Get Sundays off, though. Sucks. But I guess it'll be over in a couple of months and I'll be broke again and wishing to work Saturdays. So, I guess I can't complain."

"Did Rick work last Saturday morning, too?"

"Yeah."

"Is that right?" Wolf asked another guy looking toward them.

"What?" the guy asked back.

"Was Rick Hammes working with you guys last Saturday?"

The guy looked like he didn't want to answer, but gave a reluctant nod. "Yeah."

"Thanks."

The guy put his head down, spreading concrete with a shovel.

"You say he left yesterday morning?" Rachette asked.

"Yeah."

"Why early in the morning?" Rachette asked. "Why not the night before?"

"Because we work until dark?" Wayne shrugged. "He wanted to sleep instead of drive all the way down to Dredge, he said. Said he was beat."

"How long has Rick Hammes been working with you guys here?" Wolf asked.

"Like, ten days or so? He said he got hooked up from a friend who knew a guy at Logiwork."

"Has he gone home at all since he came to work here?"

Wayne shook his head. "No."

"So he never went home?" Rachette asked.

"That's what I said."

"Okay, then. Thanks for your time," Wolf said.

"Yep." Wayne turned and joined the men smoothing the concrete sidewalk.

Wolf crossed the street, Rachette and Cain following behind him.

"I'd call that a definitive alibi for Hammes," Rachette said.

They walked in silence over the dirt. When they came to Cain's Jeep Wolf stopped.

"I'll see you back at the SUV," he said, tossing Rachette the keys.

Rachette walked away, leaving them standing at Cain's driver's side door.

"Look, I'm sorry about what you had to go through yesterday," he said. "That was a tough thing."

Her dark eyes looked up at him. The smooth skin of her forehead creased in a web of shallow folds. Her lips parted.

"But I want to know, what exactly are you doing here?"

She looked past him and her eyes glazed over. "I kept

thinking about that dog. The way it yelped. Biting at its back leg as it sprayed blood. And the way Hammes just dropped." She shook her head. "The sound of him getting shot keeps echoing in my head." Her eyelashes brushed the tops of her cheeks.

"I'm sorry you had to go through that," he said.

Yes, sir. I like your daughter.

Look at her. She looks beautiful doesn't she?

Yes, she does look beautiful.

She looked him in the eye, catching Wolf as he was lost inside the memory. Without warning his face grew hot, probably as red as the lights on top of her roof.

"Last night I went to the bar where everybody goes to drink at in Dredge," she continued. "The Picker. I did some asking around and learned where Hammes was working."

Wolf blinked. "And you decided to keep that information to yourself?"

She looked away. "I..." she shook her head.

"You what?"

"I was a millisecond away from squeezing my trigger too, and they both would have been dead. That dog and Hammes. There's no way they could've survived two shots."

"But they're alive now," Wolf said. "You know that, right?"

She crossed her arms. "I heard the dog's all right, and I called the hospital this morning to see about Hammes. I heard he got through the surgery."

She swallowed, looking like she was fighting back tears with pure willpower. Her face turned gritty again. "I kept thinking, why would he tell the neighbor across the street that he was going to Vail to work if he wasn't really going there? It's either an elaborate ploy where he could pretend like he was out of town while he went on a killing spree, or he really was working up here, in Vail, like he said he was."

"And you went to the bar in Dredge, figured out where

Hammes was working up here, and kept the information to yourself."

"I was going to tell you," she said. "Once I learned something. It could have been wrong information."

Yes, she does look beautiful.

He thought of the way she'd touched his arm, and this time a different heat rose inside of him.

"I'm leading this investigation," he said. "I have a team of three detectives on the case with me. That's four people qualified to make that call."

"I know, sir. I'm—"

"—I appreciate the help you've given us over the last couple days, but, officially, you're not part of this investigation. You're our Dredge satellite deputy. Do you understand?"

Her eyes narrowed. She unfolded her arms, raised her chin, and nodded. "Yes, sir. I understand, sir."

He had meant the words to come out gentler. But, still, she had done wrong.

She pushed her back away from the car, standing straight. "I understand perfectly, as I did back in February. I'll head back to where I belong."

She quickly climbed into her Jeep and drove away, leaving Wolf in a cloud of dust. With her words still ringing in his ears, he walked back to the SUV and got in.

"How'd it go?" Rachette asked.

Wolf fired up the engine, ignoring him.

"That good, huh? Is she applying for a job in Rocky Points or something?" he asked, and Wolf realized Rachette had Piper Cain's resume sitting on his lap.

"Where'd you get that?"

"Saw it behind the seat. Her picture was spilling out."

"Put it back." He snatched it from Rachette and threw it over his shoulder.

They drove in silence back to the highway. Once they got up to seventy miles per hour, Rachette said something under his breath.

"What did you say?"

Rachette put a pinch of Copenhagen in his lip. "I was just saying. It's a good thing MacLean's coming back."

"Oh. And why's that?"

"Because then it won't be so awkward for you to date her. Sheriff and a deputy? Can't be done. Detective and a deputy? That's doable."

"I have no idea what you're talking about," Wolf said.

"Of course you don't. Hey, phone call." Rachette held up a finger and pulled his phone from his pocket. "What's up, Patty?...okay, he's right here...yeah"

Wolf sucked in a few breaths with little success of calming himself.

Rachette spat into his Red Bull can and lowered the phone. "Rick Hammes woke up. Surgery went well, apparently."

Wolf nodded. "We'll head back to HQ and you and Yates can go talk to him."

"Yates and I will go talk to him," Rachette relayed into the phone. "What's that? Yeah, they confirmed Hammes was with them Friday night at a bar here in Edwards until 1:30 a.m., and then he was back on the job working bright and early the next morning...yep...that's what I said...All right, talk to you soon."

Rachette clicked off the phone and pocketed it. After a few minutes of silence he said "Okay, so Yates and I will head up to County. And what are you going to do?"

"I'll return this call to Jackson Hole this afternoon, see what I can learn about our three miners from the Teton County sheriff. Then I may go back up to Dredge."

"Yates and I will go with you."

"You'll be up at County. I'll go it alone."

Rachette nodded, spitting in his can again. "Yes, sir. You could always get Cain to help you out, anyway."

Wolf eyed him. His detective hid a smirk under a thin layer of serious contemplation as he stared out the passenger window.

"One of these days you and Patterson will mind your own business."

"I have no idea what you're talking about," Rachette said.

CHAPTER 20

Piper Cain parked her Jeep in the driveway next to Stacy's pickup truck and looked in the rearview mirror. Her eyes were sore and bloodshot from the two hour drive down from the Vail Valley, all the while repressing the urge to break down into a sobbing mess.

She was never one for crying, never had been, and she'd managed to make it home without doing so this time.

"Good job," she told herself in the mirror.

Through the windshield she saw her father standing on the front porch, leaning against the railing and gazing out over the valley like he loved to do for hours a day. That was all well and good, but he looked like he was getting wet.

She turned off the wipers and let the vision of her father standing out in the rain with that lost look blur behind the drops spattering the glass.

"Buck up." She gripped the mirror and twisted it sideways, then got out and shut the door.

When was it going to stop raining every afternoon? Obviously not today. Her shoulders were soaked through to her skin by the time she hopped up onto the porch.

"Hi Honey Bear," her father said.

"Hi Dad."

Her father looked at her with surprise, and she knew he had thought she was her mother again.

"What are you doing?" she asked. "You're getting wet."

Stacy came out the front door, wiping her hands on a towel. "Oh, geez. I was doing dishes. I'm sorry I didn't notice he was out here. Back up, Peter. My gosh."

Stacy steered her father to the side and into a dry spot. Her father just shrugged her away and went to his favorite spot again.

"Don't worry about it," Piper said. "The rain's letting up." Piper pulled out a hundred dollars in twenties and handed it over. "Here. Thanks so much for coming. That's all I have for now. I know I was gone longer than five hours. I'll pay you more next time. Okay?"

Stacy stared at the money. "That's okay, Piper. Look, why don't you just keep it?"

"What?" Piper stepped forward and shoved the money into Stacy's pants pocket. "Here."

"But it was your day off again, wasn't it?"

"So what?"

"So you won't get paid for those hours."

Piper walked up next to her dad. "I told you, Jake's been helping out."

"Jake?" Her father's eyes lit up, as they always did at the mention of his deadbeat son. "When is he coming home?"

"Good question," she said.

Although her brother had been sending two thousand a month in guilt money, the truth was he'd missed his payment last week. She only hoped he would keep his word and help out this month, too. Piper's earnings and the county aid only went so far.

"I'll see you tomorrow morning, right?" she asked.

"I'll see you tomorrow morning," Stacy said, "And you're not giving me this much. I told you, I have a pension already from the hospital. I don't need this money as much as you do right now. I'm not taking this from my best friend's daughter when she needs it the most, and I don't want to hear any more about it." She came over and pushed money into Piper's back pocket as she walked by.

"Hey." Piper dug out sixty dollars. "What the heck?"

"See you tomorrow!" Stacy was already down the stairs and ducking into her pickup. For a plump woman in her seventies, she moved like a cheetah.

Fighting back yet another urge to break into tears, Piper waved with the money and put it back in her pocket. Stacy responded with two honks as she drove down the driveway.

The rain all but stopped, turning into a faint sprinkle as they watched the pickup rev down the dirt road and out of sight behind the trees.

The curtain of low fog and rain parted, revealing the panorama ahead. A spear of sunshine lanced down through a hole in the clouds on the other side of the valley, lighting a swath of forest a dozen or more miles away. She couldn't help but notice the direction the light drew her gaze—thirty to forty-five minutes of driving, depending on the weather, the Chautauqua Valley and Rocky Points huddled on the other side of those peaks.

"Let me tell you the story of how I picked this property," her father said.

Piper eyed him.

"I was driving up this road here. Right here."

"I've heard it," she said, stopping him dead in his tracks.

She stared at his eyes, watching the circuits behind them scramble.

"Excuse me?" he asked. When he looked at her it was like they were meeting for the first time again.

She turned away, looking back out at the landscape, ignoring the wave of anger that washed over her. She pushed it down, out of the way, adding to the diamond-dense ball of pent up loathing for this sliver of God's country she found herself in. The shaft of light disappeared, pinched off by the clouds.

She thought about the way the sheriff had looked down on her up in that parking lot. Just when she'd thought he was beginning to respect her, he showed his true colors. He was just like the rest of them. Just like her brother. They were all out there taking care of their own, and if anyone or anything ever threatened their climb up the ladder, they stepped on your back and shoved you down, put you in your place, leaving you behind to claw your way. Alone.

They were all cowards.

"I..." her father said. "I..."

"You what?" Her voice shook. "What!"

Her voice echoed back to her from the trees, and that broke the dam. She opened the front door and walked inside as the tears flowed down her face. "Damn it," she said, growling the words.

With blurred eyes she set to cleaning the rest of the dishes that sat in the sink, and when those were done she re-cleaned the already clean ones on the towel.

All the while her father stood out there, staring into the distance with that pathetic air.

She scrubbed the stubborn streaks of blackened steak stuck to a platter, rubbing her fingers raw on the wiry sponge. She ran the coffee mugs under scalding hot water, welcoming the burn on the backs of her hands, not bothering to lower the temperature.

She shut off the water, and with closed eyes took deep

breaths, just like she'd learned in yoga. Five seconds in, hold, seven seconds out. After a time she opened her eyes and caught her reflection in the window.

She had Tammy Faye Bakker-style twin streaks of black mascara running down her cheeks. She smiled and then chuckled at the sight. She wiped her hands, grabbed a handful of tissues, and wiped her face.

"Oh, you're a mess, Piper," she told herself.

Sucking in a deep, cleansing breath, she went to the window again and looked out on her father. His lips were moving as he stared out into the distance. *What a sad sight* was all she could think. But was he sad? It sure didn't look like it. His eyes were steely, and he had a clever smirk on his face. He was impressing whoever he was talking to right now.

She put on a fleece, pulled his off the hook, and went out onto the porch.

Again, he looked at her the way somebody does when they're trying to remember your name, but she ignored it.

"Here, Dad." She put his fleece over his shoulders. "It's cold."

"Thanks, honey."

She reached up and rubbed his shoulders. "How's the view?"

"It's absolutely wondrous," he said.

She smiled at the amazement in his voice. He'd never described it like that before.

"Have I ever told you how I found this property?" he asked.

"No," she said, lying momentously. "How?"

He smiled, a conspiratorial glint in his eye. "I came up from Summit one day. I was driving my old silver Chevy."

She remembered sitting on the center console of that silver Chevy Blazer as they drove around the dirt roads spidering through the mountains, without even a thought of a seat belt, her older brother next to her in the passenger seat.

"I came around the corner and there was this "for sale" sign hanging on a rickety old barbed wire fence." Her father smiled. "And I tell you what, behind it I could see this house right here, the one I built ten years later with my own two hands, I saw it as if it was already built. I could literally see it."

He turned to her, his eyes alight.

She smiled again and nodded. "Yeah?"

"I got on the phone and I dialed the number on the sign, and I said, 'Where can I find you? I want to sign the papers right now. I'm buying it.' The guy was down at the bar. Said to come on over. He was having a drink."

Piper smiled, picturing her father.

He continued on giving his account of the shots of tequila, the beers, sleeping in his silver Chevy on the side of the road, waking up with that wicked hangover and a signed contract to buy the land. About her mother being distraught, not wanting to leave her life in Breckenridge, but how she had been convinced with one trip to this place. This beautiful place.

Piper asked all the right questions, keeping her father on track, pausing in all the right places, sighing in awe at his retelling of the yarn that had remained constant, word for word, for seventeen years.

"It took me two years, twenty-six months," her father said. "But the dream was realized." He held up his hands and turned toward the house. "And here it is."

He turned back to the land, and his eyes glazed over again, and she knew he'd reached the end of the strand of memory.

The clouds had moved north, leaving the afternoon sun to shine brightly on most of the now glistening valley.

She threaded her arm through his and steered him around. "Let's go inside then."

"That's a good idea."

"Yes, Dad," she said. "Let's get you back in your home."

CHAPTER 21

Wolf stood up from his desk and bent over to touch his toes. When he reached the middle of his shins the pain in his hamstrings and lower back was too much, so he rose up and opted for a pace around the office instead, raising his knees high with each step.

A deputy walked past his window, eyeing him through the slatted shades.

The phone speaker pressed to his ear scratched. "Sir? Are you still there?"

"Yes."

"I'm sorry, sir. Sheriff Domino is not available right now, and he's not answering his cell phone. It's very shoddy reception around here, I'll tell you. I would say I could raise him on the radio, but he's up fishing with some friends in Idaho and not due back until Monday. But I can give you his office voicemail, which I know he checks regularly, even though he's gone. He may be catching trout, but he'll probably return your call."

"That would be great, thank you."

He was connected, and tagged Sheriff Domino in their marathon game.

He took some time perusing the new emails that had come in. It had been days and he was sure whatever servers that were holding his unread emails were bursting at the seams.

Swiveling to the window, he looked out at the rain drenching the valley for the umpteenth day in a row. Now that Jack was part of the fire department over in Carbondale, he felt a new gratitude for rain. But he also knew the weather could turn relentlessly dry overnight, sticking around for months on end. The choking, smoke-spitting blazes could ignite again, threatening the ever-growing population of the Colorado Rockies and the firefighters who fought them. It was not a matter of if, but when.

On that note, he thought of the fire he'd ignited with Deputy Cain up in Edwards a few hours earlier. Not the good kind of flames, either.

He scrolled to her phone number and stared at it.

"He's playing with his phone?" A booming voice in the doorway made him flinch.

Will MacLean stood inside his office with arms wide, as if presenting the conclusion of a magic trick.

"You're here," Wolf said with a smile, an edge of relief in his voice as he pocketed his phone.

They hugged one another, MacLean slapping him on the back.

MacLean now had the body of a different man, and Wolf's arms easily wrapped around him. Where the former sheriff had once been soft, muscle now rippled beneath his clothing.

They pushed away from one another and Wolf stared at him. When Wolf had last seen MacLean, the former sheriff had been at least sixty or seventy pounds heavier, with a pasty complexion, sunken eyes, and depressed to the point that Wolf wondered if the man had given up on trying to live. Not that

Wolf would have blamed him for riding off into the proverbial sunset. They all had to do it at some point.

But now MacLean was thin, almost skinny, but his eyes were full of light, his skin tanned and glowing gold.

"Wow," Wolf said. "You look...better."

"I looked that bad before, huh?"

Wolf shrugged.

"I did, I know it." MacLean gestured to one of the two chairs in front of Wolf's desk. "May I?"

"Yes. Go ahead. Sit. Please." Wolf sat down behind the desk. "I feel a bit awkward sitting here, when you'll be taking over in...what is it now?" Wolf checked his watch. "Thirteen days?"

MacLean smiled warmly, looking Wolf in the eyes. "How are things going?"

Wolf gestured vaguely to the building surrounding them. "Good. But I want to hear about your exploits down in Mexico. Late-stage pancreatic cancer is nothing to thumb your nose at. Seriously. How did you do it?"

MacLean swiped a hand. "Like I said on the phone before, you wouldn't believe me if I told you."

"Magic?"

"Vegetables and coffee enemas," MacLean said with a straight face. "A lot of meditation and silent contemplation."

Wolf blinked.

"I told you you wouldn't believe me," MacLean said. "So, how's it going here? I hear you're doing a decent job at keeping the fort down. The council seems impressed with you."

"They're impressed with Patterson," Wolf said. "I've done nothing productive since you left."

MacLean smiled. "Your proposal with the council made my former self want to puke."

Wolf shrugged.

"But I liked it," MacLean said. "You guys will do good with that plan going forward."

"You're fine with it? You'll have to take the training, too."

"No, I won't."

Wolf cocked his head. "What do you mean?"

"I'm retiring, Dave."

The news hit Wolf softly at first, then like a flick in the nose, and then like a drop-kick to the stomach.

"I'm going to collect my pension and fish for the rest of my life." MacLean stood up and swiped his hands together. "I can see you're not exactly thrilled with the news."

The future Wolf had been envisioning, counting on, was exploding inside his head, and at that moment Wolf realized it was outgassing through his open mouth. He closed his lips and nodded. "Okay."

"Damn right. It's better than okay. I'm excited to wake up without a care in the world for once." MacLean walked to the window and looked out. "No offense, but I will not miss this view. And I've already informed Margaret of my change of plans, in case you're wondering."

"Okay."

MacLean walked over and patted him on the shoulder. "Dave."

"Yeah?"

"It's really good to see you."

Wolf nodded. "It's good to see you, too."

"I'm sorry if I got your hopes up," MacLean said.

Wolf said nothing.

"After I called you in February, you know what? I started feeling shitty again. I could feel the stress building, breaking down my insides, as I thought about coming back to the job." He looked hard into Wolf's eyes. "Dave."

"What."

"Don't let it happen to you." MacLean pushed his face close to his. "Don't let the stress take over. Delegate. Lean on those surrounding you." He turned around, knocking on Wolf's desk as he walked out. "Let's have lunch sometime soon."

"Sounds good." Wolf's eyes glossed over as he stared through the material universe.

A moment later, two soft knocks hit his door. "Sir?"

He looked to see Charlotte Munford-Rachette poking her head inside, holding a packet of papers in her hand.

"Hi, um, is this a bad time?"

"No. Please, come in."

She entered, narrowing her eyes. "Are you okay?"

"Yeah. What's up?" He held out his hand and she passed over the papers.

She said something about a form and his signature, and he nodded, pulling out a pen from his desk.

"Of course." He opened the page, signed where Charlotte had marked with sticky notes. "Here you go. Just these three?"

"Yes, sir. Thanks." She looked through the windows at MacLean walking through the squad room and down the hall.

"Anything else?" he asked.

"Uh, no, sir. Thanks."

"Of course." He handed them back.

She left the room.

He stared at the door for what felt like a couple hours, but when he checked the wall clock it read 3:35 p.m.

He turned to the window again and stood up. The rain had subsided, leaving cloudy skies and a roll of white fog gliding up the center of the valley. People down below on Main Street walked with their shopping bags. Kids rode past on their mountain bikes. A woman who worked for the county swept the debris that had washed onto the sidewalk. Back to life as normal.

He sat back down, settling in for one last phone call. He dialed and sat rigidly upright.

"Mayor's office," the young male voice said.

"Hi, Eddie, this is Sheriff Wolf, is Margaret around?"

"Sorry, sir. She's in a meeting. Do you want me to forward you to her voicemail?"

"Yes, please."

Wolf cleared his throat and spoke for a good minute. He wondered what she would think about the message he left, but then again, he didn't care.

CHAPTER 22

WOLF LEFT the office and drove out of town up the eastern side of the valley. Twenty minutes and a few miles later he parked in a dirt lot overlooking Rocky Points.

Still stewing in thoughts stirred by MacLean's visit, he got out and stood looking down on the Chautauqua Valley below. This eastern wall of the valley overlooking Rocky Points was known as Sunnyside. Down in the bottom of the valley sunset could happen just past lunchtime during the winter. Up here the wealthy built their expensive homes on pricey pieces of land, where the sun shined as long as possible, affording wide open Rocky Mountain ski resort town views.

But it wasn't all expensive housing. There was also plenty of undeveloped forest with hiking trails snaking through the trees, often affording hikers vistas that didn't come with a mortgage.

Wolf followed a familiar trail that coiled up steeply through the woods, welcoming the way his chest heaved and his legs ached with exertion. It had been a while since he'd taken a hike. Too long.

At the top he sat on a rock and looked down, taking a cool drink from his water bottle and letting the heat wick off his body. Only the faintest whisper of the traffic leading in and out of Rocky Points up the Chautauqua Valley to the north reached his ears. The cars were tiny replicas of the real thing. The drivers inside of them, warrants outstanding or not, were inconsequential up here among the swaying pines. He would stop denying himself these types of getaways in the middle of the day, he vowed.

Taking another sip of water, he thought about Heather Patterson and her knack for paperwork and presentations to the county council. With a clear head, he was even more sure about the voicemail he'd left for the mayor a few minutes ago. The upcoming changes within the department would be good in the long run, better than good. They would be great. A new future rose from the ashes of Wolf's old fantasies, and he realized he felt at peace for the first time in a long while. And it wasn't just the hike. Everything was as it should be.

The sky above skated past quickly, heavy with moisture. The scent of rain hung in the air and he knew he would probably get wet on the way down, but he remained still, breathing gently, letting his eyes hop around the countless miles of terrain ahead.

A series of worm-like piles of rock snaking next to the Chautauqua River caught his attention. The waved piles sat next to the silver water at various intervals, barely covered in vegetation since they were discarded by the large dredges that mined the river a hundred years ago.

Even from this high vantage Wolf could see a person moving atop one of the piles, like an ant crawling on a snake's back.

A few times growing up Wolf's father had taken him there to search for gold the old-timers had missed, using a metal detector. Wolf remembered finding an old metal teacup, decayed with rust. It hadn't been a nugget, and even though he'd never found gold the old-timers had missed, finding the cup had still been exhilarating. One man's trash was another man's treasure. Especially a hundred years later.

Wolf stood up, keeping his eyes on the tailings as a thought hit him hard. He stared, thinking of the decades of time those piles of earth had sat there, undisturbed. There could have been anything under those lumps. But who would have known it? A few solitary dumpster divers with metal detectors a hundred years in the future?

Without thinking he found himself moving down the trail.

The raindrops fell sporadically at first, and then more steadily, but he felt none of them. His thoughts were back up in Dredge with those three men digging gold out of the ground. The mine was back open, life going on as normal, as if the last few days could be glossed over and moved past.

He thought of Rick Hammes lying on the road and his dog whimpering in the back of the truck.

He thought about tailings.

He picked up his pace, running down the trail. He had a long drive ahead of him.

CHAPTER 23

Wolf's SUV bucked like an angry bull as he came off the sloped road leading into the Jackson Mine and coasted into the flat area.

He parked next to the four trucks, noting Oakley's was still there.

The drive from Rocky Points had been nothing short of wet, and it was no different here up at eleven thousand feet. The air was cold as death, drizzle breathing down from the leaden sky. A thin veil of snow covered the ground halfway up the peaks, disappearing in the clouds.

Wolf ignored the majesty of the surrounding land and kept his eyes on the three men. Kevin Koling, James Sexton, and Eagle McBeth sat in camp chairs under a sagging tarp, all holding beers. Judging by the crumpled pile of cans, in the words of Wayne the concrete worker from Edwards, they were getting it done.

"Sheriff," Eagle McBeth said, standing up.

Wolf nodded. "No need to stand for me."

McBeth remained on his feet for a few seconds, then sat

down. "I have a lawyer now. He wouldn't like me talking to you."

"I don't need you three to say anything," Wolf said. "I'm just here to talk to you. If you guys want to respond, that's up to you. But I don't need your involvement."

Wolf looked at Koling, Sexton, and then McBeth again in turn.

"You figure out anything new?" Koling asked.

McBeth looked at him.

"What?" Koling asked.

"We're not supposed to be talking to this guy." McBeth turned in his seat. "Anything we say can, and will, be used against us."

Sexton sat between Koling and McBeth, staring at Wolf with unblinking, bloodshot eyes. When Wolf nodded at him he took a sip and looked away.

Raindrops popped on the tarp overhead, slapping the ground around, pinging off the metal beast of a wash plant that loomed in the growing darkness. Piles of dirt lay near the plant, but they were in a different configuration than before.

"What I keep thinking about," Wolf said, "is the dirt you guys were feeding into that wash plant when you dumped Chris's body onto that hopper."

McBeth said nothing. Sexton sipped his beer with a slurp.

Koling lit a cigarette. "What about it?" he said.

McBeth's chair creaked as he turned to Koling again. "We have to stop talking to him."

"Why? What the hell—"

"—Don't you see that he thinks we killed Chris?"

"I sure as fuck didn't kill Chris!" Koling stood up, toppling his camp chair. He loomed over his two companions. "I didn't do anything!"

Sexton's eyes clenched shut and he sagged into his chair. McBeth held up a hand. "Would you please relax?"

Koling pointed at Wolf. "I didn't do anything. I didn't kill my best friend."

Wolf nodded, otherwise remaining frozen at the edge of the open-sided tent.

Koling picked up his chair and put it down. "Sorry. I'm just...I get emotional."

McBeth nodded understanding, holding out his hand, seemingly determined to calm his friend with a mime routine.

Sexton cracked his eyes open and raised his shoulders, looking like a turtle coming out of its shell.

Wolf gave it another moment, and the three men settled into a silent stare out into the rain past Wolf.

"Like I was saying," he said, finally. "I've been thinking about that dirt that comes out the back of that wash plant. Spent. Used. Devoid of the gold that you extracted from it. So where do you put it?"

Nobody answered.

"You put it into a tailings pile, set aside from the other piles of dirt you have. You probably have an area for overburden—the soil scraped off the top before you get down to the paydirt. You put that somewhere.

"And then you get down to the paydirt, and you start digging that out, and you pile that up in a separate area. Right? That has the gold in it. You put that in a special spot."

Sexton sipped his beer. Koling sucked on his cigarette. McBeth stared out into the rain.

"But you have no use for those tailings, so you make sure that you separate them. Those piles are the kind that will stay there for hundreds of years, waiting for the next generations of men to sift through, maybe with better methods by then, seeing if you missed any gold. That would be the perfect place to bury a body, wouldn't it?"

Wolf paused for effect, taking the opportunity to watch their reactions.

Koling shook his head back and forth, sipping his beer again. Sexton stared out at the rain.

McBeth's eyes strayed away from Wolf's. He seemed lost in thought as his hand went to his jacket where he fingered a black circular hole on the breast.

"What happened there?" Wolf asked. "Is that where Chris burned you with his cigarette that night?"

McBeth ignored the question and lowered his hand back to his lap.

Wolf continued. "It was Mr. McBeth here's idea to pull all those piles up and run them through the wash plant, right?" Wolf asked. "That's what you told us. Eagle here was upset about the argument he'd had with Chris." Wolf looked at McBeth. "He had flown off the handle. He had burned you with a cigarette."

McBeth kept his eyes on the rain.

"But, in the end Chris was right, wasn't he. You guys weren't catching any gold. You needed to revamp the wash plant, and re-process that already spent ground to make sure you got everything out of it you could."

They were statues.

"Which leads to the question: if Mr. McBeth here killed Chris, put that gun up against his chin and pulled the trigger, and then buried his body in the tailings ... well, that would be just plain dumb to order everyone to rework that dirt, wouldn't it? Why wouldn't he keep the body buried where it was?"

Wolf forked two fingers, pointing them at Koling and Sexton. "So which one of you two did it?"

They looked at him.

Koling's eyes glazed over and he slowly turned to Sexton.

This time Sexton grew taller out of the chair. "No. It wasn't us."

"Damn right it wasn't us," Koling said. "Sure as hell wasn't me."

"It wasn't me!" Sexton's teeth bared. "It was that asshole Hammes. He did it."

"We figured out Mr. Hammes couldn't have done it," Wolf said. "He was up in Edwards at a construction site Friday night. We have multiple witnesses saying he was there the whole time." Wolf rubbed his hands together. "So? Which one? Who killed Chris? And then who killed Mary Dimitri and planted Chris's gun at the house to make it look like Hammes did it?"

"Then it was somebody else making it look like it was us," Sexton said. He threw his beer out of the tent and stood up. "This is bullshit! We didn't do anything." He marched past Wolf, through the rain to his trailer, and went inside.

Koling and McBeth sat in silence.

Wolf eyed them both, his gaze landing on Koling. "It makes sense, though, right? It had to have been you or him."

Koling stood up, tipping his chair back again. Wolf remained still.

"It was someone else," McBeth said in a reasonable voice. He stood up and put a hand on Koling's chest and stood between the big man and Wolf. "Look, sheriff. I told you before. We're not going to talk. This right here is exactly why I have a lawyer. To protect our rights against something like this. Now, if you would please leave."

Wolf nodded, then glanced back at Sexton's trailer. He saw fingers pull away from a crack in the blinds. "Okay, Mr. McBeth. You're the boss."

CHAPTER 24

It was 7:35 p.m. when Wolf drove down from the mine back into Dredge and parked his SUV in the parking lot of The Picker Bar and Grill. The sun was technically still up somewhere behind the mountains and clouds, but it was almost pitch dark now that the rain had socked in.

His boots crunched on wet, pebbly soil. Raindrops beaded on a herd of parked cars, reflecting the light streaming out of the windows of the establishment. Music rattled the walls, and occasional raucous laughter echoed outside.

Two men stood outside smoking cigarettes near the front entrance, eyeing Wolf as he walked up. They offered no greeting, and Wolf offered none in return.

He walked into a miasma of beer and bar food. A group of hairy, burly-looking men were playing pool while a jukebox behind them pumped out a Journey song.

All eyes went to him in his non-uniform—a buttoned-up flannel tucked into jeans, a Carhartt jacket over it, but with his badge prominently displayed on his belt next to his holster. He might as well have been wearing spurs. Everyone straightened, elbowed each other, whispered, improved their behavior by a notch or two.

He stood eyeing the bar, spotting Casey Lizotte filling a couple of beer steins behind it.

Wolf walked up and stood at an open spot along the counter, watching Lizotte work his trade. If the man had seemed out of place up at the mine last time Wolf had seen him, Lizotte was in his element here. Working like he had four arms, he slapped glasses under taps, wiping the bar top, returning to the liquid and tilting the mug just so before sliding it in front of a waiting patron and starting another order.

Lizotte nodded at Wolf between making drinks and held up a finger.

Wolf nodded back, taking in the scene while he waited. As far as hole in the wall bar and grills went, The Picker was cleaner than most. Standard décor for this half of the state hung on the walls—rusty mining tools and black and white photos of bearded men holding mining implements.

"Sheriff?"

Wolf turned around to find Lizotte leaning toward him. "I need to talk to you."

"It's kind of busy."

"I can see that. It won't take very long."

They stared at each other for a moment, until Lizotte blinked first. "Spritz!"

A man materialized from the restaurant, looking like any other patron, until he acknowledged Lizotte.

"Sup?" Spritz put an order down on the counter, eyeing Wolf.

"Can you cover for me?"

"You're Spritz?" Wolf asked.

"That's right."

"I'd like to talk to you, too."

Spritz looked like it was less than okay, but he nodded, his dreadlocked ponytail bobbing behind him. "Now?"

"Can you get somebody to cover for you two?" Wolf asked. "It'll just be a few minutes."

"Both of us?" Lizotte looked skeptical, then relented. "Maybe...Johnny!"

One of the patrons in the lounge area set down his pool stick and came over. "What?"

"Can you cover the bar for a couple minutes?"

"It's my night off," Johnny said.

Lizotte rolled his eyes and gestured to Wolf. "Kind of not my choice."

Johnny pointedly ignored Wolf. "Yeah, yeah. I'm just giving you grief. I'll cover." Johnny went behind the bar and started chatting up a patron.

"Okay." Lizotte put a bleached rag on the counter and pointed toward the front door. "Out there's probably best. Unless you want to sit at a table."

A guitar solo was wailing out of the speakers. "Outside sounds good."

Lizotte led them out the door and lit a cigarette.

"Can I get one of those?" Spritz asked.

Lizotte looked annoyed but handed one over. "You want one?" he asked Wolf.

"No thanks."

They walked around the side of the building to the edge of the parking lot. Two worn out card-table chairs had been set up next to a side door. A coffee can overflowing with cigarette butts sat on the ground.

"Right here's good," Lizotte said.

"Thanks for taking some time away," Wolf said, zipping his jacket high to his chin.

Lizotte and Spritz both wore short sleeves, looking oblivious to the chill drizzle and plummeting temperature as night set in.

"I'm sure you've heard about what happened to Chris Oakley up at the mine," Wolf said, pointing his words toward Spritz.

Spritz nodded.

"And Mary Ellen Dimitri," Wolf said.

"And Rick Hammes," Lizotte said.

"All sorts of shit going on up here," Spritz said.

"What's your full name, Spritz?" Wolf asked.

"Jake Spizzerelli." He spelled it for Wolf.

"We found some text messages on Chris Oakley's phone between you and him, Spritz. Were you two good friends?"

"Yeah." Spritz put some feeling into the response.

"I'm sorry about your friend," Wolf said, watching Spritz's reaction.

Spritz sucked his cigarette.

"Like I said we found some text messages saying that Rick Hammes and Mary Ellen Dimitri were, quote, 'hooking up behind the bar.'"

"That's right."

"Can you tell me about that?"

"I went out here to take out the trash." Spritz pointed toward the dumpster. "I saw Hammes and Mary getting busy over by his truck, which was parked right there."

"Are you sure it was Rick Hammes?" Wolf asked.

Spritz's nodded. "Oh yeah. It was him."

"It's pretty dark back here," Wolf said.

"Hammes had been coming in with Mary lately," Lizotte said.

"Is that right?"

"They both work at the casino. They come in here after work and have a few."

"Ah, I see. And what about other people? Did Mary and Rick come in with other people from the casino after work?"

"Janine."

"Her waitress friend from the casino," Wolf said.

"Yeah, that's right," Lizotte said. "I don't know, everybody comes in here. Best place in town."

Wolf nodded. "Were you two working here last Monday night?"

"I was," Spritz said.

"I wasn't," Lizotte said. "My day off."

"Was Mary Dimitri here Monday night?"

Spritz nodded. "Yep. Came in after work. Had a couple beers."

"What time did she arrive?"

"Um, like seven-thirty or something like that. She had dinner at the bar. Like I said, a few beers."

"And was she with anybody?"

"Nah. She was first cut at work. Came in alone."

"Did you speak to her that night?"

"Yeah, sure. I was behind the bar. She was sitting at it."

"What did you two talk about?"

Spritz shrugged. "We were talking about Chris. You know, how he died and all. She was pretty broken up. Crying. I was pretty torn up too, you know? We had a couple shots in his honor."

"Did anybody else join you for these shots?" Wolf asked.

"Let's see." Spritz looked up, exhaling a long drag. "Just the normal Monday crowd. Couple of guys from town."

"Derek and Larry?" Lizotte asked Spritz.

"Yeah, they were there."

"Who are they?" Wolf asked.

"A couple old dudes who drink their pension away here."

Wolf nodded. "Anybody else?"

"Not really. Not that late, when we were having the shots. That was right before I closed up."

"And what time was that?"

"Eleven."

"How about Kevin Koling or James Sexton?" Wolf asked. "Where they here Monday night?"

"No sir," Spritz said.

"Eagle McBeth?"

"Nope."

"When she left, did she drive?"

He said nothing.

"You can tell me the truth."

"Yeah. It's like five blocks."

"What did you do after she left?"

The cigarette fell out of Spritz's hand but he made no effort to pick it up. "I went home."

"And where's that?"

"Over there a few blocks." He pointed with his thumb, keeping his eyes on Wolf.

"And you drove?"

"No. I walked. I always walk. Why are you asking that? You think I had something to do with this or something?" Spritz stamped his foot on the cigarette. "I don't have to talk to you anymore. I know my rights. This is bullshit. This is bullshit, Casey. I didn't have nothing to do with no murder." He marched around the front of the building and out of sight.

Wolf kept his movements slow and measured as he turned back for fear of scaring off Lizotte, too.

Lizotte's arm was frozen, his cigarette streaming smoke across his wide eyes.

"Are you still working up at the mine?" Wolf asked.

"Huh? No."

"Why's that? It was good money, right?"

Lizotte looked like he was thinking about following after his friend, then took a drag of his cigarette. "It was until I dug a dead body out of the ground and dumped it onto the wash plant grate. Then all the money in the world wouldn't be enough to get me to work up there again."

"When you worked up there Monday morning, what exactly did they have you doing?"

"Like I told you guys earlier, I was just running the loader, putting dirt onto the hopper grate. I told that short detective guy. Hachet or something?"

"Detective Rachette. I know, I just want to make sure we have this correct. Where were the piles of dirt you were pulling those scoops from?"

"Just right there. Right next to the wash plant. They had them all lined up for me, ready to go."

"Did you ever take a scoop from somewhere else other than those piles?"

"No."

Wolf nodded. "And one more thing." He paused. "Who do you think killed Chris Oakley and Mary Dimitri."

"It's obvious, isn't it?"

"Who?"

"Rick Hammes."

CHAPTER 25

WOLF WENT BACK and sat inside his SUV. He stared out the windshield, watching the neon-lit rain streak down, his thoughts bouncing between the living and the dead, landing on Piper Cain again.

He pulled out his phone and scrolled to her number. His finger hovered there for a moment before scrolling down to Patterson's number and pressing the call button.

"Hello?" Patterson's voice burst through his car speakers.

"How's it going?" He could hear pots and pans clanking in the background, kids laughing and squealing. "Sounds like I've interrupted dinner. Can you talk?"

"I still have a few minutes. What's up?"

"I'm up in Dredge."

"Geez. You put on some miles today."

He told her about his visit to Jackson Mine and his visit to The Picker.

"Do you like Spritz as our killer?" she asked.

"My gut's telling me it's not him. But let's dig into his record. You'll need his full name, Jake Spizzerelli." Wolf spelled it out for her.

"Okay. I'll look into him tomorrow."

"I also want to know exactly what those miners did when we put them up in the hotel Monday night. Did they stay at the Edelweiss all night? Where did they eat? Dine in? Take out? Did they go for drinks somewhere? I want all three of their movements accounted for."

"We really don't have a probable to look into their financials yet. But, yes, I'll dig into it. And FYI, Rachette and Yates went to County to talk to Hammes this afternoon, but were told he was out cold again. They're going back up tomorrow to try to catch him when he's awake."

The noise behind Patterson died down and he heard a door close. "Are you okay? You sound tired. Why don't you let us go up to Dredge tomorrow? My foot's feeling better."

"MacLean is retiring."

"I know."

"How?"

"Charlotte came across some paperwork that got me suspecting. Then I twisted Margaret's arm and she told me."

Wolf squinted. "What did she tell you?"

"She told me MacLean wasn't coming back. Is there more to tell after that?"

Wolf said nothing.

"Is Wilson taking that job in Denver?" she asked.

"Why are you asking that?"

"Never mind."

They sat in silence a beat.

"I'll go to Dredge tomorrow," Wolf said. "Rest your foot and broken arm. Goodnight."

He flipped the wipers on, put it in drive, and drove down the main drag of Dredge.

He drove slowly, lost in thought, past the tiny shops converted from the ancient buildings, past the chic restaurants and the holes-in-the-walls, past a gas station and the hulking casino. At the end of the road, where it bent ninety degrees to the right and back toward Rocky Points, he slowed to a stop.

The dark and muddy county road that led to Piper Cain's house branched to the left, beckoning.

"Okay, fine," he said, turning the wheel left.

Ten minutes later he drove out of the open valley floor and into dense woods. Hypnotized by the sound of his rumbling tires, the windshield wipers, and the darkened wall of pine trees flitting past on either side, he leaned into the windshield waiting for a sign of Piper Cain's house.

He'd been driving too long, he thought. Maybe it was the wrong road altogether. Had he missed a turn that he'd taken last time? The previous drive up here had been a blur—literally—as he'd been slipstreaming her cloud of dust.

A few seconds later the road brightened from a light ahead and the trees opened up, revealing the familiar house at the top of a broad lawn.

He slowed to a stop in front, flicking off his headlights. The place stood a good fifty or so yards up from the road, up a slight rise. The windows glowed yellow, revealing the interior.

She immediately came into view, something in her hands as she passed the window, then disappeared. Then she was back, pressing her face to the glass, looking out.

Wolf waved, realizing he was invisible to her inside the cab so he flashed the brights.

She held up a hand and waved, reluctantly, then motioned for him to come up.

He drove up to the driveway and parked next to her Jeep, then got out, zipping his jacket to his chin. The rain had stopped and the air was still, smelling of cut grass.

"Is everything okay?" She said from the porch. "What are you doing here?"

He walked to the foot of the stairs. "Hi. Uh, I was just in Dredge, on my way back to Rocky Points, and I thought I'd stop by to talk."

She zipped a fleece to her chin and shoved her hands in the pockets. Her hair was pulled into a ponytail, a few strands left loose and cascading down her shoulder.

"Okay," she said expectantly.

"Can I come up there?"

"Sure. Come up." She turned around and walked to the railing as he climbed the stairs and into her now-familiar floral scent.

She walked to the railing, and looked out across her lawn.

Wolf followed her gaze. The underside of low hanging clouds glowed from the sparkling lights of Dredge in the distance.

"It's beautiful."

"Yeah." She didn't exactly ooze enthusiasm.

"Listen," he said, "I'm really sorry about what happened earlier today."

"What happened earlier today?"

He took a step toward her, catching sight of her father inside. He carried a beer to a lounge chair and sat down in front of the flickering television.

"How's your dad doing?" he asked.

"Good."

"Good." He cleared his throat. "I'm sorry about what I said to you today."

She remained silent.

"It was out of line. In the end, you were trying to help. I get that. You went through a lot yesterday, and I can see how that fired something in you to do something. I should have been a bit more sensitive to your situation. To your state of mind."

She shook her head. "No. I'm sorry. That was completely

out of line of me to drive up there and take things into my own hands like that. Like you said, there's a whole detective squad dedicated to this case, and I went behind all of your backs." She looked at him. "The truth is, I wouldn't blame you if you wanted to fire me right now."

"That's not why I'm here."

She looked at him for a beat, then back out into the valley.

"About what you said earlier," Wolf said. "Up in the parking lot. About what I made clear in February. I wanted to explain that. Back in February I was in a bit of...well, I'm not one to make excuses, so I won't. I'll just say I wasn't at my best and I made a mistake and I overlooked your resume. I know this sounds so ridiculous like, the dog ate my homework. Or, ate your resume. But I really did overlook it. With all the things I was already avoiding at work, I also avoided hiring people, too. I mean, I hired one deputy, but that was more of a personal favor and the second hire I never took care of. Now I feel foolish, and responsible for your situation up here and what happened the other day with your dad, because the truth is I would have hired you if my head hadn't been up my ass, but it was."

"It's okay," she said.

He sucked in a breath and looked at her, surprised to see her smiling.

"You can stop apologizing now," she said. "I accept."

"Okay. Good. I...accept yours too."

She nodded. "Then it's settled."

"Not really," he said. "We do have an opening for a deputy position in Rocky Points. Still. It's yours if you want it. Your resume, and the recommendation from your boss up in Gallatin County that came with it, outshines the other hire I made and any of the others in my neglected stack of candidates."

She stared at him, her eyes sparkling in the light streaming out of the windows, like they might be welling with tears. It was hard to tell, and before he could get a better read on her she turned her back to him.

"Is everything okay?" His feet pulled him toward her of their own volition. Without thinking he raised his hand and put it on her shoulder. "What's the matter?"

She turned. Her eyes were perfectly dry. Unblinking. Staring down at his hand.

"Sorry," he said, and pulled it away and stepped back.

But she followed him, reaching up and wrapping her arms around his neck.

He stood rooted as her body crashed into his.

She was firm and soft at the same time, warm and moving, a humming embrace, breath in his ear, coils of hair on his cheek and lavender in his nose.

Abruptly, she pulled away. "Sorry," she said, smiling. "Shit. Sorry. I just didn't expect that."

He smiled at the sight of her joy. "So you're happy then."

The front door opened and her father poked his head outside. "What's going on out here?" He wore flannel pajama pants and a washed-out T-shirt that said Summit County Sheriff's Department.

"It's okay, Dad, I'm just out here talking to Sheriff Wolf."

"Sheriff Wolf?"

Wolf held out his hand. "Yes, sir. Nice to meet you."

"You're the Sheriff?"

"Yes, sir."

They shook hands. Her father's grip was large and sweaty.

"Peter Cain. Operations Commander Summit County Sheriff's Department. It's a pleasure. What's the occasion for your visit?"

"I was just going over some case points with Piper, er,

Deputy Cain. It couldn't wait, so I decided to stop by the house. I hope you don't mind, sir."

"No..." Her father stopped short. His eyes glazed over and Wolf could see the moment something short circuited. He turned around and went back inside, leaving the front door open.

Piper followed and poked her head in, and Wolf could see past her as her father sat back down in his chair and pressed a button on the remote control.

She shut the door and turned around with folded arms. The earlier joy had left her face.

"Well," he said. "I guess that's all I had. I have to head back to Rocky Points."

"Long drive," she said.

"Long drive."

She gazed past him again, then locked her dark browns on his. "I have to think about it."

"Of course. Yeah." Her answer puzzled him, but he kept his face neutral. He looked in through the window at her father who was now rummaging through the refrigerator. "Well. Good night," he said with a final nod, walking to the stairs.

"Good night. And, sir?"

He stopped. "Yeah?"

"Thank you."

"For what?"

She shrugged.

"You're welcome. Take your time with your decision. It's a big one. I'll talk to you soon."

He stopped at the top of the steps. "Oh, and Piper?"

She poked her head back out. "Yes?"

"Be careful of those men up at the mine. It's them. They did it. They killed Chris Oakley and Mary Dimitri."

She stepped out onto the porch again, her eyes hardened. "You found proof."

"Not yet. But it's a matter of when, not if."

"Okay. I will."

CHAPTER 26

Piper Cain woke the next morning feeling more energized than she had in over a year. Maybe ten years, because not since her first day on the job up in Gallatin County could she remember feeling such promise for her future and such an alive buzz inside her.

She had the job.

"We're out of milk!" her father yelled from the kitchen.

"Stacy's bringing some when she comes over!" she said, buttoning up her khaki uniform shirt.

And she had her father.

She finished putting on her eyeliner, wondering if she would see the Sheriff again today.

And she had Sheriff Wolf as a boss.

All night she'd been thinking of how she'd thrown herself around his neck last night. She was half horrified about her reaction, and half glad she'd done it.

Pulling her arms around him had been like hugging a tree. The man's body was rock solid and unwavering as she had crushed him in her embrace. His face had been sandpaper, his body stiff as wood. Maybe a bit soft in the middle, but she had felt the way he had flexed when she pressed into him. He had even smelled of some sort of pine deodorant. An all-around nice wood sculpture, that man was.

She shook her head. "Easy, Piper," she said to herself in the mirror.

And then her mind drifted forward into a more realistic future, of her working in the county building down in Rocky Points, and her pathetic crush on her older, completely unavailable due to obvious professional conflicts that would land them both in the unemployment line, boss.

And what would happen to her father if she took him away from this place? Things really would turn sad if instead of looking out on Dredge Valley she gave him an apartment wall in downtown Rocky Points to stare at.

"Hello!" Stacy called as she came inside.

She blinked out of her thoughts. "Hi Stacy!"

She was on time as always. On the mark.

Piper strapped on her duty belt and went out into the great room. Light streamed in at a perfect angle, making the space sparkle.

"What happened to you?" Stacy asked.

"What?"

"You look especially chipper today."

"Really?" She shrugged and went to the kitchen and poured a cup of coffee into her to-go cup. When she turned around Stacy was still studying her. "How are the kids?"

Stacy tilted her head, eyeing her suspiciously, then beamed at the thought of her grandchildren. "Rambunctious as ever. They're going fishing with their father today."

"That's nice," Piper answered, but her mind was already on the day ahead. She was planning on doing her usual rounds around town, but she also wanted to do some snooping up at Rick Hammes's house. Sleep had come in fits last night. In between

241

vivid visions of life in Rocky Points and regrets of wrapping herself around David Wolf, and fantasies of doing it again, she'd also been cycling through the same images of Chavez shooting Rick Hammes and his dog. And then there was Wolf's certainty that the men up at the mine had killed Chris Oakley and Mary Dimitri.

If Wolf was right, that meant the men from the mine had planted that gun in the woodpile outside of Rick Hammes's house. It was brazen. Ballsy. Also stupid. She thought about when they would have done it, and realized it must have been Monday night, after they killed Mary Dimitri with the gun. That was the same night the neighbor had said he'd heard Hammes come home, because the dog had gone quiet.

Maybe there were more clues up there. As much as she despised thinking about talking to that eye-groper neighbor of Hammes's, maybe he'd seen more than he thought. He just didn't know it.

"Are you listening to me?" Stacy asked. "He-llo."

"Sorry. I've just got a big day ahead." She picked up her to-go cup. "Bye, Dad, be good for Stacy today."

"I'm always good."

She smiled at the sane response from her father and left out the door.

Stacy was right on her heels. "I have to leave here at four p.m. sharp today to be with the kids."

"Yes, I remember. I'll be off duty at three-thirty. I'll be home in time."

"Okay. Just a gentle reminder."

She stopped and gave Stacy a hug. "Thank you."

The woman stood with her hands by her sides, then pulled them up and wrapped them around her.

"I appreciate it," Piper said.

Stacy held her at arm's length and shook her head. "You

look just like your mother, do you know that?" She poked Piper's stomach. "And you're just as skinny. You need to put on some weight."

"Yeah, yeah." How easy she could do just that by skipping a couple weeks of yoga. "I'll see you later."

Piper slowed and parked her Jeep in the same spot as the last time she'd been to Hammes's house.

She turned off the ignition and sat in her silent car, listening to the incessant click somewhere inside the dashboard until that, too, came to a stop.

It had been four hours since she'd left the house this morning. After a hearty lunch at the bakery in town and a bit of stalling, she was finally here.

Her eyes went to the open window and the road next to her. Two spots still darkened the ground where Hammes and his dog had fallen.

Surprisingly little emotion stirred inside. She had been stalling for nothing, she decided.

She got out, her feet scratching on the road as she approached the spot and bent down, putting her hand down but not touching.

A low rumble of thunder came from the far distance, just at the edge of being audible. Yesterday's rains hadn't scrubbed the road clean. Maybe today's would do the trick. Maybe it would never go away, but soak its way deep in the ground, becoming part of the road, like the memory would with her.

The sky was gathering in the southwest, darkening behind the peaks where the Jackson Mine lay. The air was still. A crow cawed as it glided across the sky and dove into the trees.

She climbed back into the Jeep, fired the engine, and

coasted down to Hammes's house, parking out front of the chain link fence.

"Howdy, there!"

She started and turned to see the neighbor, Ned Larson, out in Hammes's front yard.

"You caught me!" he said, holding his hands up. He picked up something off the ground near the front door and walked toward her and the fence.

"What are you doing in there?" Her heart was racing. The last thing she was expecting was a confrontation. She hung back on the other side of the Jeep, keeping her hand close to her weapon.

Ned held up a silver bowl that glinted in the afternoon sunlight. "I told you that demon took my bowl. I figured now that they're in the hospital I'd come over and get my property back before he returns. Otherwise I'll never get it."

She relaxed a bit. "You scared me."

Ned seemed oblivious to her. He reached the chain link and dropped the bowl over the other side with a clank, and then proceeded to climb the fence with the least amount of grace she'd ever seen.

"Do you need my help?" she asked, watching him quiver on top as he pulled his other leg over.

"I didn't feed Dex that steak," Larson said, stumbling to his knees at her feet.

"Are you okay?"

Larson ignored her again and got up, brushing himself off. "He was yelling at me about that when he came home. I know what meat can do to him. I fed him only the specific blend of chow he gave me from the Tupperware. I never fed him anything else. Sure as hell not this." He reached over and picked up his bowl, then something else off the ground.

He straightened, holding the steel bowl in one hand and a

bone in the other. "I just found this. Must be what Rick was yelling about what gave Dex the shits. Like I have extra bone-in ribeyes lying around to feed a measly mutt who hates me anyway. Besides, I wouldn't be so cruel. I knew damn well about his condition."

She took the bone from his hand. "T-Bone."

"Huh?"

"It's a T-Bone steak bone." It was her father's favorite meal. "Where did you find this?"

"In there. It was lying in my bowl."

"In the yard?"

"Yes ma'am." Larson's eyes flicked to her breasts and back.

"And what kind of condition did Dex have?" she asked.

"Some sort of red meat allergy or deficiency or something? I don't know. Dog can't eat meat or it gives him the shits. Can be life-threatening, I guess. Rick told me all about it before I left. I may be a bit blind but I ain't deaf. I didn't feed him no T-bone."

She remembered back to that morning when they had come here the first time. The dog had gone to the bathroom twice while they were there. Now that she thought about it, it had seemed like it was not feeling well. She looked inside at an array of feces around the yard. She was no veterinarian, but they did not look healthy as far as dog poop went.

Ned was still going on about the steak.

"Sir," she said.

"What?"

"What usually happens when you come up to this fence? I mean, when you come over to feed Dex, does he bark at you?"

"Yeah. Barks like a guy with his nuts—"

"—Okay, yeah. And what happens when you feed him the food?"

Ned shrugged. "He eats it."

"And he stops barking?"

"Yeah. That's the only way to stop him."

"And what time did you hear Dex barking Monday night?"

"Shit, I don't know. It was late. Like midnight? One?"

She walked to the fence and eyed the woodpile standing alongside the house. At least twenty feet separated it from the fence line. All territory that would have had to be crossed by somebody planting a gun inside the property.

"Thanks," she said, holding up the steak bone and hopping back into her Jeep.

She sped away, leaving Ned Larson with his shiny bowl and a puzzled look on his face. She was so excited to get to Lonnie's Market on Main Street that she failed to take notice of the pickup truck passing her at the top of the hill.

CHAPTER 27

Wolf sat staring out his office window at the Rocky Points resort. He'd spent the morning in the gym doing a vigorous weights workout that would undoubtedly leave him immobile come tomorrow. The workout had stirred up a ravenous appetite and now he sat in a post-lunch haze.

His cell phone vibrated and rang on his desk.

He picked it up, reading a non-Colorado number. "Sheriff Wolf here."

"Hey, Sheriff Wolf. Sheriff Domino with Teton County Sheriff's Department here."

"Good to finally talk with you."

" So you have some action involving our boys down there, eh?" Domino said. "It's a shame about Chris, but I have to say I expected some sort of violent end for that boy. Kid was always a bad seed. Once you get to know his parents, you start to understand why."

"One of my detectives has been trying to get hold of them," Wolf said. "They weren't answering so he called to get you guys to help on that matter."

"Yeah. They know about his death," Domino said. "They just don't care. The two of them are career alcoholics and never lifted a finger as far as raising him went, unless it was out of anger. His father was one of those guys who opened the bar every day and shut it down every night. His mother worked at that bar."

"And now?" Wolf asked.

"Now...I don't know what they do. Drink."

"So how about Chris?" Wolf asked. "What's his story?"

"As far as I could tell, his mom and dad would whip on him pretty good. We were once called there on a domestic. His father had called us. His old lady was beating them all up. That was ... let's see ... must have been back when Chris was in middle school. He never pressed charges, and Chris had no visible marks on him. But I suspected he was getting hit by her. At the very least, he suffered major emotional abuse.

"A few years after that, when Oakley was in high school, we started having regular run-ins with him for fighting. Like mother, like son."

"And how about the others?" Wolf asked. "I was hoping you might be able to shed some light on the living."

"Right," Domino said with a sigh. "Well, first thing is, you have Kevin Koling and Chris Oakley, and then you have Eagle McBeth and James Sexton. It's not a group of four of them as much as two groups of two. Oakley and Koling were inseparable in high school, and they graduated three years before the other two. I know a lot less about McBeth and Sexton. They were good kids who generally stayed out of trouble."

Sheriff Domino took a sip of something and shuffled some papers. "I've sent you these files by the way through InterDocs."

Wolf went to his email and logged in to see the files. "Thanks, got em' right here."

"Let's start with Koling," Domino said. "You can see he had one aggravated assault when he was a senior in high school, which had everything to do with Oakley. Oakley was the bully in town, and Koling was his sidekick. Wherever there was a high school party out in the sticks, there was an Oakley assault and Koling at his side. Koling was always guilty by association.

"Oakley's record does not reflect the trouble he used to get in. Like I said, the assaults and threats to others were the main problem. I've personally put him in jail twice, and he had a DUI five years ago. He squeaked out of serving his full sentence."

"How about McBeth and Sexton?" Wolf asked. There were no links next to their names, which meant there were no official records.

"Like I said, those two were different. They're three years younger and kept their noses out of trouble, generally because they worked for a living growing up, and didn't dink around town getting in fights."

"So how do these four guys hook up?" Wolf asked. "I don't get it."

"McBeth's mother and father own—owned—the Triple-O ranch up here in Jackson. The ranch is a huge mainstay of the Teton Valley. Has been for quite a while now. James Sexton, he's an interesting fellow. He was part of the foster system up in Driggs, Idaho, and he moved over here and started working at the McBeth Ranch when he was in high school. The McBeth ranch takes in all sorts of people. Every year paying tourists come to the ranch to do the dude ranch thing. You know, like the City Slickers movie and all."

"Right," Wolf said.

"And then there are the employees of the ranch. They're quite a varied bunch, from all walks of life and from all corners of the globe. And, back then, we used to give credit for community service to those completing work programs at the ranch. That's where Chris Oakley and Kevin Koling come into the picture. Eagle McBeth was already working there, it was his family ranch. So was James Sexton, he'd come in there sometime before from the foster system. A different program I'm not familiar with. Koling and Oakley came in on a court-ordered work program for community service for beating up a kid up near String Lake."

"I see," Wolf said. "Although they still seem like opposite types of kids to me."

"I think it was the traumatizing events surrounding McBeth's father that made them close."

"What traumatizing events?"

Domino paused for a beat. "Have you ever seen McBeth's arm?"

"I have," Wolf said. "There's a big scar. Interlocking rings, or something."

"Interlocking O's," Domino said. "The Triple-O Ranch."

"Are you saying that's the cattle brand burned into his arm?"

"Yes."

"How?"

"McBeth's father. The guy was rich. Connected with the community. A tough cowboy with an American dream story, coming from a family who had nothing, somewhere in Missouri I think, who became a millionaire cattle driver. Owned a ton of land. He got into gold mining, too. Made a small fortune hitting it big at a claim in central Wyoming. Unbeknownst to most of us around town, he apparently drank heavily. He was a driven man, and when we looked into him...afterward...we found he ingested alcohol with as much fervor as any of his other endeavors."

"Afterward?" Wolf asked.

"One night he got real drunk. Or, normal-drunk is probably more like it. Anyway, apparently Eagle did something up there at the ranch that pissed him off, something about crashing a tractor or something. Costed his old man some money in repairs. So he took Eagle into the barn and taught him a lesson by putting that branding iron on his arm."

Wolf shook his head.

"You there?" Domino asked.

"Yeah. Sorry. I'm just thinking. How does that happen? I mean, wouldn't he fight back? He was in high school, right?"

"Eagle McBeth's father was huge. Six foot seven inches. Over two hundred fifty pounds of muscle, had to have been. You've seen Eagle. The kid never had a chance, as he's not the most impressively sized guy. He takes more after his mother. He was really messed up after it as you can imagine. You ask how he didn't fight back? I'm sure he fought with all his might."

"Messed up how? Mentally or physically?"

"Both. His arm was burned horribly. He was in pain. Bloodied up on his face. Bruised all over. I was actually the first responder there. Back in my green days." Domino took his time continuing. "I'm no psychologist, but he had to be pretty messed up mentally, too. They have a pretty big property there, lots of out-buildings, lots of acreage. I went out searching for his father and eventually found him dead in one of the barns."

"Cause of death?"

"Self-inflicted gunshot. I'll remember that scene until I'm dead and buried myself. That probably won't be enough to scrub that memory."

Wolf stood up. "How exactly did he shoot himself?"

"Put the barrel up under his chin. Pulled the trigger. Exit wound right clean up the top of his head. Left a neat hole in the roof of the barn."

Thick rain drops streaked Wolf's window now, but he saw none of it.

"Hello?" Domino said. "You there?"

"Did you find GSR on McBeth's father's hands?"

"Well, that I'm not sure about. Like I said, I was a rookie. It was a couple years before my time as detective. But it was my understanding this was cut and dried. Why are you asking that?"

Wolf told him exactly how Chris Oakley had been killed.

The line crackled with silence. "You there?" Wolf asked.

"Yeah," Domino said. "Holy shit. You might have just created a case for us up here."

Wolf sat down and stared at the N/A next to Eagle McBeth's name in the email from Domino.

He went down the line to James Sexton and clicked the link there. A scanned document loaded on screen with a letterhead reading Driggs Foster Families Facilities, and a logo with the letters DFFF.

Wolf stood up and paced the room. "Could you do me a favor?"

"Anything you need."

"Can you get somebody to look into James Sexton? His file is pretty sparse."

"You think he's the guy?"

Wolf thought of the way Sexton had been silent under that tarp. He'd huddled down into a protective place. When the blame had been shifted toward him, though, that protection had been blown away by defensiveness.

"Wolf?"

"Yeah, sorry," Wolf said. "I was just thinking. I have his papers here listing his adoptive home in Driggs, Idaho. His age at the time was seventeen."

"Yeah?"

"I'm just wondering, what about his natural parents? Who are they? What's his history?"

"Gotcha. That's something I don't know off hand. Like I said, McBeth and Sexton were off the radar, unlike Koling and Oakley. We'll look into him and I'll get back to you."

"Thanks for your help," Wolf said, ending the call.

CHAPTER 28

LONNIE'S MARKET sat two blocks east of Main Street. A modern building in the otherwise museum-like town of Dredge, the supermarket parking lot was still dirt.

Piper parked her Jeep along the side of the brick building, away from the other cars. Not that it was the most bustling place at...what time was it?

Her dash clock on the old piece of a vehicle the county had given her was broken, so she pulled out her cell phone and took a look. It was 3:11 p.m.

How had it gotten so late? She'd been wrapped up in real work for once, that's how. She had time, at least thirty minutes, before having to head back home and relieve Stacy by four o'clock.

She got out into cool air. Large oak trees loomed above, swishing heavily in the wind as a new wave of rain pelted down on Dredge for the thousandth day in a row.

Entering through the store's automatic doors, she went to the first checker she saw, a teenage boy with thick glasses and a mouth of huge teeth.

"Excuse me." She read his name tag. "Charlie?"

"What?" He stopped what he was doing, holding up a bag of potato chips.

"I'm looking for a manager."

"Sally or Cherise?"

"Which one of them is the manager?"

"Both of them."

"I don't care which one."

"Sally is here."

Piper smiled, but wanted to punch something. "I'd like to see Sally."

He pointed. "Down aisle seven. Back of the building."

She followed Charlie's directions down aisle seven. Ahead was an open passageway that led up some stairs. Angled mirrors were mounted on the long edge of the ceiling and back wall reflecting her image back to her from above.

When she reached the rear of the store she paused, looking both ways. There was another set of doors to the right, but they were the swing type that grocers pushed in and out of to stock the place.

Taking the stairs, she looked again at the overhead mirror. A man peered around the corner a few aisles away. He seemed to be watching her. When she turned to look at him, he ducked out of sight. Her heart skipped, fluttering into action as she stared hard at the spot. But the man was gone. Slowly, she walked to the aisle, rounding the corner as widely as possible.

The aisle was empty.

She side-stepped, checking the next aisle. A young couple with a pair of children climbing on their cart looked up at her. The man had the same color coat. Maybe.

When she noticed they were all four staring at her she smiled. "Hi."

She walked back to the stairs, eyes darting up and around.

She was either seeing things, or somebody who was

watching her had sprinted out of sight before she got there to look. Hoping it was the former, she turned the corner into the narrow corridor with the stairs.

Skipping two steps at a time, she trotted up, emerging into a small break room.

A teenage girl eating noodles out of a steaming bowl looked up at her.

"Hello," she said. "I'm looking for the manager."

Her eyes, and then a finger, went to an open door along the wall.

Inside there was movement. "Who's that?" a woman's voice echoed out.

Piper went to the door and poked her head into a closet of an office. "Hello. Are you Sally?"

"That's me." A woman sat in front of a computer screen, tapping on keys. When she turned around Piper recognized her immediately from other times she'd shopped there.

"Hi," Sally said, smiling.

"Hello, I'm Deputy Piper Cain. I'm with the county Sheriff's department."

"Nice to finally know your name. I've seen you around."

"Nice to meet you, Sally." Piper eyed the clock ticking away on her wall. It read 3:18. "Is that clock right?"

Sally looked up at it. "Beats me. No I'm just kidding. It's precisely on time. I have to keep a tight schedule, you know?"

"Right. Listen, I'm wondering if something's possible."

"Shoot."

"Is there a way to see who purchased something from the meat department on, say, last Monday?"

The manager blinked a few times. "Well, we use a new software system that monitors inventory. The purchase details are stored, in a dumbed-down version, mind you, in the system. We don't keep credit card numbers or anything."

"How about names on the credit card tied to specific purchases?"

"We would have the name from the loyalty card. Or, yes, we'd use the name that comes through on the credit card if they don't have a loyalty card."

"Could you do that for me now?"

Sally drew the frameless glasses off her nose. "Do what?"

"Check who purchased meat on Monday for me?"

"Don't you need a warrant to do something like that?"

Piper put up her hands. "Listen, I would love to just get a basic idea of what I'm looking for and see if you even have the ability to do what I'm asking. If so, the sheriff and I will come back in here with the necessary warrant."

The manager sat, thinking.

"But," Piper looked at the clock again, "it would really save me a lot of time and effort if I could just figure this out right now while we're right here in front of it. If I had something to bring to my boss, you know? He would be happy." She held her smile, not too cheery. The explanation made no sense, she thought, holding her breath.

The manager finally nodded. "Just a quick glance, to see if we can do what you need is all."

"Perfect."

Sally swiveled around and clicked an icon. A progress bar started loading at a worm's pace.

"Updates," Sally said. "They never end."

3:22 p.m.

She pulled her phone out, seeing Stacy had sent her a message.

Are you on your way home?

Piper ignored it and put it back in her pocket. She still had time. It took only fifteen minutes to make it back, maybe ten if she drove at full speed with her lights on.

Another progress bar blipped on screen, and then another. Come on!

Three full minutes later, Sally was in the system. She pointed the cursor to a 'Meats' button and clicked. A spreadsheet, and with it a list of seemingly unintelligible numbers, appeared.

Piper's stomach dropped in disappointment until Sally spoke, pointing with the cursor.

"Here we are. The sales are here. The names are here. And here are the codes for the meats."

"Which code is a T-bone?"

"Right here. Oh-eight-three."

"And where are the dates?"

"I have to enter it in to see the date."

Piper calculated in her head. "What about June 24th? That would have been Monday, is that right?"

The manager pointed her finger and touched a calendar hanging on the wall. "Yep." She entered the date in a cell on screen and tapped enter. "And you say you want to know about T-Bone steaks?"

"Yes. Please." Piper leaned into the screen, reading the name column. One name jumped out immediately. "There."

She reached over Sally's head and tapped the screen.

Sally ducked away.

"Sorry. That one, there." The name was only partial, two letters followed by three dots.

Sally clicked the edge of the column and pulled it to the side, revealing the full name.

"That's it." Her heart raced. "What time was that purchase made?"

Sally eyed her warily, looking like she knew she'd done something wrong.

"We'll get the warrant," Piper said. "But you're helping. This is a major help."

Sally rolled her eyes and pointed the cursor at the screen. "It was late. Eleven thirty-one p.m. Likes his barbecues late at night, does he?"

Piper pulled out her phone and took a photo of the screen. "Thank you."

"Now you're taking pictures?" Sally asked.

Piper failed to answer her, because she was already out of the room and down the stairs, back into the yawning space of the supermarket below. She selected the photo on her phone and texted it to Wolf.

When she got outside, she ran headlong into a stiff breeze that burrowed into her jacket. She ignored it and dialed Wolf. His phone went to voicemail after one ring.

She rounded the edge of the building. "Sir, it's Deputy Cain. I'm at Lonnie's Market in Dredge, and I think I just figured something out. Please give me a call—"

She noticed a form in her peripheral vision, and turned in time to see the dark brown coat, realizing in a flash it was the man she'd seen inside the store.

For a fleeting instant, a fraction of a heartbeat, she recognized him. And then something hit her on the back of the head with a dull thud. Her vision contracted, nothing but stars swimming in from all sides. The last thing she saw was her phone drop onto the ground, falling from her fingers, and then everything went black.

CHAPTER 29

"SHE SAID GROUND FLOOR..." Wolf pulled the phone away from his ear and checked what the vibration had been.

Piper Cain was calling.

His thoughts went back to her porch the previous night. Just when he'd pushed that out of his mind, here she was calling him, reeling him back in. He would return the call in a minute. He declined the call and pressed the phone back to his ear.

Patterson was still talking. "...three rooms. There's no—"

"Sorry," Wolf interrupted her. "I just had another call. Can you repeat that, please?"

"Yes. I said I went to the Edelweiss Hotel and spoke to the owner."

"I heard that part," Wolf said. "You went to the hotel, the owner said McBeth checked them in using his credit card. And then I missed what you said."

"I said that even though we paid for it, they put McBeth's credit card on file, but there were no charges made to it by the motel when they checked out the next day. All three of the men had single rooms on the ground floor. They all filled out a registration form for the parking lot. But that's about as far as I got for information. She did not know if any of the trucks left, or if any of them left. And besides asking her, she was on duty that night, there's no way of knowing."

"Security cameras?" Wolf asked. His phone dinged, notifying him of a voicemail.

"No, sir."

Wolf stood and stretched his free arm overhead. His clock read 3:30. It had been a long day jockeying behind the desk.

"If we could find a financial transaction for Monday night up in Dredge around the time of Mary Dimitri's murder," Wolf said, "we could prove one of them left the hotel in Rocky Points and went back up there."

"I'll work on getting the records."

"I know you're working on it," he said. "Thanks. Talk to you soon."

Wolf hung up and yawned, looking out at the bleak weather pressed down on Rocky Points outside. His muscles hurt from the workout he'd done that morning, just as he'd predicted. Maybe a brisk walk to the coffee shop would loosen him up.

He put his phone onto his desk and hit the voicemail button, putting it on speaker while he slipped on his jacket.

"Sir, it's Deputy Cain." She sounded excited, out of breath and higher-pitched than he'd remembered. "I'm here at Lonnie's Market in Dredge, and I think I just figured something out. Please give me a call—"

The phone call cut out in a blast of static. She said something else but it was distorted by the wavering signal, a single syllable coming out of her mouth drawn out into a haunting wail. Then the call ended.

He pressed her number and put the phone to his ear as he walked out of his office, smiling as he heard her voice. "Hello, this is Piper Cain, please leave me a message and I'll get back to you as soon as I can. Have a great day." Though the words themselves were ordinary, the musical lilt in her voice made it worthy of a Grammy. "Hi, this is Sheriff Wolf, I got your message. Give me a call back."

Seeing he had a text from her as well, he opened it as he entered the elevator. A picture, and nothing else.

The image was of a computer screen. The flash had washed out the middle of the photo, though he could make out a jumble of numbers on a spreadsheet.

The elevator doors opened at the ground floor, but he stood frozen, staring at the screen. The numbers were coded, accompanied by abbreviations and the occasional complete word.

She had come across a financial transaction at Lonnie's Market up in Dredge. Did it involve the miners? She'd been excited.

He stepped out of the elevator and called her again, again getting her voicemail.

She wasn't answering. She would certainly call back. But he'd also been handed a perfectly legitimate excuse to make the drive up to Dredge now. To see what she'd gotten firsthand.

To see her again.

He walked down the hall to the back of the building and out into the parking lot. The rain swirled down in sneeze droplets. The sky was low enough his head was leaving a wake in the clouds. It was already almost four o'clock and he was dead tired. But he decided it was going to be a decent day after all.

CHAPTER 30

SOMEONE TAPPED Rachette on the shoulder. He snorted awake and wiped a stream of drool from his chin. "Hey, yeah."

The blurry form standing in front of him solidified into Yates. Hanson was standing next to him.

"He's awake now," Yates said. "Let's go."

Rachette stood up from the row of plastic chairs in the Sluice-Byron County Hospital waiting room and stretched his limbs, checking his watch. He'd been sleeping for an hour.

Deputy Hanson had been tasked with guarding Hammes's room overnight up on the third floor, and also letting Yates and Rachette know when the big man woke up again so they could question him.

"You guys want coffee first?" Hanson asked as they passed the vending machine.

"Nah," Rachette said, allowing the deputy to escort them through double doors to the main hallway.

They rode the elevator to the third floor and walked down the hall to an open doorway, where Hanson sat down on a plastic chair and began looking at his phone.

Rachette and Yates entered the room, knocking softly on the

door. Inside, a doctor and two nurses stood at Rick Hammes's bedside.

"Hello, detectives" the doctor said. "Just give us one moment, please."

Rachette recognized the nurse as one of Wolf's ex's friends. She seemed to be ignoring them, and good riddance to that, he thought.

Hammes's eyes were half opened. Tubes snaked from beeping machines into his gown and one side of his abdomen. Liquids dripped into his veins from IVs hooked into one arm, which was handcuffed at the wrist to the hospital bed.

The doctor came over and nodded.

"Hi, doc. I'm Detective Rachette. This is Detective Yates."

"My name is Doctor Bates." He looked back at the hulking, tattooed man lying on the bed. "Let me start by saying that Mr. Hammes is not in good shape right now. We've removed his spleen. His stomach was perforated by the bullet, and there was significant internal hemorrhaging, along with half a dozen other complications from the gunshot. Talking too loudly or for too long will be hard on him."

"Ah, we won't keep him too long," Rachette said.

"If you could please keep his recovery in mind when you speak to him, I would appreciate it."

"Yeah, doc, no problem. We've got our silk gloves on. Don't worry about it." Rachette winked at Hammes, who stared back through puffy eyes, a blank expression on his face. His gown was open at the chest, revealing a pentagram and other symbols on his muscle-bound flesh. His arms were covered in more ink than a comic book. The tats even climbed up his neck, stopping just below the chin like some kind of insane turtleneck.

The doctor and nurse left quietly, closing the door with a soft click.

Hammes flicked his eyes to the door, then back to Rachette and Yates. "What the hell do you guys want?" he croaked.

"We just have a few questions for you," Yates said. "And then we'll be on our way and we'll let you get back to healing."

Hammes picked up a remote control next to him with his free hand, slid his eyes to the television, and pushed the button. Over Rachette's right shoulder, the television came to life, canned laughter blaring. He set the remote down and settled in to watch an episode of "Friends."

Rachette smiled, then grabbed the remote control and turned it off. He then held it up for a moment before letting it drop to the floor. Bits of plastic skittered across the tile.

"I said we had a few questions for you. Then we'll be on our merry way."

A noise, something like a chuckle, came out of Hammes's mouth. It turned to a squeal in pain. The machine behind him made a loud beep.

The nurse came in. "Everything okay?"

Nobody responded as she looked at the readout on the machine. "Is everything okay in here, I said?"

Rachette shrugged, looked at Yates. Yates shrugged back.

"Is everything okay with you?" she asked the patient.

Hammes nodded. She walked out without another word.

Outside the hospital window, the wind kicked up, and rain streaked sideways across the glass.

"You're looking good," Rachette said. "Pretty lucky to be alive, pulling that gun on our deputies like that."

"I wasn't going to do nothing."

"Oh really." Rachette snorted. "Then next time you might not want to pull a gun on them."

Hammes stared at the window. "What happened to Mary?"

Rachette frowned. "Mary Dimitri?"

Hammes's eyes locked on Rachette's. "What happened to her?"

"She's dead."

Hammes's eyes closed, and he leaned his head back against the pillow.

"You didn't know that?" Yates asked.

"Nobody told me anything. I've been asleep. Drugged up." He kept his eyes closed. "I drove back into town from Vail and saw there was a bunch of cops at her house when I passed by. But I didn't know what for."

They sat in silence for a beat.

"Then I saw you guys at my house," Hammes said. "And then I thought it all had to do with me."

"But you just said you didn't know she was dead."

"I didn't."

"Then why did you think anything had to do with you?" Rachette asked. "I'm not following."

"I don't know. Chris was dead. She was dating him. I was dating her behind his back. I have a history, shooting at those pissants a few years ago. I thought she was telling you I killed Chris. I thought she was, you know, giving you guys DNA evidence or some shit. Something you could match to Chris's killing or something. Something she set me up for."

"You think she set you up for that?" Yates asked. "You think she was involved with Oakley's death and pointed us to you?"

Hammes shook his head. "I don't know. I have no clue what's going on. I came home from working up in Vail, and now I can't eat solid food for months, and that's if I heal good."

Rachette held up his phone. "This is a picture of the wood-pile on the side of your house."

Hammes said nothing while Rachette swiped to the next photo.

"Do you recognize this gun?" Rachette asked, showing the photo of the G21 with the attached suppressor.

"Nope."

"We found that gun in your woodpile," Rachette said.

"In the pile?"

"Between the pieces of wood."

"Well, it's not mine."

Rachette nodded. "Where were you on Monday night?"

"Up in Eagle. The Motel 6 right there. Also downtown Edwards. Ask any of the five other guys I was with from the Edwards Downtown Construction Project. I was out drinking with them. I stayed all night in the motel afterwards." Hammes looked around. "I don't know where my phone is."

"We have it. And we talked to the workers up there," Rachette said. "They corroborated your story."

"Yeah?" Relief looked to wash over Hammes. Then he twisted his handcuffed arm, pulling the slack in the chain.

"Why did you come home this Tuesday morning?" Rachette asked.

"I took the day off. I had to go back and make sure my dog was doing all right."

"You haven't asked about your dog," Yates said.

Hammes shot him a glare. "The doctors told me he was all right. He's okay, right? That's what they said. They said it was a graze to his leg. They said he'd have a limp and—"

"—He's fine," Rachette said.

Hammes closed his eyes and leaned back. His chest rose and fell fast. The machine beeped once, but otherwise did nothing out of the ordinary as Hammes continued to relax.

"I was going to pick Dex up and bring him up to Eagle for the rest of the month," he said. "Work was going well and I was going to stay up there. That's why I came home that morning."

"You never told your parole officer about the new job," Rachette said.

"I was going to, if things went well. But the cops came over and shot me in the stomach."

"I'm not feeling any sympathy for you, Hammy," Rachette said. "In fact, I'm holding back from punching you in the stomach right now."

Yates put his hand on his shoulder. Rachette took a step back.

Hammes shook his head, closing his eyes. "I'm not going back to jail."

"I'm sorry to say you're wrong on that count," Rachette said.

Hammes said nothing, keeping his eyes closed. After a few seconds he opened them and said, "Something isn't right, though."

"What?" Yates asked.

"I said something isn't right."

"What isn't right?"

"The steak bone."

"What steak bone?"

"When I came home, Dex had diarrhea."

"Yeah," Rachette said. "We noticed."

"There was a T-bone steak bone that Dex was chewing on. I asked the neighbor across the street if he fed it to him. He said no. I was pissed off, but I believed him. That guy doesn't lie. Not really in his DNA. Especially since I gave him specific instructions not to do that or I would rip his arms off. Dex has a meat protein allergy. It could kill him. Put him into anaphylactic shock."

"Okay," Rachette said.

"Okay," Hammes repeated. "So, somebody planted that gun in my woodpile."

"If anyone was trying to get near my house, Dex would have

chewed off that person's nuts. He was outside the whole time I was gone. But you give him a steak? That would keep him occupied."

Rachette had to admit it made sense, and he'd been thinking along the same lines. That's why the gun was shoved into the woodpile. If it was actually Hammes's gun, why wouldn't it have been inside? Why in the woodpile outside? Or, like he'd said before, why not in a lake or a river? It was too sloppy and stupid.

The machine beeped again, and the nurse returned. "Excuse me," she said, pushing past Rachette. "I have to get to the machine."

"No problem," Rachette said. "We were just leaving anyway."

CHAPTER 31

Wolf's cell phone vibrated as he drove into the aspen-tree covered clearing on the near side of the pass leading to Dredge.

The *cell service vortex,* he had dubbed it in his mind, because passing through this section on the way to Dredge always injected his phone with the service needed to download whatever Wolf had missed in the thirty minutes of dead zone on the outskirts of Rocky Points.

He pulled to the side of the road and saw he had a new text message and voicemail from Rachette.

Give me a call when you can. I left a voicemail.

He clicked the voicemail button and Rachette's voice blared through the speakers.

"Sir, we were just at the hospital and finally got a chance to talk to Hammes. I wanted to talk to you about something he said. Remember how the dog had the shits when we were there talking to his neighbor?"

Wolf turned down the volume and listened to Rachette's explanation about Rick Hammes finding that a T-Bone steak had been fed to the dog, flaring up a reaction from a meat protein allergy.

"That gives us probable cause to look into everyone's financials," Rachette said. "We find who bought that T-Bone, that's gotta be our killer."

Wolf zoned out, thinking of the way the neighbor had been talking about how Hammes had been yelling at him about the steak. Wolf had dismissed his ramblings at the time. He pulled up Cain's text message again, and the picture on screen.

He studied the numbers and letters on the spreadsheet this time. The letters STK jumped out at him from a spreadsheet cell underneath a column labeled *product*. A number filled the next cell, the column labeled *Price*. The column name to the left said *Customer*, but if there was any name associated with the transaction, it was concealed by the blur of light.

"... so give me a ring when you can and we'll talk about it." Rachette finished his voicemail and hung up.

Wolf called Cain again, realizing she still hadn't called him back. It rang six times, then went to voicemail.

He pressed her voicemail message again. As her voice came out of his speakers, he cranked it up, her voice filling the cab.

"Sir, it's Deputy Cain. I'm at Lonnie's Market in Dredge, and I think I just figured something out. Please give me a call—"

Again her words cut off, but what came out of the speakers at full volume sounded much different this time. He suddenly realized there had been no digital distortion after all. With sickening clarity he heard a thump, accompanied by a sharp yelp of pain, followed by a long drawl of unintelligible noise. It was the sound of a body shutting down, completely taken over by unconscious reflexes.

He shook his head, wondering if he was hearing things with an overactive imagination.

She wasn't answering her phone. He listened again, but he was already convinced. He had already pressed the gas pedal to the floor.

CHAPTER 32

PIPER'S HEAD slammed hard against something and her eyes fluttered open. Her nose whistled with a spastic sucking in of air, then crackled with mucus as she exhaled.

She tried to open her mouth to take a breath and found it stuck shut. She tried to bring her hand up to her mouth to unblock whatever was there, then realized her arms were bound behind her.

She lay still, then tried it all again. Thoughts moved sluggishly in a head pounding with pain.

What is this?

There was a deep, guttural rumbling coming from somewhere. Her body vibrated with the noise.

So cold.

Popping sounds overlaid the rumble. She blinked, trying to focus, but something was right in front of her face. She adjusted her focus and realized it was a blue plastic sheet. Raindrops were pelting it, rivulets running down on the other side as wind fluttered it against her face.

When she twisted her hands, she felt a pliable plastic cord

that terminated in a knob with three prongs, and she realized it was an electrical extension cord wrapped around her wrists.

Whatever she was lying on bucked and jumped, lifting and slamming her down. She straightened, hitting the back of her head on a metal retaining wall of some sort. Her fingers groped down, feeling a cold, wet, dirt-covered metal floor.

So cold. Her chin bobbed up and down as she shivered.

Her head hurt so much.

A memory of leaving the supermarket wriggled its way through the pain. She'd seen a man. A man who had attacked her.

Her legs were free, but she couldn't feel a thing. She tried moving her right leg and heard the scrape of metal. She moved her foot, then her other leg and foot. All she felt was cold.

She shivered some more, and heard the high-pitched squeal as she slid forward, hitting her head again. And then it dawned on her she was in the back of a pickup truck, covered by a tarp.

The engine cut off. The sound of a door shutting. Footsteps crunching. Then just the popping of the rain.

She opened her eyes wide, waiting, then jumped as the blue covering lifted off her. Icy drops hit her face, landing inside her ear. A man's visage filled her vision and their eyes met. She recognized him and tried to speak, remembering too late she had the duct tape over her mouth.

His eyes were wild, nothing like they'd been the first time she'd seen the man a couple days ago, reminding her of a cat's on the hunt. He put a finger to his lips. "You be quiet, all right?"

She tried to speak again.

"I said, shut up."

She glared at him and screamed behind the duct tape.

He flinched backward, turning his head.

Again she screamed. The sound was futile to her own ears but it built in intensity as the panic within her redlined.

"Shut up!" he hissed.

Her throat felt like she was gargling razorblades as every effort to yell was jammed back into her by the tape, but the man was growing distraught at her increasing volume, however pathetic it was.

Something in his eyes changed and he ducked away and out of her field of vision.

What about dad?

The thought stopped her. She sucked in breaths through her nose, thinking of her father.

She wanted to check her watch, but her arms were bound behind her back. She already knew that. Her sluggish brain worked in fits and starts. She thrashed against her restraints. This was stupid, she thought. Stacy was with Dad, and that's the least of my worries.

Footsteps sounded again, this time down by her feet. The tailgate clicked, squealed, and dropped open. The truck sagged down as someone stepped on the tailgate.

She let out the loudest scream yet.

"I said, shut up." The world flashed as there was another tremendous blow to her head, and she fell back into the darkness.

CHAPTER 33

WOLF KEPT one eye on his cell phone, the other on the road in front of him as he descended into the Dredge Valley. He had been driving out of the cell vortex when he'd last spoken with Patterson. His call had been cut off by three beeps early in his rant for help. Despite the disconnection he continued to drive, certain Patterson had heard his request for backup. But as

he drove on, doubt had crept in and set up camp inside him.

His phone still read No Service. Damn it. He should have turned around when the call had gone out, but something told him every second counted right now.

There! The No Service indicator disappeared, replaced by a single bar of reception. His phone began vibrating as missed call notifications and messages rolled in. Ignoring them, he poked Patterson's number.

"There you are," she said through the speakers. "You cut out."

"Are you on your way?"

"Yes. I have people heading up," she said. "We're all heading up. I tried to get a chopper up there, but they're saying the radar indicates it's impossible."

Wolf's windshield wipers slapped back and forth at the highest setting but it was still not enough at the speed Wolf was going. Still, he kept his foot on the gas.

"The radar's not lying," he said.

"What's happened to her? You said somebody attacked her. Who?"

"I don't know that yet." He told her about the text message that he'd gotten from Cain, and the voice message. "She was onto something, though. Something about a financial transaction at a place called Lonnie's Market."

"Where?"

"Dredge? I don't know."

Wolf passed a sign reading Dredge—2 miles. He wanted to jam the accelerator all the way down, but the road veered to the left and the windshield already looked like he was inside a carwash.

"I can look it up," she said. "I can call and speak to a manager. Maybe figure out what she was—"

"Good. Yes. Call. Call me back."

"On it."

He dropped the phone in the console and concentrated on the road, blurred by the shifting stalagmite raindrops hitting the ground.

He poked Cain's phone number again, willing her to answer and prove his paranoia as unfounded, but again it rang six times and then went to her voicemail.

Wolf pecked his Toughbook, entering a search on the digital map for Lonnie's Market. By the time directions came up he was inside the town limits, driving past the Casino's glowing lights. He hit the brakes hard, the rear of the SUV fishtailing as mud and rock rained upward from the spinning wheels, pinging off the underside and spraying the side windows with maroon streaks.

Lonnie's Market came into view on his left. He flew into the lot, seeing Piper's vehicle parked alongside the building. He jammed the brakes, shut off the engine and got out in one fluid motion.

Just then his phone rang in the center console. He reached in and pulled it out, taking the call as he went to Piper's vehicle and looked inside the windows. It was empty.

"It's me," Patterson said. "I can't get ahold of the manager. They put me on hold and it keeps going to voicemail. I called back, and they put me on hold again."

"I'm here, forget it."

"Keep me posted."

Wolf looked at the ground. It told him nothing. If there had been any indication of a struggle it had been erased by the rain now pelting the back of his neck.

He sprinted through the front door of the supermarket, heading straight to the first cashier.

"There was a cop in here, a woman, her name was Deputy Cain."

The man behind the register stood straight, wide eyes. "I...I don't know anything about that."

"Where's the manager's office?"

"I'm the manager." A woman said, walking quickly toward him. "What's going on? I was just told you guys have been calling."

"Did you speak to Deputy Cain this afternoon?"

"The woman with black hair?"

"Yes."

"I did."

He pulled his phone and flashed the picture. "I need to know the name behind this blur here. I need to see this screen in person."

She put her hands on her hips. "I told her I probably needed to see a warrant to show her that. And she reassured me that if there was a next time, you guys would—"

Wolf cut her off. "I need to see this screen, and I need to see it now. Deputy Cain's vehicle is still out in the parking lot, but she's gone missing. I believe it's a matter of life and death that you show me this."

The manager's eyes bulged wide. She swallowed and nodded. "Back here. Aisle seven." She started walking, then began running when Wolf passed her at a full jog.

One of his feet slipped out from under him and he landed hard on his knee.

"Oh my gosh, are you okay?"

"Keep going." He got up, limping hard on one foot, feeling like his kneecap had split in half, following her up the stairs and into a small room.

"Shoot. I just turned it off. I was going home."

Wolf was unsure what that meant until she turned on and watched the snail's pace at which the thing booted up. With each progress bar that appeared the tension ratcheted in his chest.

"She was checking the financial records," the manager said.

"Look at T-Bone steaks," Wolf said. "Monday."

She typed in a date and the familiar spreadsheet appeared on screen. "That's what she said, too. Here. We were here when she took the picture. I extended the name cells like this."

There it was. Eagle McBeth.

Wolf bolted out of there, burying the pain of his knee.

CHAPTER 34

At some point Piper became aware of the noise.

Then her consciousness returned to her body, and with it a dull pain filling her skull.

When she opened her eyes she saw the familiar blue tarp again, but this time it was darker, almost black. A light flitted through the plastic, then disappeared. Then it came back. Vanished again.

With each shift of the light came the roar of a giant beast, some sort of prehistoric animal that howled with repetitive sound as it moved.

She clenched her eyes and opened them again, coming back to the moment. It was a diesel engine. She could smell it. And then there was the sound of metal scraping and clashing with the hard ground.

Again she felt the pull of tape around her mouth. She pulled her mouth open as wide as she could, which was not very much. She thought she might have felt a bit of give on the right side of her cheek. She pushed her tongue through her lips, tasting the adhesive as she pressed outward as hard as she could, but it was no use. The tape held.

The light swung in and out of view again, and the panic rose in her fast and hard as she realized exactly what she was listening to.

She began hyperventilating through her nose, sucking in shallow doses of the sickening diesel fumes. An earthmover was digging a hole, and the opening would be for her. Her next exhale became a whimper.

Another clank of metal on rock, this time even harder. She heard a pile of earth hit near the truck and felt it in her bones.

She pulled at her hands to no avail and tried to kick her feet, which were now bound as well.

Wriggling like a dying fish, she screamed beneath the tape, but her voice was a fly's wings over a rock concert.

And then she stopped. She closed her eyes and inhaled, practicing the yoga breathing. She thought of David Wolf. Of his hard eyes and harder jaw line. Of his soft words.

Her eyes popped open as she remembered she'd been leaving a message for him when she was attacked. Hope surged through her, quickening her breath. Maybe he was coming to help her. Yes, he had to have heard her attack and he was coming.

Then again, maybe he had heard nothing out of the ordinary on the call. Maybe he thought it was just a bad connection. That something was wrong with her phone. The thought slapped down her optimism.

Tears flowed across her face and over the bridge of her nose. She sobbed, lost in misery. She was going to die. She was going to be put in the ground, probably so deep she would never be found again. She shut her eyes and saw her mother's face, wrinkled with concern. She smiled reassurance and Piper wept even harder, pleading for her mom to wake her from this nightmare.

And then the image of her mother faded. There was nothing she could do.

The thought made her eyes open. Her sobbing stopped.

Her mother couldn't save her. Wolf wasn't coming. It was her and this sicko, and that's how it was going to be. She had only one thing left to do, and that was to die with dignity, or somehow kill this bastard first.

Buck up!

Pushing her legs straight she realized that sound of the diesel engine had become a steady growl. The swiveling light was now a constant glow.

The tarp ripped back again. She blinked, surprised to see the clouds above. It was still daylight but just barely. She must not have been out for too long since the blow to her head.

"I can't shoot you," he said. "I don't have a gun for that this time."

He looked out into the distance as he spoke, not at her.

"I don't care," he said under his breath. "No, forget it. Stop." He hit the side of his head with his open palm, looking as if he was trying to eject inner voices speaking to him out of his opposite ear.

"I'll knock you out again so it's not so scary," he said, eyes looking into another universe. "I'm sorry."

The man ducked away and the tailgate lowered again. Again the truck sagged down as he stepped up.

Feeling him brush against her knee, she kicked up and out as hard as she could with both feet lashed together, a ramrod powered by all her might and fear. But she connected with nothing. Her feet slammed hard back down onto the truck bed.

Wrestling her like she was a captured rodeo animal, he turned her over and pulled her by the legs, scraping her face along the chipped, dented truck bed as she slid back. Her hip banged hard over the threshold, then the side of her face slammed against the tailgate as he yanked her off the truck bed's edge.

The breath barked out of her lungs and she lay on the ground trying to inhale through her nose, but the air wouldn't come. The familiar bug-like stars swirled at the edges of her vision.

Giving her no reprieve, not a second, he dragged her with frightening speed across the wet earth.

Her face and head slid over rocks, her chest scraped, sharp pain turning to cold numbness. She tried to turn, giving the side of her face and shoulder the full brunt of the attack.

Lightning flickered overhead, illuminating the entire area around her in one flash. She saw the giant earth mover standing like a monster looming high above. The bolt of electricity crawled across the sky and then back again, giving her plenty of light to see something else: a gaping black hole.

Her breath came back with a squealing noise as it filled her chest with agonizing slowness. There was the sound of a thousand tinkling bells in her ears. She was going to pass out. Good. She didn't want to be conscious for this.

Suddenly, the man stopped and dropped her legs.

"What is it?" he asked nobody. "Shit." He walked away with quick, crunching steps, then came back and knelt down next to her.

Again, she was not here as a human, it seemed, just a thing he had to deal with. She pleaded through the duct tape.

"Shut up," he said, this time putting his face close to hers.

She lurched forward and head-butted him in the face. It was hardly a knock-out blow but she felt ultimate satisfaction at finally getting a lick in.

"Ah!" he put his hand on his cheek. Another flash of lightning showed his grimacing mouth.

She expected retaliation to come hard and swift, but instead he turned and looked at something far away.

Blinking away her tears, she followed his gaze to a pair of

headlights barreling down the road. She let out a squeal of excitement seeing the light bar affixed to the top and the SBCSD paint job.

With the injection of adrenaline spiking her bloodstream she rolled to her side, onto her back, and then her other side. Using her momentum she kept rolling, again and again, away from the open mouth in the earth waiting to eat her.

"Stop!"

He was already on top of her, slapping his hand on her shoulder, but she didn't care. She thrashed as hard as she could, ignoring the pain shooting through her wrists as she pulled her legs up again to kick.

"Stop it!"

He swatted her feet away, knelt on top of her chest, and punched her twice in the face with the force of a dropping boulder.

She felt one of her teeth loosen behind the duct tape. Suddenly, she couldn't breathe. Blood clogged her nose, choked it. She snorted hard and swallowed, and then she sat motionless, feeling the darkness close in even harder now. She concentrated on her ragged breathing, slowing, slowing...

Her head slammed on a rock. She was gliding along the ground again. No, she was still conscious.

Don't do it!

She tried to scream but no sound came out this time.

Then it was too late. Her body went weightless for a moment, then she landed impossibly hard onto ground. The darkness completely engulfed her.

And the monster roared again.

CHAPTER 35

WOLF's SUV finally dipped out of the clouds as he descended the ski slope-like grade road into the mine. His unsafe speed seemed to double as he saw the final turn leading into the flat zone of the mine yard coming fast.

He pressed the brakes and took his eyes off the road to assess the situation down in the mine yard. In the fading light and aided by a single flood bulb mounted on top of one of the trailers, he saw two blue pickups parked next to a couple of ATVs.

Two pickups were missing. What did that mean?

Down the valley, toward the cut, he saw the faint glow of another light, but it was hidden behind a slope.

Whatever they were doing to Piper Cain, the first step was to get them to stop and come deal with him. He turned on the overhead lights and siren.

In a spectacle of light and sound the SUV shuddered and turned sideways as Wolf mashed the brake pedal and bounced into the flat, catching air before crashing hard into a deep puddle. The SUV lurched up with the sound of rending metal. He slammed hard into the seatbelt and then back into the seat.

And then he skidded to a halt. He shut off the howling siren and flashing lights and got out, waiting for a welcome party.

But none came. There was no movement. No flicking on of lights. No people. Nothing.

His knee screamed in pain from the fall inside the supermarket, but he ignored it and marched toward the trailers, his gun pulled and aimed forward.

His eyes snapped from point to point—the trailer doors, the tent where he'd talked to them the night before, the wash plant, the abandoned tractor near it, the parked ATV.

But no one was there.

He turned around and saw the glow behind the slope had disappeared. Somebody was down there. That's where the two missing trucks were. That's where they had her.

Another noise came out of the silence—first a crunching of car tires high up on the road, then a long squeal of brakes. The fog glowed for a second and twin headlights appeared.

McBeth's black pickup truck coasted down at normal cruising speed. Wolf had seen headlights in his rearview mirror much earlier, but they had disappeared into the fog as he'd begun climbing the mountains toward the mine.

He had been ahead of them the whole time. Was this a play? Had he just barreled into a trap?

He reached the other two trucks parked in front of the trailers and ducked between them, waiting. There was no movement near the trailers, tent, or other machinery, but the light had appeared again down at the cut.

The truck inched its way down and stopped at the final turn into the mine, its headlights illuminating Wolf's SUV, then it continued inside toward Wolf's position. He saw two men inside—Koling in the passenger seat and McBeth behind the wheel. They were talking to one another, eyeing Wolf's vehicle.

Another set of headlights swung into view, bobbing up the

interior mine road, coming from the direction where Wolf had seen the glow. The twin points of light were closer together. It must have been one of their ATVs.

When the truck lined up to park next to the others, Wolf came out into the open, ran up to the passenger window and aimed his gun inside. "Stop right there!"

Koling's eyes went wide behind the glass and he put up his hands. The truck lurched to a stop and McBeth put up his hands, too.

"Stop the truck and get out right now!"

McBeth shut off the engine and they got out, leaving the headlights on.

"Hey, hey, hey," Koling said, stepping out. "What's going on, Sheriff?"

"Get up against the hood, now!"

McBeth and Koling went to the front of the truck and put their hands on the hood, their long shadows stretching across the trailers.

"Lift up your coats!"

The ATV was now only fifty yards away. Wolf stepped close to McBeth and Koling, keeping them in between him and the approaching ATV.

Koling pulled up his coat and so did McBeth.

"Turn all the way around."

"We're not armed," Koling said.

"Do it!"

They did as they were told, exposing their gun-free waistlines.

"What's going on?" McBeth asked.

The ATV came closer, the engine still revving hard.

"Where is she?"

Koling looked at him with a puzzled expression. "Who?"

Wolf aimed his gun at the mountainside and shot off a

round. "Stop right there!" he screamed toward the approaching ATV.

Koling and McBeth jumped, putting their hands back on the hood.

"Whoa!" McBeth said. "What are you talking about?"

The ATV slowed to a stop and James Sexton climbed out. His eyes were wide, both hands up. "What's happening?"

"Hands up where I can see them!"

Wolf went quickly to Koling and McBeth and frisked them with his free hand, keeping his eyes on Sexton.

"Whoa, watch it," Koling said.

"Shut up and keep your hands there." He went to McBeth and frisked him. "You too!" he yelled at Sexton. "Show me your waistband!"

"I'm not armed," McBeth said.

Down the road, Sexton lifted his own jacket and turned full circle in his ATV headlights, showing he was unarmed as well.

"Where is she?" Wolf asked again, rounding the truck. He looked into the cab, seeing nothing but fast-food trash inside. He checked the truck bed and found nothing but a case of light beer and mud.

"Where were you just now?"

"At the liquor store," Koling said. "Getting beer."

"Get on your knees, hands behind your back."

"Shit, brother."

Wolf fired another shot. They did as they were told.

"We know about how you bought a steak at Lonnie's market Monday night," Wolf said. "I said down on the ground!"

McBeth and Koling were frozen, staring toward the ATV.

Wolf saw why. Sexton had just finished ducking back into his ATV and came out with a pistol. Wolf's talking had given him the split second he'd needed.

"Drop your gun!" Sexton's voice was high-pitched and shrill.

He stepped toward them, leading with his gun. The light from McBeth's truck and the trailer flood illuminated his feral eyes.

Wolf put his hands out to his sides, but kept his gun in his grip.

"I said drop it."

Wolf hesitated, thinking of how quickly he could roll, aim, and fire.

Sexton's gun flashed. A bullet zipped past Wolf's head and ricocheted off the ground behind him.

"Okay! Okay!" He dropped his Glock.

"I knew it was you, asshole," Koling said. "I knew it."

"Where is Deputy Cain?" Wolf asked. "What did you do to her?"

"You son of a bitch!" Koling's voice echoed off the mountain walls. "You killed him. I knew it was you this whole time."

"Be quiet," Wolf said to Koling.

But Koling was shaking his head. "You're a sick bastard. I always knew you were a sick bastard. I knew it. I knew—"

Sexton's gun popped twice. Blood fountained from Koling's chest and his body went limp instantly, falling onto McBeth.

"Shit," McBeth crawled out from under his downed employee.

Wolf held his breath, waiting for two more shots to kill him next. But Sexton lowered his weapon, tilted his head, and stared at the scene in front of him.

Wolf lowered his hands to his side slowly. "James. Where is Deputy Cain?"

"Where is she, Jimmy?" McBeth asked. "Come on, man, what did you do with her?"

Sexton's eyes locked on McBeth's. "I had to shut her up. She's okay. I knocked her out first so she wouldn't be scared. Nobody will find her, I made it deep enough so the cadaver dogs can't even smell it."

McBeth exhaled in exasperation. "Jimmy, what did you do?"

Jimmy stared.

"You killed Chris?" McBeth asked. "You killed Mary? And look what you're doing now, Jimmy."

"He hit you," Sexton said. "He called you names. He tried to burn you, Eagle. He made you feel weak again. Nobody gets to do that to you. Nobody should ever do that. I stopped him. He was just going to keep going if I didn't. It was just like your dad."

Wolf fingered the key chain in his jeans pocket, finding the bulge of the key fob through the fabric. He pinched the button and held it down. Two seconds later his vehicle fired to life next to Sexton. Sexton swiveled fast, aiming the gun at Wolf's vehicle.

Wolf wasted no time. He bent down, picked up his own gun off the ground, took aim, and fired.

Sexton spun and ducked out of sight behind the four-wheel vehicle. Wolf followed, sprinting around the ATV. His feet thumped loudly, telegraphing his approach to Sexton, but Wolf was ready.

When Sexton's leg came into view he fired, then shot the hand that held the gun, then his chest, his throat, and his head.

Spinning around, he marched back toward McBeth, gun pointed and teeth clenched. "Get in your truck right now."

McBeth was on his hands and knees, staring at him with an open mouth.

Wolf shot past him. "Now!"

McBeth jumped up and got in his truck. Wolf got into the passenger seat, aiming his gun. "Get down there now."

"Okay. Okay." McBeth nodded, firing up the engine and spitting gravel as they sped down the mine road past the ATV and Sexton's corpse.

Wolf thought about what was ahead. It had been years since he'd operated a tractor, and he'd never operated an excavator like the one Wolf knew was parked down here—the one that must have been used to bury Cain.

My God. He'd said he'd knocked her out first so she wouldn't be scared. She was either dead or in the process of suffocating right now. He looked at McBeth, trying to assess the man in the faint light of the dashboard. His eyes were wide, shell-shocked, yet he kept the truck true and straight on the dirt road.

"You bought that steak," Wolf said.

"What steak?" McBeth shook his head. "No, I didn't. I don't know what you're talking about!"

"You planted the gun at Hammes's house. You fed the steak to the dog so you could do it. We saw your credit card transaction under your name."

"No, I swear. All of us use the same credit cards. My credit cards. Jimmy had one. I told you, I pay for everything in the operation."

Wolf looked out the windshield, watching as another pickup truck came into view, parked next to a giant excavator. The scoop was dug halfway into the ground next to a gaping hole.

He held his breath, hope welling up inside. He'd been picturing the hole covered with dirt. Here it was, wide open. Maybe Sexton hadn't covered her yet.

"Stop here!"

While McBeth's tires scraped to a halt, Wolf was already out the door and running.

He slid to the edge of the hole and looked down. It was too deep and dark to see the bottom so he pulled his flashlight off his belt, clicked it on, and pointed it down.

She wasn't there.

At least, not topside. The hole's sheer walls led down to a mound of what looked like freshly laid dirt.

McBeth ran up behind him and stopped at the edge of the hole, looking over. Wolf shone his light in the man's face. McBeth still looked in shock, trying to comprehend what was going on.

Wolf made the only choice he had. "Get in the excavator. You can pull out the side of this hole, right?" He put a hand up in karate chop position, signifying the overall linear hole shape. He put his other hand up against it, perpendicular, making a T. "If you dig out the side and then past the bottom of it, we have a place to push the dirt that's already in the bottom."

McBeth stared, frozen stiff.

"Did you hear me? Get in the excavator and pull out the side of this hole!"

McBeth nodded, jolting into action. "Yes. Okay!" He ran into the dark toward the machine, climbed up and inside, and fired it up. It rumbled to life and the boom arm lifted off the ground.

The beast's tracks churned as it lumbered forward, then sideways, then forward again. McBeth was shifting the machine into position, but Sexton's truck was in the way. He finally pushed it aside with the boom, the truck bouncing and screeching as it was cast aside. The excavator drove forward, this time much faster.

Wolf looked down again. He couldn't take it anymore. She could have been under mere inches of the dirt, waiting for air to fill her lungs. Every second counted.

He slid over the edge, landing hard on the corner of the hole, hoping she hadn't been underneath his bodyweight as he slammed hard into the soft ground.

He dug frantically with both hands, probing as deep as he could, moving in a line side to side. He moved up a couple feet and tried again, getting his arm in all the way to the elbow. His fingers jabbed into something hard. He opened his hand and clasped around a rock. He moved forward and started another line.

His right hand felt something. There! His fingers pinched around fabric, and underneath it he felt soft muscle.

The sound of the excavator grew louder while one wall of the hole lit up.

It was her. Her ankle and calf muscle. The outline of her body materialized in his mind. She was face-down and he was kneeling at her feet. He squatted and started digging like a dog, ejecting dirt back through his legs. He had to get to her face as quick as possible, but he didn't want to stand on her, making any trauma that might have happened already worse.

There was her hip.

He moved up and to the side, estimating where her head was, and continued digging. His arms burned, his hands numb from the scraping wet cold earth. He felt a loop of her hair, then the shape of her skull.

"I'm coming, Piper! I'm coming!"

Wolf doubled, then tripled his efforts, ignoring the cramps seizing his arms and shoulders.

When the overhead light dimmed he looked up to see the excavator was in position. The underside of the massive, gouged metal scoop loomed directly above.

Wolf kept digging, but kept a curious glance at the scoop as it remained motionless for another beat. And then with a sickening twist of his stomach Wolf realized his mistake.

The scoop slowly swiveled downwards, dumping a full load of earth onto his head.

CHAPTER 36

Wolf covered his head with his arms and felt the brunt of a hundred bowling balls slam onto his back. Rocks, dirt, and mud covered him in an apocalyptic whomp.

Then there was silence. The dirt was packed in his ears, up against his face, every curve and crevice of his body pushed by the heavy earth lying on top of him. Pushing down on Piper Cain.

He opened his eyes and immediately regretted it as dirt pressed in, packing underneath his eyelids. He tried to take a breath and dirt shot into his lungs. He nearly went berserk, trying with all his might to free himself from death's stranglehold.

His body felt like it was packed in concrete. With each moment he was frozen in place, the more panic built inside of him.

Ryan's smiling face flashed in his mind. His grandson running to kick a ball and falling onto his butt. He started crying. He needed help getting up. He needed comfort.

Wolf flexed every muscle in his body. A muffled grunt sounding a thousand miles away bellowed from his chest. He arched and pushed up with his legs, and he felt the earth slide off of his back.

He had to breathe!

He freed one of his legs, propping it up to the side like a kickstand, and rolled sideways.

With agonizing slowness, a tremendous weight slid off his back, sloughing away. He felt cool air caressing his face. He took a deep breath, again coughing on dirt. On his hands and knees he tried to clear his lungs, only faintly aware of more dirt raining down, the deafening sound of metal on rock, close to his head. He suddenly realized he had to move fast to avoid the next load, or he wouldn't have the energy to fight again.

But it was too late. He felt another slam against his back and he was flung into the hole wall in front of him.

With stars swimming in his vision, he watched as the metal scoop pulled away from him and then disappeared up and away. The light of the machine pierced his tearing eyes, then it snuffed out again as the scoop with its glinting metal teeth came back down.

He put both hands up, brought up his legs, clenched his jaw, tensing every muscle in his body as he prepared for a grisly death.

Then the dirt underneath him shifted and dropped forward.

He opened his eyes and saw the scoop pull up and away again. The light was on him one more time as the bucket swiveled to the side on its retracted boom.

Wolf brushed the dirt off his face and blinked, seeing the side wall had been completely removed.

McBeth's silhouette came into view as he stumbled down into the new hole he'd created. "Shit! I'm sorry! I didn't mean to dump that first scoop on you! I didn't realize it was still half-full!"

Wolf got off the dirt and kicked his feet into the new section of hole. Pushing McBeth back, he turned around and began digging again.

McBeth got next to him and helped.

Wolf went straight for Cain's head. It was much easier now that they could pull at the dirt and get it out of the way in between their legs into the new hole.

There's no chance. She's dead. It's been too long.

He dug harder.

A few seconds later they heaved, grunting with all their might, and Cain's body spilled out sideways. Wolf sat back, catching her on his lap.

She lay face-up over his thighs, her eyes closed, her lips covered by a strip of duct tape. An extension cord wrapped around her wrists and behind her back, and another one around her ankles.

He put one hand behind her head, brushed the dirt away from her face, and peeled off the duct tape.

It's been too long.

He put his lips to hers and breathed in twice. Her lips were cold and sticky from the tape's glue. Her chest rose and fell with all the life of a CPR dummy. He started chest compressions.

"Get out! Move!" A male's voice yelled.

McBeth was ripped away by someone who had climbed down. Wolf realized there were now red and blue lights slashing into the hole from above.

"Is she okay?" Rachette was next to him now, Yates crowding in beside him.

Wolf checked her carotid and felt nothing. His hands were numb. "I can't feel anything."

"I'll check." Rachette reached over and put his fingers under her jaw. "I feel it! It's weak, but it's there!"

"She's not breathing." Wolf put his lips over hers and pushed air into her lungs again. "Untie her hands."

Rachette slipped his hands beneath her back and got to work. "Shit. It's tight."

Wolf breathed in again. The air escaping back out of her lungs made a sighing sound as if she was consciously making a noise, but her eyes remained closed.

"Piper," he said. He gently slapped her cheek.

"There." Rachette pulled out the extension cord, flinging it aside, and then checked her pulse again. "I'm not sure if I'm feeling a pulse anymore. Shit."

"Get her flat," Yates said.

They picked her up and laid her back into the hole Wolf had just pulled her out of. Now lying on her back and not Wolf's lap, he began chest compressions again.

"I'm getting the AED!" Yates climbed up and out of the hole.

"One, two, three, four..." he whispered the numbers with tiny exhales, trying to ignore the grave-like appearance of where she lay. Rain began pelting inside the hole, running down Wolf's neck and back.

After thirty compressions Wolf did two more breaths. "Come on, Piper!"

"Shit," Rachette said again. "Where's the ambulance, damn it?"

Yates dropped down into the hole holding the defibrillator machine. "Here!"

"...eleven, twelve, thirteen." Wolf kept going as Rachette ripped open her shirt, exposing her bra. He pulled his knife and cut the center, exposing her breasts.

The AED machine was talking now, belting out instructions in a woman's voice.

"...remove pads and place on bare skin exactly as shown on the diagrams on each pad."

Wolf continued his compressions. "...twenty-three, twenty-four, twenty-five..." He blanked his mind, going through the motions.

Rachette pressed the pads into place.

"*Analyzing heart rhythm*," the machine said. "*Stop chest compressions.*"

Wolf let go of her and sat up on his knees. Rachette kept clear next to him.

"*Electric shock not advised*," it said.

"What?" Rachette breathed.

Piper lurched, and Wolf wondered if the machine had inadvertently delivered the ill-advised shock after all.

She coughed and her eyes flew open. She sucked in a desperate, long breath.

"Piper," Wolf said, as he closed her shirt and put his hand on her ice-cold forehead. "It's okay, it's okay. Get a blanket!"

Her eyes latched onto his as she convulsed with more coughs.

"I got some," Yates said. "Here."

When the blankets landed on her she squirmed, flinging them off with a grunt. "No!" she cried. "No!"

"It's okay," Wolf said. "You're okay, Piper. It's us. It's Wolf, and Yates, and Rachette."

Her manic eyes stopped darting and rested on his. Her heaving chest relaxed and her breathing slowed.

"It's okay."

Wolf put a thermal blanket on her, this time gingerly. "Let's get her out."

Her lips moved.

"Wait!" Wolf bent close, putting his face inches from hers. "What?"

She reached up and put her hand on his face. Her fingers were icicles against his skin.

They stared at each other. Then she laid back onto the dirt, closing her eyes.

He checked her pulse one more time, and even with his numb hand he found it strong.

"All good?" Yates asked, bending down to get a grip on her.

"Yeah," Wolf said. "All good."

CHAPTER 37

FIVE DAYS LATER...

People walking down Main Street wore shorts and short-sleeved shirts. Sunglasses. Flip flops. Summer had officially arrived in Rocky Points.

The sun pierced a cloudless blue sky, showering rays full bore onto the town outside. But because of the triple-paned and tinted glass of his office, Wolf barely had to squint. Here he remained cool to the point of nearly shivering as more Jetstream-fresh air blasted out of the floor vents.

"Not bad outside. It's hot as shit in Denver." Undersheriff Wilson sat at a chair in front of Wolf's desk, picking a thread off his pant cuff. "Seems like that place gets hotter every time I visit."

Through the squad room windows Wolf saw Deputy Nelson march toward Wolf's door. After two knocks he poked his head inside. "He's here, sir."

Wolf nodded. "Thanks. I'll be right there." His desk phone trilled and he felt a twinge of pain in his back when he raised the phone to his ear. Bruised ribs—a side effect of a couple hundred pounds of rock and dirt being dropped from an excavator onto him from ten feet up—were mending on his right side.

"He's here, sir," Patterson said through the receiver.

"I'll be right there." He hung up and walked to the door.

"Good luck." Wilson scratched his blond walrus mustache.

"Margaret will be here in fifteen minutes," Wolf said.

"I know. Go, I'll keep her occupied until you're back. We can talk about the exploding real estate market for the ninety-ninth year in a row up here in Rocky Points, or something."

Wolf left the office and went down the hall to interrogation room two. Eagle McBeth and his lawyer sat in chairs in the hallway, talking softly to one another.

"Hello, Eagle," Wolf said.

McBeth and his lawyer rose, the attorney whispering in McBeth's ear as they both stood.

"John Lessiter, I'm Mr. McBeth's attorney."

Wolf nodded and shook his hand. "Let's head in, shall we?" They walked in through the observation room where Patterson, Yates, and Rachette stood in front of the one-way mirror.

"After you," Wolf said, letting them pass at the threshold of the interrogation room and inside. "You two can take a seat on the right there."

Patterson handed Wolf a thick manila folder as Wolf followed McBeth and Lessiter inside and shut the door. They had decided beforehand Wolf would handle this alone.

He sat and placed the folder on the table. "This interview will be recorded with audio and video," Wolf said, tapping the recording device in the center of the table and pointing to the cameras mounted on the ceiling. "I appreciate you volunteering to come in, Mr. McBeth."

McBeth nodded, looking at him with weary, haunted eyes while Lessiter pulled out a legal pad and gold pen. He checked his Rolex, smoothed his dark gray suit and crossed his legs.

McBeth wore the same flannel he had the first time he'd been in this interrogation room, but it looked like he'd since washed it. No mud clung to the sleeves and the wrist buttons were fastened tight. The scar poking out of the one sleeve was already safely tucked away under his other hand. His hair was freshly cut to a couple inches all around.

Lessiter cleared his throat. "I've advised my client to not answer any questions that may implicate his involvement in the deaths of Chris Oakley and Mary Ellen Dimitri. He will be conferring with me before answering each question."

McBeth shook his head slightly. He looked like a teenager whose father has made a stupid joke in public.

Lessiter flicked his eyes to his client, then jotted another note on his legal pad. After another few seconds of silence Lessiter waved his hand with a flourish. *Proceed.*

Wolf nodded. "Eagle, we asked you here because the more we're learning about Mr. Sexton after his death, the more questions we have. We're wondering if you might be able to clear things up for us."

McBeth kept his eyes on the table.

Wolf picked up the remote control on the table. He pointed it at the flat screen television on the wall and pressed play.

A black and white video popped up on screen, showing the inside of a grocery store from a ceiling camera. There were empty check-out counters and empty aisles. The movement was the running ticker in the bottom right corner showing the date as June 24th and the time as 11:35 p.m. and counting.

"This is the inside of Lonnie's Market up in Dredge on the Monday night of Mary Ellen Dimitri's murder," Wolf said.

A figure walked into view and down an aisle. The camera changed, showing the back wall of the market. The figure walked into view, straight to a meat case. He picked up a package, turned it over, set it down, then went to another package and picked it up.

Wolf paused it and used the arrows on the remote control. The image on screen zoomed in on the man's face, enlarging it to fill the screen. It was a bit blurry, but clear enough to be unmistakable.

"As you can see, this is James Sexton."

Sexton's eyes looked just like Wolf remembered that night, the minute before he'd shot him. Animalistic. Feral. "He's at Lonnie's Market up in Dredge when he's supposed to be at the Edelweiss Hotel. This is the night before you came in to speak with us."

"We're well aware of the timeline of events, sheriff," Lessiter said.

"I'm just lining out the events for clarity's sake."

"I understand—"

"Keep going," McBeth said, his robotic tone overpowering his attorney's.

Wolf opened up the folder and pulled out copies of credit card receipts. "Here we have your signature for the hotel rooms' security deposit. Here we have Sexton's version of your signature for the T-Bone steak, which he purchased at Lonnie's Market."

Wolf pressed pause on the video, leaving an image of Sexton walking through an aisle of the market with a packaged T-bone steak in his hand.

Wolf looked between Lessiter and McBeth, then tried his first question. "Did you know Sexton had left the hotel that night?"

Lessiter turned to his client. "Do not answer that."

"I did," McBeth said, putting up a hand in Lessiter's face. "But I thought he was out getting a drink."

Lessiter sat back in his chair making another note.

Wolf considered the dynamic between these two. Why have a lawyer if he was only a hindrance? Wolf had learned the McBeth family money had paid for the last three losing years up at the mine. The lawyer must have been paid for by the Triple-O ranch as well.

Both Wolf and Sheriff Domino up in Jackson Hole had no luck speaking with Eagle McBeth's mother, the sole beneficiary of McBeth's father's many holdings. She had her own lawyers that had kept her silent up to this point. Eagle McBeth, however, was rebelling. He was here of his own accord. Mrs. McBeth and her firewall of attorneys up there in Jackson Hole couldn't stop that.

"I thought he was at a bar, you know?" McBeth said, his eyes meeting Wolf's for the first time. He was sincere. "Koling was out drinking. I thought he had gone out with him."

"What did you do that night?"

"I stayed in the room."

Wolf nodded. "Thanks for telling me that."

Lessiter blew a puff of air from his nose.

Wolf ignored him. "We've since tested this jacket he's wearing in this video and we found gunshot residue matching that of Chris Oakley's silenced G21. We also found blood spatter that matches Mary Ellen Dimitri. We know now that he fed this steak to Rick Hammes's dog minutes after this footage was taken in order to get into the property and plant the gun in Hammes's woodpile, making it look like Rick Hammes killed Mary Dimitri."

McBeth stared into nothing, shaking his head slightly.

"Were you with him?"

His eyes latched onto Wolf's. "No, sir. I was in the motel room."

"Okay." Wolf nodded, pulling out another sheet of paper from the stack. "We have your GPS phone records here that indicate you might be telling the truth. Your phone stayed in Rocky Points all night."

"Might be?"

Wolf shrugged. "You could have left your phone in the motel room."

McBeth shook his head. "I wasn't there." There was no anger in his voice.

"Okay." Wolf flipped to the next page, pulling the folder closer. "We got extensive background information on James Sexton from Sheriff Domino up in Teton County. He did some digging over in Driggs, Idaho with the foster care agency that worked with James to find him a home.

"We learned he's originally from Pocatello, Idaho. We learned he was in the foster care system because his birth parents had died. His mother died in a car crash when he was thirteen. Two years later his father died of a self-inflicted gunshot wound."

McBeth's eyes darted to the sheet of paper, to Wolf, and back to nothing in particular. "I never knew that."

"You didn't?"

"No."

Wolf nodded. "Okay." Wolf licked a finger and removed that sheet of paper, revealing the next. "I'd like to talk about the night of your father's death."

McBeth closed his eyes.

"I know your father burned you with the ranch brand," Wolf said.

McBeth's hand moved, but remained beneath the other.

"Do you think your father really killed himself that night?" Wolf asked. "Or do—"

"Eagle, we need to end this line of questioning right now," Lessiter said.

McBeth opened his eyes, letting out a flood of tears. He turned to his lawyer. "Will you shut up?"

Lessiter backed away as McBeth leaned into him.

"I don't want to keep...not talking about this anymore! I don't want to live with this anymore!" His shrill voice echoed off the walls. "I don't want to cover things up!"

The door opened and Rachette and Patterson stood in the entryway.

"It's okay." Wolf put up a hand to them.

"I don't want you here." McBeth's wet eyes bore into Lessiter. "Does he have to be here?" He turned to Wolf, his voice pleading.

"He's your lawyer, Eagle."

"I don't want him here. I want him to leave."

"Your mother hired me to be here with you, Eagle."

"You can tell my mother she doesn't need to worry about me anymore."

"You'll be defenseless against these people. You might end up in jail. Don't you get that?"

"Get out!"

Lessiter closed his notes, put them into his attaché and left without another word.

Wolf nodded at his detectives as they parted and let Lessiter out, closing the door behind them.

McBeth's hands shook on his lap. But both of them were out in the open now, and he pointedly kept them that way, staring down at his scar with widened eyes. He slowly unbuttoned his shirt sleeve and rolled it to his elbow, revealing a trio of intertwined circles of scar tissue. He ran a finger across the raised flesh.

"My father used to drink himself to sleep every night, and he started first thing in the morning. Not many people knew that about him. I did, though. He never hid it around me. He used to give me pulls of the stuff as early as I can remember."

Wolf remained frozen in his seat for fear of changing McBeth's trajectory.

"There was always a point when the monster would take over," McBeth said. "It could have been any time of day. It just depended on how much he was drinking and who was around. If there were friends and family at the house he could keep it caged up until they left. If he was just working around the ranch and none of the other help was around it could have been by lunchtime.

"He was real big. Used to play lineman in college. I learned to be quick on my feet." He looked up at Wolf. "I learned to dodge and run, you know?"

Wolf nodded and kept silent.

"Anyway. My mom was smart. She knew that when other people were around the monster kept away, so she started the work program at the ranch, which kept people there all the time. We made one of the barns near the main house into a dormitory. We brought in travelers from around the world. Europe. Australia. And then we started taking in misfits that needed straightening out with good old-fashioned hard work. People like Chris Oakley and Kevin Koling."

"How did James come to you guys?" Wolf asked.

"Jimmy was different. I met him through a sheep farmer he had been working for. Just got to talking one day when I was delivering feed and we became friends. I told him about our ranch and the dorms and everything. Next thing I knew he showed up. He told me he quit the other job and would rather work for us.

McBeth smiled at the memory. "Anyway, since he wasn't part of the work program my parents didn't want him around, but I begged and got him a job with us. Like he was a stray dog or something. He was cool, though, you know? Something about him. We connected."

"Tell me about the scar," Wolf said. "What happened?"

McBeth ran his finger over it again. His eyes glazed over, looking like he was staring through time. "Jimmy broke a tractor. Ran it into a ditch in a place my dad told everyone to avoid because of the risk. That got the monster real mad that day. And since I'd fought for Jimmy to stay with us, my dad saw it as all my fault.

"It happened late in the day. Right at sundown. I was in one of the barns when Jimmy came running in and told me about what he'd done. My dad wasn't too far behind him because he'd seen what had happened."

McBeth's voice softened. "Dad yelled. He made Jimmy leave. Jimmy left. And my dad went to the workbench and plugged in the electric branding iron." Tears fell down McBeth's cheeks. "I begged. I ran. He caught me before I could get out." McBeth shrugged and held up his arm. "And he beat the shit out of me and got me with the iron."

"I'm sorry," Wolf said.

McBeth wiped his cheeks and chuckled. "Yeah. It was quite a thing. But..."

"But what?"

McBeth looked at Wolf. He looked at the empty chair sitting next to him. "But he got what was coming to him."

"He received justice," Wolf said. "Is that what you're saying?"

"Yes."

"How?" Wolf asked. "How was justice served?"

McBeth shook his head. His eyes were calculating now. "But...I didn't know any of this at the time."

"You didn't know what?"

"Back then I thought my dad shot himself. But, now...now I think now that Jimmy did it."

Wolf uncrossed his legs and leaned an elbow on the table, decreasing the distance between them. "Is that the truth, Eagle?"

McBeth's breathing quickened and he closed his eyes.

"I wonder if it is," Wolf said. "And I'm curious if you're absolutely sick and tired of hiding the truth. You just kicked your lawyer out. Jimmy is dead. So is Kevin. So is Chris. So is Mary. A lot of people paid with their lives in service of hiding the truth."

McBeth said nothing.

Wolf took the leap. "I think you knew that Jimmy shot and killed your dad back then."

McBeth looked at Wolf.

"Am I right? Did you know back then that Jimmy killed your father?"

"I...I..."

"Stop fighting for something that doesn't serve you," Wolf said. "I know from experience. It's not worth it. That sickening feeling inside? That's the truth trying to get out. It's draining you."

McBeth's shoulders sagged. "Yes."

"Yes, what? Yes you knew back then that Jimmy killed your father?"

"Yes."

Wolf stayed frozen, watching McBeth draw in a breath.

"Yes," McBeth said. "I did. I knew he killed him. In fact I saw him when I left the barn. I was bloody. I was staggering. I was holding my arm. Jimmy was right outside. Just standing there in the dark. He didn't help me or anything. He just told me he would take care of it. He had a gun in his hand. I saw it. And I said, 'Good.' That's what I said. I just walked away into the field, toward the house. When I got back I heard the shot.

"Later that night the cops found him in the barn. It looked like he had committed suicide. They said that he'd shot himself. They found me the way I was—bloody and burnt on my arm. I told them what had happened. All of it. Except for the end. Except for seeing Jimmy with that gun." McBeth nodded and closed his eyes. "Yes. I knew exactly what happened."

Wolf placed a hand on the table. "And when Casey dumped Chris's body on your wash plant hopper grate," he said, "this time you didn't tell the cops everything, either. You didn't tell us that Chris had burned you with a cigarette during that argument you'd had."

McBeth opened his eyes.

"Koling told us in his interview about that," Wolf said. "That was the mark on your jacket when I came up to visit you guys at the mine, wasn't it?"

McBeth nodded.

"What was he saying when he burned you? Was he mocking you? Was he being a bully in typical Chris Oakley fashion? Did he mention how your father had burned you?"

McBeth closed his eyes again. "Yes. I could tell it really pissed off Jimmy. But I didn't think he was going to do anything. I mean...he didn't do anything. We all just went to bed after that."

Wolf waited a few moments and then continued. "So that Monday morning when Casey dumped Chris's body onto the hopper grate, you saw that gunshot wound. You must have known right then and there that Jimmy had done it. Again."

McBeth clenched his eyes shut and rubbed his forehead. The scar squirmed as his forearm muscles flexed underneath. When he lowered his hands his face went slack. Again he looked at the vacant chair next to him, and then he nodded.

"Yes. I knew. When I climbed up there and saw the blood under his chin I checked the top of his head. I saw it was a gunshot. I knew right then."

"And then what did you do?" Wolf asked. "Did you talk to Jimmy about it? Did you ask if he had done it?"

"No." McBeth shook his head and closed his eyes again. After a beat he looked at Wolf. His eyes were half-closed. Resigned. "Fuck it. Yes. I did. I asked him. He told me 'I took care of it.' I told him that everyone was going to find out. He told me 'I'll take care of it again.'"

"Did you know he was going to kill Mary Ellen Dimitri and try to frame Rick Hammes for everything?"

"No. I swear I didn't know that."

Wolf nodded. "That Monday night you stayed in Rocky Points at the Edelweiss while he went to Dredge alone?"

"I stayed in my motel room. Kevin went out drinking. I knew that Jimmy left, too. Shit, I didn't know he was killing another person so he could try and cover up what he'd done."

"But you knew he was 'taking care of it.' What did you think he was going to do?"

"I don't know."

Wolf nodded. "You know you're in trouble now, right?"

"Yeah. I know."

Wolf got up.

"What's going to happen to me?" McBeth asked.

"That part's not up to me, Eagle."

Wolf left, shutting the door behind him.

CHAPTER 38

HEATHER PATTERSON WATCHED McBeth's confession from a stool in the observation room. When Wolf finished and opened the door, he made eye contact with her first.

"We have to speak in my office," he said, glancing at his watch. "You two can book him," he said to Yates and Rachette.

"What's up?" Patterson asked.

Wolf ignored her question, leading her out into the hallway.

She was on her own two feet now, without crutches. She still felt a spasm of pain in her ankle every now and then if she made a sudden movement, but all in all she was healing fast. Wolf was walking quickly, probably testing her. She kept up easily.

He knew *she* knew. Wilson had gotten back into town from Denver this morning and those two had been speaking behind closed doors for hours. Things were playing out exactly like she expected they might. Wilson had gotten the job with the Denver PD, which meant there was a vacant spot that needed to be filled.

Butterflies took flight in her stomach. Why was she nervous?

Probably because it wasn't every day she was promoted. How would she do as Wolf's right hand?

The butterflies disappeared. She would do fine. Wolf would be better with her working closely with him. The department would do better.

She'd gotten little sleep the last few nights just thinking about it. Not because of anxiety for what might come, she had since realized, but because she was genuinely excited. When she had started her criminal law courses back in Boulder she'd dreamt of moments like these: moving up. Not that she had ever considered herself a ladder-climber before. That wasn't it. It was what she'd always wanted, making a difference—doing her best and being acknowledged for it.

My gosh, how had she come so far so fast? she thought, following Wolf out under the vaulted ceilings of the squad room and towards his office. She was only thirty-four years old.

But she deserved it, she thought. Was that being egotistical? Not really. Not with all the hard work she'd put in.

The blinds of Wolf's glass-enclosed aquarium space were screwed shut, making it look like a bomb bunker instead of the sheriff's office. That was normal for big meetings. News of the undersheriff leaving and the chief detective moving into his place was cause for closing the blinds.

Wolf's door was open and he stopped before it, motioning her in first.

Wilson sat in a chair inside the office. Suddenly, she had a thought: If Wilson is leaving and I'm taking his place, who's going to be Chief Detective? Yates or Rachette? And, if so, why aren't they in this meeting, too?

Wilson stood up, as did DA White next to him. So did her aunt, Mayor Margaret Hitchens, and her husband Scott.

"Hello, Heather," Wilson said.

Patterson stopped inside the doorway. "Hello," she said

slowly, as the door clicked shut behind her and the group took their seats.

A single chair sat vacant next to Wolf on the other side of the desk. Wolf motioned to it.

She walked behind Wilson and White. *Why are Margaret and Scott here?* Her husband was avoiding eye contact, which was a tell for when he knew he was doing something wrong. Or, at least, knew he'd done something she would disapprove of.

Margaret's face had the same blank half-smile she wore when she was holding back a tirade against somebody who pissed her off.

Now she felt like she was attending an intervention and she was the guest of honor.

What is this?

She sat down next to Wolf. The butterflies were back.

"What's going on?" she asked.

"Heather." Wolf turned in his chair towards her. "I've called this meeting to discuss some changes that are afoot here in the department. Changes that will involve you centrally, or...not."

"Okay." She smiled at the absurdity of the sentence. "Hopefully they involve me. I'm not going anywhere anytime soon. Unless...you have plans that say otherwise."

Wolf stood up and pushed his chair in, then started pacing.

She frowned. Shit. Maybe she was getting fired. Or somehow relocated? Is that why Scott was here?

Uncertainty swirled inside her, and suddenly her life was flashing before her eyes, only the moments she saw were ones where she'd snapped at Wolf, or made a snide remark to DA White, or been too harsh with Wilson.

She looked to Scott. Her husband was now looking at her in the eye. His eyebrows were peaked with concern, and then he smiled like everything was going to be alright.

"What the hell's going on?" she asked.

"Heather, we want to talk to you about this November," Wolf said.

"What about it?"

"Elections," Margaret said.

Wolf looked at her aunt like she'd said something wrong. Margaret hid a smirk.

"Yeah. Okay. Elections." Patterson upturned her hands.

"This is a tough subject to discuss delicately," Wolf said, "so I'm just going to come out and say it. I don't want to be sheriff anymore. I'm not going to run for sheriff in November. Wilson doesn't want to be sheriff, we know he felt that way last year and he still feels the same way now. As of yet no other candidates have come forth. We've gathered here today to tell you we'd like you to be sheriff of this county."

Her vision went blurry for a few moments as she wondered if she was actually conscious.

"Wait," she said. "No. Wilson, I thought you got the job with Denver PD. I thought you were leaving and you wanted me to take the Undersheriff position."

Wilson straightened. "What? No, I turned it down. I'm not moving to freakin' Denver."

"She's gonna pass out," Margaret said with a chuckle.

"What?" Patterson shook her head. "Me? Sheriff?"

"Yes, you," Wolf said.

She felt her face burn red, her chest pounding. She stood up and walked to the window as she composed herself with some deep breaths.

"Heather," Wolf said, "You're the best we have in this building. And I know I've said it before, and that wasn't just because I wanted you to complete that budget proposal. That was the truth."

"You're the best we have in this county," Margaret said. "Not just this building."

The wave of panic passed through her and cold logic settled in. She turned around. "Look. Guys. I'm not sure if you've noticed, but I'm thirty-four years old."

"So what?" Wolf said.

"So, that's young. Thirty-four years old is young."

"You're most qualified for the job," Wolf said.

She scoffed at his dismissiveness. "It's not just that. I'm also a w—" she stopped herself and looked out the window again.

"What?" Margaret asked. "You're a woman? Is that what you were going to say?"

Her ankle sparked with pain as she spun around. "Yes, damn it! I'm a woman! I'm thirty-four years old and I'm a woman. Doesn't that seem like it might be a little bit tough for the citizens of Sluice-Byron County to swallow? Doesn't that for one moment give any of you pause?"

Blood roared in her ears.

DA White raised a finger. "The thought of you becoming sheriff most definitely gives me pause, but not because you're a thirty-four-year-old woman. You would be a political pain in the ass. But you'd be effective because you're hard-headed, you get stuff done, and you don't take shit from anybody. It gives me pause, but just because, you know, it's you."

White picked at his cufflink.

"Uh, thank you, District Attorney," Margaret said.

"You're welcome."

"Heather," Wolf said, sitting on the edge of his desk, "I could stay on as sheriff, put Wilson on as chief detective, and bring you up as undersheriff for four years where you could learn the ropes, and then you could run as sheriff after that with a lot more confidence."

"Yeah," she said. "Sounds good to me. That's exactly what I thought this meeting was about."

Wolf shrugged. "But you've been pretty much doing my job

this whole time. In looking out for me over the last year, you've taken it upon yourself to learn every squeak in every wheel of this huge machine. And when you see something that needs greasing, you hand me the bottle and tell me where to apply it."

"Excellent metaphor," Margaret said.

"Shut up." Wolf stood and karate chopped one hand with the other. "Let's cut through the unnecessary steps here and get you where you belong. These deputies, these people above and below us," he pointed at White, "they need you. You will do such a good job and you know it. Me? I'm a detective. I'm meant to be out there." He waved a hand to the window. "I solve crime. I don't do spreadsheets. I don't manage a thousand people. I don't do well spending this much time with Margaret and the county council. I don't write proposals. I cannot stand to look at another 10-65-G report for every single sub-depart—"

"F," Heather said. "10-65-F reports. You don't deal with the Gs."

"She's right," Wilson said.

"Shut up." Wolf shook his head like he was getting attacked by a swarm of bees. "Heather. You *would* be great at this job. And if you need help that's what we're here for. That's why we're all gathered here now to talk to you about this. You need political knowledge? Margaret has your back. You want procedure help? Wilson knows everything better than I do. You need anything else? I would be down the hall. In the Chief Detective's office."

She looked at Scott. "You knew about this?"

He shook his head. "They called me in for the meeting. I had no clue what for."

"We wanted him to hear this, too," Wolf said. "Obviously this is a big decision and it involves your whole family. We don't expect you to have an answer right away."

"But I suspected it was something like this," Scott said,

ignoring Wolf. "I always knew you were going to be big time, from the moment I met you."

"O-kay," White stood up, looking at his watch. "I have a four o'clock. Heather. I'll support whatever decision you make. You'd be running unopposed so I'm not sure an official endorsement would help you or not. But you know where my office is if you need to talk about it. Everyone. Have a good day."

White left and shut the door behind him.

"Is he always that much of a prick?" Margaret asked.

"Yes," Wilson said.

Heather was still looking at Scott. He shrugged his shoulders. "I'm fine with it if you are. But we can talk about it. Like Dave said, you don't have to make a decision right now."

But the wheels were already turning. And to use Wolf's metaphor, they were well-greased, chugging along at high efficiency. And she knew now it wasn't the thought of becoming undersheriff that had kept her up with excitement these last few nights. It had been the step after.

Sheriff Heather Patterson. She tried on the name and felt a wave of energy pass through her, like seltzer water being poured down her spine.

"I'll do it," she said.

Wolf smiled, standing tall. "Good." He walked to her and gave her a hug.

Scott stood and walked over, and Wolf passed her off to her husband.

Wolf looked at his watch and walked to the door. "I'll see you guys later."

"Whoa, whoa," Margaret said. "What the heck? You have some place better to be?"

"Yes," he said, leaving out the door.

CHAPTER 39

"What does she look like?"

Wolf ignored the question as he shaped another buffalo patty and slapped it onto a piece of wax paper.

"Come on." Cassidy stood with her hands on her hips, a pouty look on her face that reminded Wolf how young his daughter-in-law still was.

"Leave him alone." Jack entered Wolf's kitchen and wrapped his wife in his arms.

"Where's Ryan?" Cassidy asked.

"Out there."

"Geez, Jack." She wrestled away and bolted from the kitchen. "There could be a mountain lion out there!"

"I meant out there in the family room!"

"Oh, hey buddy!" she said, her voice receding. "You want to go play some soccer?"

"Yeah!"

Wolf washed his hands at the sink, cleaning off the meat residue but unable to wipe the smile from his face as he watched Ryan run in giggling circles on the front lawn.

"I'm glad you guys could make it," Wolf said.

Jack ducked into the refrigerator and pulled out a beer. "You want one of these? Or are you still on the wagon? Or off it? Or whatever."

"No, thanks. Those are all yours." Wolf dried his hands and leaned up against the counter, appraising his son's physique. "Geez. You guys do anything besides lift weights in the firehouse?"

"Yeah." Jack took a sip and smiled. His green eyes twinkled in the late afternoon light streaming into the window. "Pull ups. How about you?" Jack eyed him. "You exercise anymore?"

Wolf smiled. "I plan on getting back into it."

"I was just kidding. You look good."

"Don't patronize me," Wolf said. "I'm a fat-ass. But I'm going to get back to my fighting weight."

"You seem determined." Jack waggled his eyebrows. "It must be this new woman, then."

"I told you, this woman is nothing like that. Geez, I hope you two are more subtle when she gets here." Wolf walked out of the kitchen to the front door.

Jack slapped him on the back, walking by his side out to the front deck. "I'm not the one you have to worry about."

They stood watching Ryan chase a miniature soccer ball while Cassidy chased after him. The sky was still cloudless. The sun hung low above the mountain to the west, almost kissing the tip of the peak. The air was still and dry, filled with the scent of pine mixed with the charcoal briquettes waiting to be lit.

The sound of crackling tires drew their gazes down the drive to the headgate, where a shining windshield crested the hill and drove toward the house.

Wolf and Jack went down the steps to the lawn. Ryan ran over and latched onto Wolf's leg and he picked him up. Cassidy joined them and they stood still, watching the vehicle approach.

"Remember to keep your mouths shut about everything," Wolf said, looking at Cassidy, who

made a key-twisting motion at her lips.

Wolf's stomach danced with nerves. It had been a while since he'd seen her last. That would change once and for all.

The brakes squealed to a stop and the engine shut off.

With Ryan in his arms, he walked over to the passenger door and popped it open.

The woman in the seat looked up with beaming brown eyes that matched his own. "David!"

"Hi Mom." He reached down and took her hand. It was frail and thin. Her grip was strong, though, as she lifted herself out of the car on sure legs.

"And there's my little Ry-Guy!"

They embraced in a three-way hug until Wolf was forced to give up his grandson to her waiting arms.

A taller woman, thin with her long white hair pulled into a ponytail, stood up from the driver's side. "Hi David."

"Hi Harriet," Wolf said. "How are you?"

"Not bad. Not bad. You're mother's driving me crazy of course. But not bad." Over the last decade Harriet had become his mother's favorite competitive bridge partner down in Denver. Both of them being widows, they had become fast friends, and then eventually roommates in the same apartment. More recently, Harriet had taken it upon herself to watch over his mother as her mental acuity began to slip.

"Yeah?" Wolf chuckled. "What's going on this time?"

Harriet ignored him, popping the trunk on her Prius. "Kat! Leave that kid alone and come talk to your son!"

His mother put Ryan down, kissed him, and released him back into the wild. "How are you, David?" she said, coming over and wrapping him in a hug.

He winced as she latched onto a bruised rib but rode out the pain and hugged her back. "I'm good, Mom. How about you?"

"I'm excellent."

"Keeping busy?"

"Busy as ever. Racking up those Masterpoints."

He smiled. "They have a pretty raucous bridge scene up here, you know."

She swiped a hand.

Wolf unpacked their bags from the car and brought them inside while his mother followed. They made some pleasant small talk, only briefly skimming through the part where they had not seen each other in too long. And only briefly did Wolf feel a tinge of shame. They were here together now, and that's all that mattered. Besides, things were going to be different from now on. This time he wasn't seeking her approval of his plan, either.

But for now he didn't mention the condominium he'd bought for her in downtown Rocky Points. He didn't mention that he wanted her back up here where he could keep a close eye on her. He didn't mention the in-home nursing services that he'd lined up to visit her three times a week. He knew his mother, and knew the memories of this place haunted her. That news would have to be slow dripped over the next few days of her visit. At least, that was the plan.

Wolf went inside with the luggage and put it into the spare bedroom, then went back into the kitchen where Jack and Cassidy were finishing food preparations.

"She's here," Cassidy said in a sing-song voice as she leaned into the window. "Wow." She opened her mouth and looked at Wolf. "Wow. She is beautiful."

Wolf had been too busy to notice Piper Cain pull up in her Jeep Cherokee. She was already parked and out of the door, approaching the house with her father next to her. She carried a

Tupperware in her hands and was bending down to say hi to Ryan.

Wolf had to admit he agreed with Cassidy. Piper wore a pair of jeans and a long-sleeved floral-patterned shirt. Her dark curls were pulled back and cascading onto her shoulders. Dangling earrings glinted in the evening light, accentuating her sparkling eyes and smile.

Wolf's stomach lurched when he heard his mother's voice outside.

"Who's this?" His mother walked at her. "My goodness. Who is this beauty? David. Is this your girlfriend?"

Wolf rushed to the front door and went outside.

"Mom! This is Piper Cain and her father!" He spoke loud, trying to smother the words coming out of her mouth. "She's a deputy with the department. Hi Peter." Wolf shook her father's hand.

"Oh, hello, Piper." His mother got in on the action, shaking her hand and then her father's. "What was your name?"

Piper's father beamed. "I'm Peter Cain."

Harriet swooped in from nowhere. "Hi Peter. I'm Harriet."

"Hello, Harriet."

"What happened to you?" Wolf's mother asked, reaching out and touching the cast on Piper's arm. "And your face. Honey. Are you all right?"

"Mom."

"It's okay," Piper said. "I was just a little banged up on the job."

"Geez, David. What are you letting happen to your deputies?"

"Kat!" Harriet said, pulling her by the arm. "Come on!"

"Yeah, okay. I'm coming."

A smiling Peter Cain allowed himself to be swept into the house by the two women.

"My God," Wolf said. "Here. I'll take that." He took the container from her.

Cassidy came up and introduced herself. Jack nodded hello, too. Piper shook their hand then introduced herself to Ryan, who started out shy, then told a thirty-second story about his running and kicking abilities. Maybe. It was tough to tell.

"My goodness, this guy is so cute," Piper said, playfully poking a finger into Ryan's armpit.

"Thanks," Cassidy said. "O-kay, buster. Let's go. We'll be inside." Jack took the containers from Wolf and Cassidy led her family in through the door, leaving Wolf and Piper alone outside.

Wolf toed a rock and looked at her. The scrapes had darkened where they had scabbed over. The bruises were fading now.

"You look good," he said.

She put her hand up to her face. "Yeah. Right."

"The swelling has gone down," he said. "You looked like you were on death's door back in the hospital."

"I didn't put makeup over all this. 'Cause, you know, then I'd look like I had five pounds of makeup on."

"You look good."

She smiled. "Thanks. You look good, too."

They both kicked some rocks.

She turned around and looked toward the dipping sun. "This place is beautiful. Wow."

"Thank you. I love it."

He looked back at the house and saw three heads looking out at them from the kitchen window. "Hey, why don't we take a quick walk."

"Okay. Sure."

He led her past the barn, onto a narrow game trail that had

become one of Wolf's favorite hikes to the north side of the property, where there was a lookout to Rocky Points.

She walked gingerly. A few days ago he had seen the x-rays of her chest, and the two fractured ribs high on her ribcage.

"How are you feeling?" he asked.

"Not bad."

"Thanks for making the long drive," he said. "That couldn't have been that fun with your injuries."

"Oh, no." She smiled. "It was fine. And it's not that long."

He nodded. "Yeah. Not that long."

They walked in silence for a beat.

"And your arm?" he asked. He'd also seen the picture of her fractured ulna, either broken from her thrashing against the restraints or from the fall into the hole.

"Better. A little sore. But not bad."

He nodded, continuing to walk next to her.

The sun had dipped fully behind the peak where they were, but the rays still blazed down on Rocky Points up the valley. The trail sloped up toward the top of a low rise.

"It's just a little more," he said. "I want to show you something."

"Great."

They made it to the top of the hill and Wolf stopped.

"Oh, wow." Piper nodded, gazing north into the Chautauqua Valley.

The silver river wound up the valley, cutting its way through the vast landscape and into the town of Rocky Points. The town's lights shimmered silently. The mountains beyond were painted in layers of fading blue, some of their tops still beaming with sunlight.

"It's beautiful," she said.

"Yeah," he said, standing next to her.

They stood in silence for a while. Wolf breathed in her floral scent.

"So," he said. "What do you think?"

"About?"

"About working here in Rocky Points with us?"

She looked down. "I would love to."

He kept his face neutral, but the anticipation of seeing this woman day in and day out filled him with electricity.

She looked up at him. "But I can't."

"Oh." The word came out like a sound comes out after a blow to the gut. "Okay."

"Listen, I really appreciate the offer." She turned to him. "I really do. But, my father built that place. It's the only thing that gives him any consistent joy day in and day out. It's the only thing that's...I don't know how to explain it."

"That's permanent?"

"Yes. That's it. Exactly." She picked at her cast. "And I don't want to take that from him."

"I understand. That's very noble of you."

"Or stupid," she said. "I can't tell."

"No." He touched her shoulder. "That's not stupid to love your father like that."

She looked at his hand and he dropped it away, feeling his face flush.

They stood in silence again, Wolf trying to come up with something to say.

Then he saw out of the corner of his eye as she raised her hand and brought it to the back of his neck. She got up on her toes and pulled him down at the same time, looking like she was aiming to peck him on the cheek.

But he turned his head and their lips collided, bouncing hard off one another.

She reached up and touched a scab on her mouth.

"I'm sorry," he said.

She smiled. And then her face went dead serious as she leaned up again.

This time she leaned sideways, aiming true to his lips and they kissed. It was a soft and gentle peck. Then their mouths parted and their tongues caressed. Their breath mingled. Their bodies leaned into each other.

When they were done the rays of the sun over Rocky Points had dimmed—the only proof that time had existed for those moments.

He cleared his throat. "Okay, then. You're declining the job."

She chuckled.

"I guess we'd better head back," he said. "I can see they've started the grill."

A tendril of smoke rose from behind the trees towards his house.

"Yeah," she said. "Good idea."

They began walking side by side down the hill.

"Oh yeah," Wolf said. "I have some interesting news."

"Oh? What's that?"

As they wove their way down through the trees he told her about Heather Patterson's ascension to sheriff that would occur in the months ahead.

"Oh," she said, appraising him.

"Yeah," he said.

"And you're fine with all that?"

"Yes. I am."

They stepped together in silence, until she said, "So, you wouldn't be my boss anymore."

"That's right."

A smile pulled on her lips. "Which makes what we just did less awkward, doesn't it?"

"Considerably so."

When they came around the barn Jack was in a handstand on the front lawn. Ryan kicked a soccer ball and hit him in the face, toppling him onto his back. The girls watching screamed in delight, which scared Ryan, who ran to Cassidy crying.

"Oh no," Piper said with a laugh.

"They're back." Jack walked to the grill and flipped the meat. "Are you guys hungry?"

The outdoor table on the front porch was set with a variety of place settings Wolf didn't know he owned.

His mother and Harriet sat down, flanking Peter Cain and pointing Piper to sit in a designated spot across from them. Cassidy sat Ryan in the highchair next to her and settled in.

Wolf and Jack gathered the buffalo burgers onto a plate and joined them. By random chance a spot opened up between Cassidy and Piper so he took it.

Cassidy elbowed him in the side. With a mischievous smile on her face she asked, "All good?"

"Yeah," he said. "All good."

Thank you for reading In the Ground. I hope you enjoyed the story, and if you did, thank you for taking a few moments to leave a review. As an independent author, exposure is everything, and if you'd consider leaving a review, which helps me so much with that exposure, I'd be very grateful.

CLICK HERE TO LEAVE A REVIEW

. . .

I love interacting with readers so please feel free to email me at jeff@jeffcarson.co so I can thank you personally. Otherwise, thanks for your support via other means, such as sharing the books with your friends/family/book clubs/the weird guy wearing no shirt and suspenders sitting next to you right now, or anyone else you think might be interested in reading the David Wolf series. Thanks again for spending time in Wolf's world.

Would you like to know about future David Wolf books the moment they are published? You can visit my blog and sign up for the New Release Newsletter at this link – http://www.jeffcarson.co/p/newsletter.html.

As a gift for signing up you'll receive a complimentary copy of Gut Decision—A David Wolf Short Story, which is a harrowing tale that takes place years ago during David Wolf's first days in the Sluice County Sheriff's Department.

Made in the USA
Las Vegas, NV
22 December 2020

14599023R00194